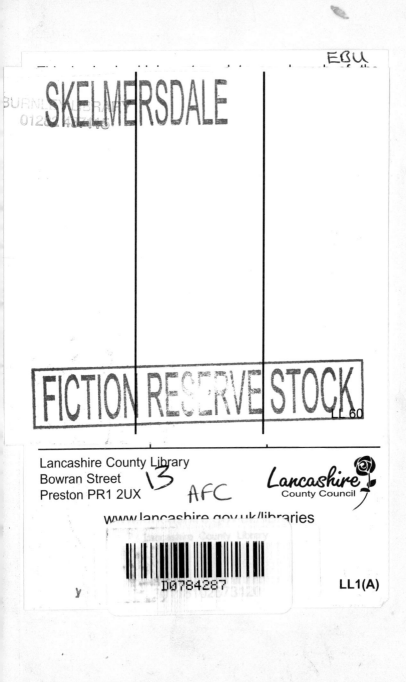

Baby Love

Maureen Carter

CREME DE LA CRIME

First published in 2006
by Crème de la Crime
Crème de la Crime Ltd, PO Box 523, Chesterfield,
Derbyshire S40 9AT

Typesetting by Yvette Warren
Cover design by Yvette Warren
Front cover illustration by Peter Roman

ISBN 0-9551589-0-7

A CIP catalogue reference for this book is available from the
British Library

www.cremedelacrime.com

For Peter Shannon

Acknowledgements

I am fortunate to have a wonderful editor in Douglas Hill. Douglas offers generous support, unerring advice and acute vision. I thank him enormously.

I am also hugely indebted to Lynne Patrick for her faith and focus, and to her inspirational team at Crème de la Crime.

Writing would be a lonelier place without the endless support of some pretty special people. For 'being there' even when miles away, my thanks, love and affection go to:

Sophie Shannon, Corby and Stephen Young, Suzanne Lee, Paula and Charles Morris, Frances Lally and Helen and Alan Mackay. And my 'sister-in-crime' Sarah Rayne.

www.maureencarter.co.uk

The plain woman in beige trailed wistfully along rail upon rail of tiny baby clothes, pausing here and there to bestow a tender touch, a gentle stroke. Imagining. Anticipating. Knowing.

This time nothing would go wrong.

More than anything in her drab life, the woman ached to nuzzle the delicate skin of a baby's nape. She pictured it all the time, breathing in the glorious scent, tasting its uniqueness. She wanted it so badly it hurt. Surely a newborn's neck was the most wonderful, most innocent place in the world?

Her acquisitive glance lingered on a line of tiny pastel-shaded sleep-suits, soft as lamb's fleece, with exquisite hand-stitched teddy bears. It was a new range, or not one she'd noticed. She wandered closer, impulsively reached out a hand, reluctantly drew it back. The drawers in the nursery at home only just closed as it was. How many clothes could one baby wear?

She moved on, a flicker of a smile adding a fleeting interest to her bland features. At school, the other children had called her The Mouse. Thirty years on, she rarely attracted a second glance, often not even a first. It no longer rankled; going unnoticed had advantages.

As she headed for the soft toys, her fingers slowly circled her swollen stomach in a gesture that had become habitual and was probably unwitting. She visited the store sometimes twice a week, had done so for months. It wasn't the nearest to where she lived; she drove fifteen miles to this much larger branch. It was worth the trip. She revelled in sharing knowing looks with other women, that conspiratorial glint that boasted approaching motherhood.

Surely, she thought, a woman wasn't complete until she'd had a child? The days were over, thank God, when it was torture for her even to glimpse a baby. Again, she ran a gentle hand around her stomach.

This time nothing would go wrong.

By now she was on nodding terms with a few of the staff. She suspected one or two of the sales assistants looked out for her. They were probably on commission. She rarely left without a bulging bag or two. Bulkier items like the cot and the changing unit had already been delivered to the house.

The mousy woman smiled hesitantly as she passed the counter. Lorraine and Sue were on the tills. Not that she was on first-name terms; the staff wore badges on their uniforms. That was how the woman knew it had been Sue who'd made the cutting remark all those months ago.

Sue of the pointy stained teeth and flat Midland vowels had blithely assumed the purchases were for the mousy woman's grandchildren. At the time it was completely crushing, but that was in the summer when her bump had barely begun to show. Five months on, she was able to laugh it off. Just.

Now the time was so close.

Today the woman bought a huge golden teddy bear and half a dozen white vests to add to the collection at home. As she paid in cash, she recalled the positive outcome of Sue's thoughtless faux pas.

Though she had left the store shaking with pent-up rage and humiliation, at home she'd taken a long appraising gaze in the mirror. It was true. She was old before her time. After Richard's death she'd lost the will to live, let alone bother with the way she looked. It showed in the face of the dowdy stranger staring back.

Only the thought of the baby had pulled her from the brink. It was unspeakably sad that Richard wouldn't be around to see the little one grow up. But she could do it. She had to do it. She had to look to the future, not the past.

She'd bought new clothes, even coloured her hair, but the transformation wasn't cosmetic; she'd always look mousy. The real changes weren't visible. She was no longer cowed at the prospect of bringing up a baby alone; she looked forward to it with energy and excitement. She'd make Richard proud of her, proud of them both.

Today's trip had exhausted her. On reaching home, she breathed a sigh of relief and happily, avidly, closed the door on the world. She really ought to rest a while, put her feet up and relax. Later, she whispered, as she slipped off her shoes and carried the bags upstairs to the nursery.

The room never failed to lift her mood. Everything was pristine, everything perfect. It was entirely white: walls, carpet, curtains, each lovingly chosen item of furniture. The only splash of colour was a vibrant rainbow mobile suspended over the cot. As always, she gave it a gentle tap. Tiny sequins stitched into the fabric reflected the light like myriad raindrops. She watched in delight until the swaying was barely perceptible.

As she bent, to pack away the vests and place the bear on the floor by the window, she felt a twinge at the base of her spine. It was the extra weight. There was no cause for alarm. She gently massaged the area before applying the same gentle treatment to her stomach. She smiled; it was so nearly her time.

With difficulty, she reached both hands round her back. The straps were quite tricky to unfasten, even though she'd created the harness herself and had carried out the procedure on countless occasions. She was rather pleased with the design. She'd ensured it could expand to accommodate increasingly large amounts of padding. This she now removed, placing it gently under the white satin quilt.

Her head brushed against the mobile, sending it into a gentle spin. She gazed at it, mesmerised again by the twinkling raindrops.

This time nothing could go wrong.

1

The rape suite at Highgate police headquarters had six hundred and seventy-six off-white tiles.

Probably.

The number was different every time Detective Sergeant Bev Morriss counted and she'd lost track of how often she'd started. She curled a lip. Tarting up the grim surroundings with primary prints and pot plants didn't change the ambience. Pain and shame lingered here, almost tangibly.

Bev slouched back in a not-so-easy chair and blew out her cheeks in a sigh. She was acutely aware that counting tiles wasn't the most productive use of her time but she couldn't talk to the victim, Laura Kenyon, until the police doctor cleared it. He'd been in the examination room with the teenager for two hours. Bev glanced at her watch. It was 9.05 already. Make that two hours twenty.

She picked at a few strands of fraying fabric on the arm of the chair. If the day had panned out according to the best-laid et cetera, she'd be down the Bullring flashing plastic with her best mate, Frankie. A burger at the Hard Rock Café and Johnny Depp at the UGC had been on the cards for later. Mental note: call Frankie. The girl was going to kill her. Again. Working on a Saturday was a concept Frankie had yet to grasp.

Missing out on a day off Bev could live with, but she deeply regretted eschewing a bowl of bran or a bacon roll during her hasty departure from a house she still couldn't quite think of as home. Her stomach was making gurgling sounds reminiscent of faulty plumbing or a dodgy balti. She rummaged through the pockets of her denim jacket for chocolate or chewing gum. Nada.

Earlier, en route from the incident room, she'd grabbed the Operation Street Watch files. A bit of light reading while she waited for the action. She skimmed the reports again. It was ninety-nine per cent certain that Laura's rape was the latest in an on-going inquiry that had touched just about every officer on the force. Bev knew the top lines by heart. Not surprising: she'd written most of them. She'd been assigned the lead interview role from day one.

Her mouth twitched as she recalled how well that had gone down with Mike Powell. DI Powell reckoned empathy was his middle name. Fact was, he had the sensitivity of a morbidly obese rhino in a suit of armour. Her relatively high profile on the team was the governor's call. Detective Superintendent Bill Byford rated her interview technique. He claimed she could get Trappists to talk among themselves.

She suspected, too, it was a message to the troops that he still had faith in her. She'd cocked up big time earlier in the year, been all ready to jack in the job. The guv had persuaded her to stay, but she was under no illusion: there were still acres of ground to landscape, not just make up. Either way, Byford wanted consistency. It was why she was here now.

And given the inquiry's complete lack of progress so far, consistency was about the only thing they did have. Unless Laura Kenyon could give them a break.

Laura was the third city teenager to be raped in as many months. In each case they'd been dragged off the streets in the early hours, then dumped like trash. Bev had only caught a glimpse of the latest victim but it was enough to confirm that Laura fitted the profile. Like the others, she was pretty with long blonde hair, blue eyes and flawless skin. All three were slender and below average height, slight young women barely capable of landing a punch, let alone winning a fight.

There was another factor that couldn't be ignored. From the back Laura Kenyon, Rebecca Fox and Kate Quinn could be mistaken for much younger children. Bev shook her head, but the disquieting thought was still there. As was another: there was little doubt the attacks were down to the same offender.

With hindsight, the signs had been evident back in September. Then, a month later, another attack with an almost identical MO. SOCOs were still at the scene of Laura's rape, but Bev was sure they'd find the same sick signature. The first two victims had each been missing an earring. It could be coincidence; Bev thought not. Serial sickos often took trophies, pathetic reminders of what big brave men they were.

She shook her head, conceded there was a sliver of doubt on the jewellery angle. But there was none on what he did to his victims' pubic hair.

The weird stuff had not been released to the media. The reporters didn't know the half of it. Not that it had stopped the speculation. They were already going big on what they'd dubbed the Beast of Birmingham. They'd hooked up with a couple of women's groups and a Tory honourable member to get daily comments that were invariably swipes at the police. It was all a bit rent-a-quote and it wouldn't satisfy the media lust for salacious detail. Bev pursed her lips. Sooner or later there'd be a leak. Sure as eggs are eggs.

"I'm Martha Kemp. Are you with the police?"

A leak on legs? Bev wiped the thought off her face. There could be a reasonable explanation why Martha The Mouth Kemp had been granted access to the rape suite. Bev just couldn't come up with one right now. She rose and tried to make eye contact, but Kemp's gaze was sweeping the room, looking for someone more important.

Bev was still trying to get her head round the fact she was face to face with The Mouth. She'd never seen Kemp in the flesh but the woman presented a talk show on Birmingham Sound, the city's commercial radio station. Provocative and outrageous, Kemp focused on big news issues, encouraging listeners to call in, then baiting them mercilessly when their views didn't coincide with hers. Shock jock wasn't in it. The Mouth was vicious, offensive and utterly compulsive. She got away with murder, mainly thanks to the sexiest voice this side of Mariella Frostrup. Talk about vocal Viagra. Bev only sounded that hot when she had a sore throat. Actually, Bev never sounded that hot; hoarse, maybe.

She offered a hand. "Bev Morriss. Detective Sergeant…"

Kemp lifted a finger and scrabbled in her bag, eventually taking out a sleek black mobile. Presumably it had been on vibrate and clearly it was a message, not particularly welcome going by Kemp's furrowed brow.

Bev tried not to stare but it was a shock to find that her mental picture of the woman had been so not right. For years, she'd imagined early Anna Ford. This was late Betty Ford. The severe salt-and-pepper crop was like a skullcap. The skin tone was the shade and texture of old newspapers, probably due less to the lighting than the lighting up. Bev suspected a forty-a-day habit. The long brown woollen coat had no style and little shape.

Kemp returned the phone and Bev tried again. "Bev Morriss, Detective…"

Though standing nearer now, the gap widened as an unsmiling Kemp flapped a dismissive hand before wrapping hostile arms round a spreading waist. "Not now. I need to talk to Laura."

The urge to mirror Kemp's body language was strong. Bev settled for clenching her fists. "Are you a doctor as well, Mrs Kemp?"

A tendon stiffened in Kemp's neck. "Ms Kemp."

"And the answer to my question is?" Bev's trainer was tapping the floor tiles.

Kemp made eye contact for the first time. The whites were bloodshot, the irises light blue, almost grey. "Has anyone ever told you that you have an attitude problem?"

Once or twice. It was a sore point. "You still haven't answered the question. Not that I give a toss. 'Cause unless you're doing a spot of medical moonlighting with a rape kit, you can get off my case."

Kemp's smooth delivery carried an edge of menace. "Who's your superior officer?"

Red flag. Raging bull. Shame it hid the warning light. Bev snorted. "Don't pull that one on me, love. As soon as Laura Kenyon's fit enough to talk, there's only one person going in there. And that's me." Bev jabbed a finger in the direction of Kemp's breastbone and took a step closer. "You shouldn't even be in here. Who the hell was stupid enough to let you in?"

"I guess that'd be me."

Bev didn't need to turn. The governor's voice, in its own way, was as distinctive as Martha Kemp's.

2

There was no premonition, no inkling of any kind. Natalie Beck's morning was starting like a bunch of others during the bumpy course of her sixteen-year life: bleary-eyed and bad-tempered. Her slow reluctant surfacing wasn't prompted by the garish Mickey Mouse alarm clock. She'd forgotten to set it again. Erratic bursts of heavy rain needling the window eventually roused her as cartoon hands pointed to a tardy ten past nine.

The not-so-early riser grabbed the clock and squinted at the dial in disbelief. The sour expression on her sleep-softened features suggested the rodent was deliberately giving her a hard time. She slammed the clock on to a flimsy orange box pressed into service as a bedside table. The off-key ping echoed in the stillness of the house.

Natalie chewed a pierced lip and frowned. The place was like a morgue during a lockout. No blaring radio. No telly. No crocks clattering. She lay motionless, held her breath, listened again. Still silence. And in a mid-terrace with tissue-thin walls, that was saying something. Especially now with the baby.

Her maternal instincts were still in the embryonic stage, but even Natalie knew it was unusual for a newborn to sleep so long. To date, little Zoë Beck had managed no more than a four-hour stretch in a three-week existence. Natalie sighed, gave the faded England duvet a truculent kick, then paused, grabbed by a cooler idea. Her mum, Maxine, must be doing her doting granny bit. On past performance, *bit* was the operative word. Still, gift-horse and mouth and all that.

Natalie retrieved the cover and snuggled back into its warmth. A lie-in was rare these days; a girl might as well make the most of it. And, boy, did she need one. It had been a late night, a first since the baby. Natalie had been down Broad Street with a few mates on the pop and on the pull – just like the old days. Old days? Christ, she sounded like her ma. Whatever. At sweet sixteen, Natalie was plenty old enough to hit on Mr High and Mighty Gould. She still couldn't believe she'd made out with a teacher. Gouldie had barely given her the time of day when she was at school.

School. What a joke. The head had written suggesting she go back, sit the exams next year. As if. She wasn't a kid any more; she had a nipper of her own. What use was a bunch of poxy GCSEs?

She reached down, fumbling for a ciggie from her bag on the floor; swore as she brought out an empty pack. As she moved, she caught the spicy scent of Gould's aftershave. Not surprising, really. He'd been all over her. She recalled some of the more hard-to-reach places, smiled; she'd certainly taught Sir a thing or two. Bastard had buggered off, then. Didn't even walk her to the bus.

"Nat'ly! Nat'ly!" The girl sighed and rolled her eyes. Maxine Beck's voice could dent concrete, never mind daydreams. "I'm off now, our kid. Get your ass in gear."

Yeah, yeah.

"And you shouldn't have the baby in bed with you. It's not safe."

Whatever.

Natalie counted the seconds until the front door slammed. Yep. Seven. You could set your watch by Maxine and her dull little routines. The bossy clack of heels on pavement would fade by thirty.

Natalie hit twelve before registering her mother's words.

The girl's bare feet skimmed freezing lino as she dashed across the landing, heart pounding. Halfway across the cheap carpet she halted, dizzy with relief, closing her eyes briefly and mouthing a silent thanks to any passing god. The baby was asleep, the top of her head just visible above the pink quilt. Her mum must have fed Zoë, then put her down before leaving the house.

Natalie took a calming breath to slow her racing heart. Maxine's mean trick had forced her out of bed all right. Into a state of shock.

She tiptoed to the tiny cot and gently pulled back the covers. The macabre sight turned her insides to ice. She cupped a hand over her mouth to stem the bile rising in her throat, not able to make sense of what she saw.

Zoë wasn't in the cot. It was a doll. A stupid doll.

Natalie flung it across the room, angrily snatched at the pillow, yanked the covers aside and up-ended the mattress. It had to be another mean trick, a nightmare hide-and-seek. But in her heart she knew Maxine wouldn't be that malicious.

Her panic rose as her breathing quickened. She stared wildly round the room before turning back to the cot. All that remained was a white cotton sheet, a little crumpled and so very cold. Natalie lifted it to her cheek, inhaled the scent of her beautiful baby. She lost it, then. Screaming, unable to stop, she clamped her hands over her ears. She needed to think straight but couldn't think at all over the appalling noise she was barely conscious of making.

In the street, the sound stopped Maxine in her stilettoed tracks. She was vaguely aware of furtive stares from passers-by, but no one else halted. Why would they? It'd just be the estate kids mucking about again. Except Maxine Beck knew it wasn't. Her daughter's anguish was clamouring in her ears. Rooted to the spot, she felt her blood run cold.

3

"How was I meant to know?"

Bev had been kicking her heels in the corridor while the guv did his best to placate Martha Kemp. He'd just emerged from the rape suite and it turned out the presenter wasn't a media queen on the sniff for a scoop. She was Laura Kenyon's mother.

Byford waited as Bev tried to get her head round the fact that Ms Kemp had kept the Happy Families card extremely close to her chest. "She didn't say a word, guv."

"Maybe she couldn't get one in," he suggested. "Cut her some slack, sergeant. She's in shock. That's her daughter in there."

She shrugged. Kemp could still have said *something*. Bev felt she'd been deliberately wrong-footed, like it had been some sort of test. And she'd failed.

"Uniform had a hell of a job getting hold of her to break the news," Byford said. "She wasn't answering the door. A neighbour had a key. They found her on the bathroom floor. She'd got bladdered at some awards do. So she's feeling guilty as sin on top of everything else."

"Yeah, well, I'm not a mind reader."

"Clearly. Or you'd have an idea why I'm here."

She hadn't given it a thought. Her entire focus was on Laura Kenyon, how soon she could talk to the girl. How soon she could elicit every fact while staying alert to every nuance. The Street Watch squad badly needed pointing in the right direction, any direction. There was an outside chance the girl had caught a glimpse of the attacker. It hadn't happened yet; he'd been smart, or lucky. But grey cells died off and luck ran out. There was always a first time. A visual was probably too much to hope for but there was more than one way to skin a cat – even the most repulsive tom on the block. An accent, for instance, could give away loads; a distinctive smell; the way he wore his hair…

"You all right?" Byford asked. God knew what her face was doing. His was full of concern.

"Just thinking."

"Don't let me stop you." Her look spoke volumes. "Let's sit down a minute, sergeant."

He indicated a heavy wooden bench lining one of the custard-coloured walls. Kilroy had been there, and his mate Elroy. And they'd carved their names with pride, and a blunt penknife. Bev traced the letters with a finger, reluctant to meet the big man's gaze. He'd used the s-word, for one thing, and she didn't like the way he said it. A quick glance confirmed her suspicions. She could read his eyebrows like a book. The left had almost disappeared into the hairline: something was bugging him.

She let the silence stand and sneaked a few more covert glances. She reckoned he'd aged a bit in the last couple of years. The grey flecks among the still-thick black hair were more snow-scatter than sprinkle. And the lines down the side of his mouth had become a permanent feature rather than the by-product of late nights and early mornings, often back to back. He was early fifties, nothing these days, but he'd had a health scare earlier in the year, had even toyed with the idea of early retirement.

That had sent shock waves rippling down Bev's vertebrae. The guv was on her side, almost the only suit at Highgate that was. Without his metaphorical arm around her shoulder the world would be a much colder place. Not that he didn't call a spade an earth mover, and not that he was afraid to tell her to her face what a lot of the Highgate neanderthals only whispered behind her back. Whatever the reason for the current uncharacteristic shilly-shallying, it was neither fear nor concern for her sometimes fragile self-esteem.

"It'll probably all be over by the time you get there."

Where? The only place she had the slightest intention of going was the room at the end of the corridor where Laura Kenyon was waiting to be interviewed. The guv still hadn't looked her in the eye. She folded her arms, slumped back against the wall. She wasn't going to make it easy for him. "Like I say, I'm no mind-reader."

"I'm taking you off Street Watch." He lifted a hand to quell a Morriss outburst. "Just till we know how this thing pans out. As I say, by the time you get there, it'll probably be sorted."

"What will?" Her gaze fixed on a peeling poster extolling safe sex. Given the state of her love life, any sex would be a fine thing. Oz had been giving her so much space lately she could rent rooms.

"We got a call-out. Looks like it could be a missing baby."

Her heart skipped a beat as she abandoned the slouch. "Missing?" Her senses were on red alert. Baby-snatch, kidnap, abduction, call it what you like. A dictionary couldn't come close to describing the horror, the emotional fall-out when a baby's taken, a young life's at stake. Priority didn't get much higher. So why the shifty look?

"Uniform's there," Byford said. "Les called it in. He reckons there's something fishy. Wants another pair of eyes."

Les King. Laziest copper on the force. Christ, if Kingie thought it was fishy, there must be shoals of the bloody things. It was a time-waster. And there was none to spare. Byford knew it. She knew it. "With respect, guv…"

"Don't even go there." He stood, mentally elsewhere

15

already.

"But…"

"But nothing." He handed her a slip of paper. "I want you to take a look."

She clocked the address and snarled. Blake Way, Balsall Heath. Better known as Asbo Alley. What fun. She gave a theatrical sigh, tapped fingers on thigh.

"And you can stop that soon as you like." Byford read bodies as well as minds.

"What I'd like is to talk to Laura Kenyon."

"You should have thought about that before inserting yourself in her mother's nostrils."

"That is so unfair."

"That's life." He shrugged half-heartedly. "Think yourself lucky she isn't filing a complaint."

In his office on the fourth floor, Byford watched through the window as Bev crossed the car park. Even from this distance, he could read the signs. The slumped shoulders and head down had nothing to do with heavy rain falling from a leaden sky; she was seriously pissed off. He sighed, absentmindedly tipping the dregs of a canteen coffee on to a parched cactus languishing on the windowsill. The plant was the latest in a long horticultural line of Morriss peace offerings. Indeed, had all the cacti flourished, he could have opened a garden centre. Was the choice of plant significant?

He gave it a passing thought, his focus still on the woman sending smoke signals from below. Detective Sergeant Beverley Morriss didn't need to open her mouth these days. Learning to button it – which she had by no means mastered – never helped when she had one on her, so to speak. And she'd had several during the spat with Martha Kemp.

Byford rubbed his eyes as he recalled the radio presenter's threat to have a word with her mate, Ronnie: Big Chief Constable Ronald Birt. Thank God she wasn't pally with the Queen's Constable as well. Kemp had taken exception to Bev's slack attitude and sloppy appearance. There'd been no percentage in pointing out the sergeant's early shout on a day off; that only explained the denims and trainers. Anyway, when Kemp was in full flow, on or off the air, The Mouth was unstoppable. Only an apparently reluctant agreement that a more senior officer would be assigned to her daughter's interview had halted the diatribe.

Ms Kemp had looked suitably gratified, not to say smug, at what she perceived as a victory. In reality there'd been no agreement, reluctant or otherwise. Byford had already made the decision to take Bev off the interview. His wayward sergeant could and did ruffle feathers; she could also soothe entire flocks of birds. If a baby were missing, he could think of no better officer to deal with the family.

Especially the Becks. He was surprised Bev hadn't picked up on the address. Still, it would register soon enough.

Right now she was alongside the Morriss-mobile, an ageing MG Midget that she loved even though its erratic performance occasionally drove her to distraction. Byford watched her waggle her fingers and mouth a greeting to someone out of his field of vision. Glossy curtains of chin-length Guinness-coloured hair drew back to reveal a warm smile that lit her entire face and widened the bluest eyes he'd ever seen. It had never occurred to him before but when Bev looked like that, she was almost beautiful.

The senior detective who'd shortly be questioning Laura Kenyon was currently trying to answer a few being put to him. DI Mike Powell was perched precariously on the muddy slope of a disused railway embankment off the main road into Moseley. Gnarled oaks provided a dense overhang of twisted branches glistening with slimy moss. Natural light struggled to penetrate the gloom, which explained the battery of police lights and a tableau that at first sight resembled a film set. The inspector had been carefully positioned camera-left. The scene of Laura Kenyon's rape – almost certainly the latest in a series – provided a damp and dismal backdrop.

In the distance two white-suited figures were on their knees, steel cases full of fine-tooth combs, a steadily growing pile of small see-through bags on the ground beside them. It looked like a *CSI* shoot or something out of *Doctor Who*. As for the plastic bags, they could contain evidence or detritus; people had been dumping rubbish in the cutting for years. A few litter louts were probably among the motley crew of extras that had congregated at street level and were now lining a wire-mesh security fence, agog at the activity below. Clutching the fence and faces pressed against the wire, they could have been spectators at a zoo. Powell half-expected to be tossed a banana. A notice exhorting trespassers to keep out had earlier been ignored. Or maybe the rapist couldn't read.

It was wet under the inspector's expensive Italian loafers and fat raindrops were flattening his recently coiffed locks. The pose was both uncomfortable and fairly ungainly but Nick Lockwood, the BBC's safest pair of hands in the Midlands, had been extremely persuasive. It helped that Mike Powell was as keen to get his face on the box as the old TV pro firing the questions was to put it there. Though at this precise moment Lockwood was itching to tighten his fingers round the inspector's neck.

Powell wasn't being deliberately obtuse; it came naturally. But on this occasion, he either didn't have the information Lockwood was after or he couldn't or wouldn't give it. He'd hummed and hedged like a musical privet. Maybe the officers he'd put on house-to-house might come up with a whisper. He'd heard nothing yet.

The only known fact was the girl's name and even Lockwood knew that was a no-no. A rape victim's identity was rarely released to the media, even without the current three-line whip demanding anonymity that Martha Kemp had apparently issued. Powell hadn't spoken to the woman, but he'd had an ear-bending from Byford who clearly had. What a nightmare: a female control freak with friends in high places.

Lockwood took advantage of Powell's wandering thoughts, hoping his casual delivery of a loaded question would slip by unnoticed. "So there is a link with the previous attacks?"

"I didn't say that."

Can't win them all. Lockwood bowled another. "So there isn't a connection?"

"I didn't say that either." Powell regarded Lockwood with renewed interest. The man might look like a crumpled sofa but the journalist brain was sharp as a razor and equally cut-throat.

"So what *are* you saying?"

The newsman had let local radio and the print guys do their bit first so they wouldn't be around to pick up any exclusive gems Powell might drop during Lockwood's turn. It wasn't working; this was more swine before pearls. Powell, or Blondie as he was commonly known among the hacks, wasn't singing at all, let alone from the same crime sheet.

"At this preliminary stage in the inquiry, it's not possible to indicate whether this incident is related to..."

Blah-de-blah-blah. Lockwood tuned out. Apart from a complete lack of anything worth using, at this rate he'd be lucky to hit *Newsnight*.

"Finito?" the inspector asked with a smile that bordered on smug.

"Yep," Lockwood agreed. "That's a wrap." He'd wasted enough energy on this blond twat. He'd give Bev Morriss a bell; she didn't do police-speak and often had something worth saying.

He'd been surprised not to see her out here. He sensed she wanted a collar particularly badly on this one. They'd bumped into each other quite a bit in the course of Operation Street Watch. He'd even financed a pinot or two in the Prince of Wales. It was a police pub, good for contacts. Lockwood made it his business to drink there regularly. When Bev Morriss was around it was pleasure as well. Off the record, he reckoned she was well fit and a fucking good cop. And she'd tossed the occasional snippet his grateful way. Question was, could he sweet-talk the delectable DS into parting with a quality steer?

Lockwood was still mulling it over as he reached the top of the slope and heard a string of expletives ring out from behind. The newsman didn't actually see Powell's tumble; the inspector was already down when Lockwood turned. Blondie had landed slap-bang in what looked suspiciously more pungent than a puddle of mud. The newsman watched as one of the SOCOs raced across to lend an arm.

A red-faced Powell flapped a hand in angry dismissal and immediately lost his footing again. Lockwood had to turn away. Shame the camera hadn't been running. The crap might wash off the fancy footwear eventually, but it'd be a bugger to get the stains out of what looked like a brand-new Barbour. As for the smell… Lockwood smiled. Had there been cattle around, he'd swear it was bullshit.

4

Travis was spouting *Why does it always rain on me?* Bev flicked off the CD with a finger and gave a heartfelt sigh. "You and me both, mate." The downpour was now a deluge but she wasn't talking weather; she'd turned into the Wordsworth estate. She was chasing a wild goose on Balsall Heath's Little Gorbals, where you washed your motor on the way out. Assuming it still had wheels.

Way she saw it, the whole business was a non-starter. No one snatched babies on the Wordsworth. Girls popped them out like peas, swapped them for a pack of fags. With a bit of luck, she'd be back at Highgate within the hour. End of.

She peered through the windscreen, half-expecting to see animals in pairs forming an orderly queue outside the nearest ark. What she saw was an ugly, graffiti-scarred, derelict high-rise. Tennyson Tower's smashed windows and rusty grilles dominated an ominous gunmetal sky. She lowered her sights. Blake Way? Was that the one off Keats Avenue? They all looked the naffing same to her: mean streets of redbrick council semis, with scrubby front gardens and grotty nets at grimy windows.

She took a right into Coleridge Drive. And what joker had come up with the names? Poor sodding poets would be turning in their urns, Grecian or otherwise. As for daffodils, you'd be lucky to spot one in March, never mind a bunch in mid-November.

Blake Way? Why's it ringing a bell?

A bunch of hoodies, on the other hand: you'd be spoilt for choice. There was one lot now, hanging round the chip shop. The little shits gave her the finger as she cruised past: synchronised obscenity. Class. She'd nicked one of the bastards for dealing a few months back. Not a hand of poker.

She tapped her fingers on the wheel. The asbo kids and druggies round here were responsible for a significant portion of south Birmingham's crime figures. Cops nationally took sixty-six thousand complaint calls every day, three every four seconds. Bev reckoned most of them hailed from the Wordsworth. Low-level stuff, mostly: muggings, intimidation, verbal abuse, music blaring all hours.

But it didn't always stop there. Shootings were on the increase and kids carried blades like old women carried handbags. It was a miracle there weren't more killings. Bad news for the handful of decent law-abiding families who still lived on the estate, clinging like hairs round a scummy sink. God knows what their quality of life was like. Stuff anti-social orders; give the sleaze-balls a good kicking.

The car was steamed up as well. Bev opened the window a touch, letting in faint traces of cabbage and curry. She opened it a tad wider and caught a whiff of dog shit.

Why does it always rain on me?

Closure came quickly along with a generous squirt of Opium, a present from Oz in the days he still bought her things. Blake Way? Of course. Maxine Beck. The guv wouldn't do that to her, would he? She'd find out soon enough; it was next left, opposite a patch of wasteland laughingly known as The Green. Yeah, right. How green is my valley of rotting bin bags and rusting bike frames?

Bev's wry smile vanished as she spotted a police car straddling the kerb a few doors up and Les King having a crafty smoke huddled on the doorstep of number thirteen. Thank you so much, guv.

Someone should tell that Travis. If it's only raining, why's he whinging?

Maxine Beck had been one of Bev's first collars. Over the years, she'd taken the silly cow in more times than laundry. Shoplifting, soliciting, scamming the social, you name the pie and Maxine's digit was in it up to the knuckle. More often than not some bloke would have pushed it in on her behalf. Maxine was a looker, not a thinker: sexy, sensual and borderline stupid, apart from the odd flash of acuity. Women's lib had never hit her pretty radar. She needed a man like a fish needs fins. Generally she landed sharks.

Maxine had been cautioned, fined and given a suspended sentence or four but never served a custodial. Until she took off on a two-week jaunt to the sun with her then lover-boy piranha, leaving her daughter, Natalie, to sink or swim. The kid was ten years old at the time. Maxine swore she'd made childcare arrangements but either they fell through or were a figment of her lack of imagination. Whatever. The kid was lucky to pull through after going down with what turned into double pneumonia. Natalie Beck went straight from home alone to intensive care. Bev made damn sure Maxine went down: the sentence was six months in Holloway.

WPC Morriss – as Bev then was – received a good deal of correspondence from Prisoner Beck during the four months Maxine had kept Her Majesty happy. None of it was fan mail, most of it was threatening. Indeed, if Bev's memory served her right, Maxine's last written words had included the phrases: see you, my dead body, over. That had been getting on for five years back and since then, as far as the police were concerned, Maxine had kept her fingers to herself. Even so, Bev did not anticipate a warm reception at the Beck residence.

"Took your time, didn't you?" Les King's thick Brummie drawl dribbled contempt. And that was before Bev was over the threshold. Not that she could get over. King's lard-arse was still spread across the step.

"Congratulations, Les." Bev's tight smile was dangerous. Taking lip from a lazy incompetent git she could do without. The git looked like she'd told him to split the atom. "The sergeant's exam?" she asked pleasantly. As if she gave a fuck. "When did you pass?"

"Never took it. Couldn't be arsed." The smug leer revealed a black hole with stumps.

"That's 'Couldn't be arsed, sergeant,' is it?"

He shrugged. "If it makes you feel better, love."

She took a step nearer, recoiled at the baccy breath and hint of body odour. "Tell you what'll make me feel better – you getting off your butt and running the facts past me. You know? Like a professional?" The lip-curl was deliberate. "Drop that fag, man, sort yourself out."

She rarely pulled rank, but she was sick of Highgate tossers like Les King: time-wasting clock-watchers, drifting to early retirement, treating women as bikes or dykes. Or both. Women bosses especially. The old slacker wouldn't be here at all if they weren't so stretched these days. It wasn't just Street Watch. They were on constant terror alert. And it was the soccer season. Saturdays were bad enough anyway and a derby at the Blues' ground made it even worse.

Rising with a couple of exaggerated winces, King stubbed the cigarette under a size ten boot, then made great play of extracting a dog-eared pocket book from his tunic.

Bev's trainer was tapping Morse. She de-coded anyway. "Just talk." Tosser.

He ignored the remark, continued to riffle the pages

with a fat hairy finger.

"For fuck's sake, out of my way!"

Bev couldn't have put it better herself. But the words had been spat by a blowsy, busty blonde who sent Les flying as she stormed out of the house. Bev recognised the retreating figure instantly, reckoned the years had not been kind. The woman was in four-inch heels but Bev had to lengthen her stride to keep up. "Where you off to, Mrs Beck?"

"Where d'you think? I'm looking for Zoë."

Bev put a hand on the woman's sleeve. "Let's get some details first."

"That fat sod's got the details…" Maxine suddenly stiffened, stopping mid-pavement. Bev watched as rain-drops dripped from the bleached bird's nest and trickled down wan cheeks. The face was easy to read. Maxine was scanning her memory bank and clicking on Bev when she'd been in uniform. The penny dropped. Bev caught its flash in the coffee-coloured eyes. "You're the cop what got me sent down."

Bev braced herself for a good slapping. The woman was already as wired as a junction box.

"I'm putting in a complaint," Maxine snapped.

As quick as that? Bev tried not to show her feelings. Signally failed.

"Not you." More snapping from Maxine. "That bastard." She jabbed a thumb over her shoulder. King was lighting up again. "Been here nigh on an hour. Done nothing but drink tea and make stupid cracks." Maxine sniffed, wiped her nose with a sleeve. "I can't stand the sodding sight of you. But at least you'll get the job done."

Bev tucked her hand under Maxine's leopard-print elbow and gently led her back to the house. She'd made a mistake. It wasn't rain running down Maxine's face. It was tears.

5

"It's just routine, Mrs Beck. We have to make sure."

Two uniforms were upstairs searching every inch of number thirteen. Maxine Beck was unaware the men had been instructed to remove bath panels, lift floorboards and check for false partitions. Bev seriously doubted they'd find a body; but grief didn't necessarily preclude guilt, and children – including three-week-old babies – are more likely to die at the hands of a supposedly loving parent than a paedophile.

That there was grief in the house was not in doubt. It had moved in, taken over, dripped off the walls.

"Whatever needs doing. Whatever it takes. We just want her back." Maxine Beck looked like a stuffed doll that had been in a fight. And lost. She was cradling her daughter in her arms. Bev hadn't recognised Natalie at first. Not surprising. The girl had been at death's door last time she'd seen her. She looked only marginally better now, though that was caused by emotion, not lung infection.

Within minutes of entering the place, Bev had assessed the girl's story and initiated a full-scale hunt while Highgate rang every news desk in the Midlands. If ever the media were called for, it was when a child went missing. In the meantime, every available officer and dog handler was either on or en route to the Wordsworth estate.

And Les King was already on gardening leave. Bev had heard on the Highgate grapevine that the guv had come close to decking the lazy slob. There'd be an inquest later as to why King had dragged his feet. But if Byford had any say, the suspension would be permanent. Les King had lost them precious time. How much more had been wasted was unclear. What Bev knew, or had been told, was that Baby Zoë had been asleep in her cot at 3am. By 9.10am the baby had vanished. Now the nursery looked as if it had been ransacked, but that was because Natalie had up-ended everything in sight to find the one thing she couldn't. The empty cot told its own story. God knew what it was doing to the Becks. Bev knew it would loom large in her nightmares.

"Let's run through it again, Natalie."

The girl was sixteen going on thirty. Think scrawny Britney Spears on a bad hair day. Bad everything, Bev reckoned. Lank blonde locks framed sullen features dotted with spots. Natalie mumbled a few words into her mother's neck. Maxine looked as if she'd never let her go. They were cuddled up on the sofa opposite, a brown mock-leather affair scarred with cigarette burns and stained with what looked like red wine. A baby's dummy was wedged at the back of a cushion.

"The time you got in? Can you narrow it down at all?" Bev looked her notes. A rare occurrence: Oz usually took care of the written word. DC Khan – lucky best man – was at a wedding in Brighton. According to Bev's scrawl, Natalie had arrived home after midnight but before 2am. Talk about window of opportunity.

Natalie eased herself from Maxine's embrace and sat clutching her bare mottled legs. "Can't remember."

"Why's that?"

She shrugged, concentrated on her toenails. "Just can't."

Bev wondered why girls Natalie's age, any age come to that, thought it was cool to have pierced eyebrows. Ears yeah, nose maybe. But eyebrows? It was painful just thinking about it. She tried another tack. "Did you notice anything out the ordinary? Door unlocked? Window open?"

"Nah. Nuffin'."

Blood. Stone. Out of. Bev didn't think Natalie was being deliberately obstructive or evasive. She reckoned the teenager had been on the piss. Alcohol fumes were wafting across. On the other hand, they could just as easily be emanating from Maxine.

"What about your mates? Anyone see you back?"

It was an innocent question, so why the furtive look? Guilt? Shock? Bev wasn't sure. The recovery was too quick for further pondering. "Yeah, my friend and me got off the same stop. That's right. We walked back together."

Bev jotted down the friend's address.

"How about you, Mrs Beck? You reckoned it was three when you got up. Anything strike you as odd?"

"No. Like I say, I went to the loo. Poked me head round. The baby was fine. I give her a bottle…"

"You didn't mention a bottle." Bev checked her notes. Unless she'd missed it first time… nope, nada. "Did you or didn't you?"

It didn't take a lot to confuse Maxine. She dropped her head into her hands.

"Leave her alone. It's no big deal." Natalie was only looking out for her mother. But the hostility was unnecessary. Bev was looking out for a three-week-old who could be starving to death, assuming she was still alive.

Still, Bev thought, it wasn't surprising the Becks' recall was a tad hazy, since it was clear they were both out of their heads with worry. Everywhere they looked was a reminder of what they'd lost. The small sitting room was littered with baby gear; Mothercare meets the Disney Store.

"Is it just the three of you here?" Natalie and Maxine seemed to avoid each other's eyes. Bev wasn't sure what to read into it, but her antennae twitched. "Well?"

She got a yes from Maxine and a no from Natalie. She sighed, while they sorted it.

"Terry's my bloke, like," Maxine said. "But he don't live here."

Natalie's snort suggested otherwise.

"He don't," Maxine whinged. "He's got his own place over Selly Oak way."

Another snort.

"He stays over once in a blue moon." Maxine conceded.

"And last night?" Bev asked. "Was the moon blue?"

"No." Maxine was adamant.

Bev turned her gaze on Beck junior. The girl shrugged. "Weren't here, was I?"

Bev added Terry Roper's name and address to the pot. Dear God, let it come to the boil soon.

"Is Zoë's dad round, love?" As if. Round here, lad-dads were called feafos: fuck-'em-and-fuck-offs.

"She hasn't got a dad," Natalie snarled.

Bev nodded. "Immaculate conception, then?"

"Don't be a smart-arse. You know what I mean. I don't need a bloke. I'm bringing the kid up on me own." The words' import registered and the girl's face crumpled like a soggy kleenex.

Bev regretted the snide remark. It had done neither of them any good. "I'm sorry, Natalie. But we need to speak to Zoë's father."

"Leave her alone," Maxine hissed. "Look at her."

Mascara-stained tears trickled through Natalie's fingers and down her wrists as she shook and sobbed.

Bev sighed. They needed the man's name and address. A breather, that's all she could spare the girl. "Have a think about it, love. It could help us find Zoë. That's what we're all after here, isn't it?"

"'Kay."

It wasn't a yes, but it wasn't a no. For an hour or two, she'd settle for an OK. "I'm almost done," she smiled. "Can one of you sort that picture for me?" Baby Zoë. Not happy snaps. Not right now.

Maxine hauled herself off the sofa. Natalie was picking her nails again. Bev ran back through her notes. It was a start, but she had a feeling she'd be seeing a hell of a lot more of the Becks over the next few days.

Sounds of police activity drifted in from the street: radio static, slamming doors, barking dogs, raised voices. She heard the guv's. She was itching to get out there but had to hang round to brief the family liaison officer, Mandy Forsyth, who'd be babysitting the Becks. Though no one would use the expression within earshot.

"Nat, have you moved them photos?"

Natalie had not. She abandoned her pedicure to lend a hand in the search. Mandy Forsyth turned up twenty minutes later; the photographs didn't. Great, Bev thought. The media circus was in town to show off a missing baby, and they didn't even have a black-and-white still.

Big questions were: who did? And where were they?

Brindley Place was ten minutes from Balsall Heath and about a million miles. The canal-side development was one of the coolest jewels in Birmingham's burgeoning crown. Vibrant and bustling, it boasted the top bars and clubs, the chicest restaurants and galleries. It was bright lights and big-city buzz. If you were really lucky – and loaded – you lived there. Helen and David Carver had held their apartment-warming three years ago.

Now framed in their big picture window, Helen gazed

down on the activity below. Garishly painted narrow boats bobbed or glided on the surface of the water. A few hardy tourists juggled umbrellas and Nikons, snapping the pub where Bill Clinton had sipped a pint and inhaled chips. Helen remembered when dumped prams and dead rats were about the only entertainment on offer around the canal, and in it. Brindley Place, like Helen Carver, had come a long way.

Gently, very gently, she eased the baby into a more comfortable position. The last thing she wanted was Jessica to wake and cry again. But she was like a dead weight, hot and sticky, on Helen's neck. Holding her breath, she carefully laid the baby on the settee, watching anxiously as an incipient protest faded and Jessica drifted back to sleep.

Helen tugged at the long sleeves of her high-neck blouse, trying to relax. She'd seen the story about the missing baby on the TV news. It was shocking, of course, but she'd virtually tuned out when the location was mentioned. The Wordsworth estate was notorious across the country, let alone the city, for its sky-high crime rate and dysfunctional lowlifes. Helen shuddered; it was no place for a baby.

She gazed down at her own child. She and David had tried for years to start a family. They had a gorgeous home, exotic holidays, top-of-the-range cars, but it had begun to pall without a baby. And now? Helen dabbed angrily at a drying patch of milky sick on the shoulder of her blouse. It wasn't that she didn't love Jessica; but why hadn't the books mentioned the *mess*, and the draining, seemingly endless exhaustion?

Shaking her head as if to banish the negative thoughts, she stroked Jessica's cheek. The blemish was barely noticeable, really. Her mouth tightened as the child farted, rigid and red-faced. Another smelly nappy. Wrinkling her nose,

Helen drew back a cuff, checked her Gucci watch. It could wait until her mother-in-law, Veronica, returned with the shopping.

She picked up a copy of *Vogue,* leafed desultorily through a few pages. Jessica writhed and grizzled. Helen threw the magazine petulantly across the room and went to lift the child just as a key turned in the door. Thank God. Veronica would deal with it. Helen could sleep for an hour, maybe two. That was all she needed. She was so tired these days, what with her hormones and everything.

6

"My daughter's shattered, inspector. I'll grant you a few minutes. And I'll sit in. Naturally."

Mike Powell, accompanied by DC Carol Mansfield, was paying an unscheduled house call on Martha Kemp. He was spitting spikes but smiled politely and made sure his eyes did as well. Body language was Morriss's big thing but he reckoned he was more fluent. Take Kemp's rigid stance, tight lips. They screamed that she was in the wrong and knew it.

The radio presenter had insisted her daughter's questioning take place at home. After clearing it with the police doctor, she'd whisked Laura away. No problem with that. Except she hadn't bothered to inform anyone at Highgate. For nearly an hour, Powell had hung round the place waiting to talk to the girl. Now he was being spoken to as if he was some bloody tradesman at the door. The only surprise was she hadn't ordered them round the back. Mind, it was a classy pad. Moseley was full of them, more precisely Ludgate Hill was. Kemp's castle, so to speak, was a double-fronted, three-storeyed Edwardian spread.

She led the way up a curving carved staircase as Powell checked out marble floors and big mirrors, Regency stripes and old paintings. Carol, who he reckoned was nursing a cold, was bringing up the rear. She shouldn't have much to do. Sitting-in job really, like Martha Kemp. He'd do the talking.

Laura Kenyon, bolstered by pillows, was sitting up in a four-poster bed that was covered in candyfloss. Netting and drapes, actually, but Powell didn't do soft furnishings. He did know Laura looked like a princess, the fairytale kind. Stick a petit pois under her mattress and she wouldn't get a wink of sleep. She'd had none last night. There were coffee-coloured smudges under double-glazed eyes. She didn't even try to stifle a yawn.

Given Laura's fragile state, Powell tried to cover the main points first; mop-up sessions would follow. It appeared Laura was grabbed from behind as she walked home from a friend's house in Fair View, half a mile from the rape scene off the Alcester Road. The attacker dragged her through a gap in the wire fencing, then down the slope to the abandoned rail line.

"What time was this, Laura?" he asked.

"I kind of lost track, sorry."

He let it go for the moment, concentrated on physical details of her assailant. He was taller and heavier than her – she was probably a size eight – but she couldn't estimate by how much. He'd put some sort of bag over her head and tied her hands behind her back. And threatened to kill her if she screamed.

"What about the voice, Laura? Young? Old? Any accent?"

She shook her head. "The mask... Everything was muffled."

And she'd been so terrified she could barely breathe. He had a knife. And scissors. As with the other victims, he'd further violated Laura by hacking off her pubic hair. For Laura it was almost the worst moment in an ordeal that had lasted... how long? Powell still hadn't got a fix on the timings. The triple-nine had come in at 5am after she'd dragged herself up to the wire fence and been spotted by a shift-worker. She'd either left her friend's house way too late to be walking home alone or she'd lain around down there for hours.

"You're doing really well, Laura." There was a warm smile in Carol Mansfield's voice. Powell had forgotten she was there.

He asked Laura if the attacker had said anything before fleeing.

"He warned me not to move. Said he'd cut me. He untied my hands. Ordered me to close my eyes. Removed the bag…"

Powell pounced on what that could mean. "And you saw…?" The prompt came out more like a prod.

The tears that had threatened throughout coursed down her cheeks. "I was scared. My eyes were closed. I was tired… So very, very tired…"

And she fell asleep? Powell found that hard to believe. Unless she'd been on the jolly juice. "Were you…?"

"That's enough for now." Martha Kemp's voice brooked no argument. Hands tucked under her armpits, she'd listened to every word from the foot of the bed. Carol Mansfield thought the woman would be better occupied comforting her daughter. Laura was in bits.

They were at the bedroom door when Mansfield turned. "Just one thing, Laura. Did your attacker take anything? An earring, perhaps?"

"No." A trembling hand shot to her earlobe. "No. I wasn't wearing any."

The answer was quick. Too quick? "You're sure?" Mansfield asked.

"She's sure," Kemp spat. "Look at her. Don't you think he took enough?"

Mike Powell was behind the wheel. He wanted another look at the crime scene and it was always good to keep the guys on their toes. It was a bit stop-start; traffic was generally slow through Moseley on farmers'-market Saturdays. He glanced at his passenger. Carol Mansfield was dabbing her nose with a tissue. As well as the sniffs, her eyes were streaming. He hoped to God he'd not come down with it as well. Aside from the cold, he reckoned she was well fit. He liked his women with curves. He preferred petite blondes and Mansfield was tall and very dark but at least she wasn't lippy. Like Morriss.

"What were you going to ask Laura, sir?" There was a blank look on his face. "You didn't get the question out. Ma Kemp called time."

Of course. He'd made a mental note to check with the medical man. "Blood tests. Jot it down, would you, love?"

Patronising prick. "Blood tests?"

"Yeah. I was going to ask if she'd been drinking. Could be why she was out of it for so long. And how she ended up in it in the first place."

"How d'you mean?" As if she didn't know.

"Girls nowadays, go out of a night, get tanked up. Alcohol lowers the resistance. And a few other things, if you get my drift."

She was beginning to understand Bev's deep antipathy for the guy. She bit her tongue.

"I'm not saying they ask for it…" He checked his hair in the driving mirror.

"That's exactly what you're saying. And it's bollocks." It just came out.

The lack of a comeback suggested he suspected he'd gone too far; he was certainly taken aback. He cast a surreptitious glance: bloody woman was probably on the rag.

The continuing silence was punctuated by the odd sniff. He switched the wipers off, wondering how long ago the downpour had ended. He sighed. The rain would've played havoc with the crime scene. It was a quagmire down there and only a slim chance of lifting a decent cast. Fucking lethal as well. At least he had his boots with him this time. He glanced again at Carol, who was looking queasy – probably feeling a touch contrite.

"Meant to mention it before, love." He was good at people skills. "The earring? Good question. Joined-up thinking."

The eye-roll was hidden beneath a tissue. "It was Sergeant Morriss's," Mansfield offered. "She's convinced he takes them as trophies."

"Word in the shell-like, love. Morriss isn't exactly flavour of the month. I'd keep your distance if I were you. The lads call her…"

Lonely. "I'm fully aware what a handful of wankers call her. And know what? It's double bollocks. Can you open the window, sir?"

"Sure thing." Change the subject. "Need some fresh air."

"Yeah. The car stinks of shit. Did you step in something?"

7

Few crimes are bigger than child kidnap. Child murder is one. While there was the slightest chance of finding Zoë Beck alive, every available body was out there hunting. Blake Way and adjoining streets were teeming with police officers, dog handlers and squad cars. Off-duty uniforms and detectives, who'd offered their services, were swelling the ranks. Volunteers were being briefed and would be employed on non-specialist tasks. Every householder had to be interviewed; every shed, out-building, garage and lock-up searched. If Baby Zoë wasn't found quickly, leave would be cancelled and unlimited overtime up for grabs. It would be taken eagerly. Crimes against kids touched every copper. Those who committed them were scum.

Bev registered the action with a glance as she stepped out of number thirteen. The fresh air was welcome after the suffocating atmosphere inside. And it had stopped raining. Puddles still pooled and pavements glistened but a weak sun appeared, determined to shine.

At six-five, Superintendent Bill Byford was a head above most of his officers and head and shoulders above the press pack. Bev spotted him, standing out against a roiling sea of pushy hacks shoving mics and camera lenses in his face. The notebooks had been shunted to the back.

With half an ear and growing incredulity, she listened to a string of questions that at this stage no one could answer and at any stage no one should ask. It was a close call, but most crass was: how's the mother feeling? The usually unflappable Byford was riled. She saw it in the tightened jaw and raised palms. The journalists must be fully aware nothing further would be released before the one o'clock news conference. She checked the time: 12.15. Three hours since the baby was reported missing. She closed her eyes, mouthed a silent prayer.

Unless God now answered prayers via a mobile, someone else was trying to get through. She ferreted for her phone in the depths of a seemingly bottomless shoulder bag. The number displayed didn't ring a bell. She adopted her I'm-a-busy-woman-don't-bother-me voice.

"Nick Lockwood here."

"Nick?" Beeb bloke. Boyish fringe. Brown eyes. Beer gut. Not exactly a pleasure but it could be worse. "What can I do for you?"

He laughed. "Don't sound so suspicious."

"It's in the job description, mate." She listened to the newsman's take on events at the crime scene in Moseley that morning, realised that the baby snatch had pushed Street Watch on to one of her many mental back burners. Powell's pratfall was a laugh but she had the nous to know Lockwood was after something in return.

"I'm after a new line, Bev."

At least he was up front. "I'm not up to speed, mate. I'm on the missing baby. I'll have a sniff round, get back to you if I come up with anything." Hacks weren't her favourite people but she knew the old saying about tents and urine.

"Appreciate it." She sensed there was more. "Don't fancy a drink tonight, do you?"

It would be a miracle if she was off before midnight. "Prince of Wales 'bout eight?"

No harm in keeping him sweet. She felt a hand on her shoulder as she stuffed the phone back into her bag.

"Sergeant?" Byford, fresh from the media mauling,

wanted the top lines from the Beck interviews. He'd listen carefully to every word, keep his thoughts to himself until she'd finished. That was his way. Like lowering his voice when he was about to erupt. Like making his face a blank screen. Bev often tried copying the technique. Hers was an open book with pop-up illustrations.

After digesting the gist, his neutral knack appeared to have deserted him. The big man's screen was showing a double feature: frustration and fury. Not surprising. He had two grown-up sons, third grandkid on the way.

When he heard there were no photographs of Zoë, Byford shook his head and sighed. The image of a missing child had immense impact on the emotions of a telly-viewing, newspaper-reading public. Some may already have seen something significant; others might, over the next few hours and days. With thousands of potential witnesses out there, the importance of a visual was impossible to over-estimate. "For Christ's sake, Bev. A baby's only got to break wind and its parents shoot a roll of film."

In Perfect Land maybe, where mummy and daddy live happily ever after. "That's another thing, guv. We haven't got a steer on the kid's dad yet. Natalie won't say who he is."

"We'll see about that." He stroked an eyebrow. Ominous.

She didn't fancy Natalie Beck's chances in a run-in with the big man. Not in his current frame of mind. Given how long the guv had been around, it was odds-on he'd been one of the officers on the Baby Fay abduction in the late eighties. The tiny body – burned and abused – wasn't discovered for three weeks. The kidnapper never found. As a schoolgirl, Bev had followed the news coverage with equal degrees of horror and fascination. Details were hazy but going by the guv's grim face, now would not be a good time to ask him to share.

"You the cop been talking to Maxine Beck?"

She swung round, eyes flashing, as a hand tapped her bum. It was attached to one of the best-looking blokes she'd seen in a long time. But it wasn't aesthetic appeal that saved him from a verbal hammering. It was what he clutched in his other mitt.

Bev took it from him without speaking. The photograph was probably a good likeness; shame the baby's eyes were closed. Little Zoë was asleep on her back, tiny perfect fingers loosely splayed, wisps of pale blonde hair only just discernible on a head fragile as eggshell. Bev bit her lip. The line about newborns all looking like Winston Churchill was dead wrong.

"Where's the rest?" she snapped. The pic was lovely but not brilliant for publicity posters and handouts.

The guy shrugged. "Can't help with that. Sorry." It was the only photograph around because it was the only one Maxine Beck had given away. Terry Roper – Mr Blue Moon – said he'd driven over with it the minute he heard it was needed. Max had phoned and told him to look out for a woman cop in blue with a chin-length bob and a mouth on her.

"She was right." Roper winked. "'Bout the blue."

Bev arched an eyebrow Byford-fashion, didn't return the cheeky grin. She had him down as Lovejoy meets Jack the lad: an alumnus of easy-charm school. His soft black curls looked just washed and striking slate-grey eyes glinted from a face that could sell skin-care products. He was only five-six but every inch looked as if it visited health clubs. Daily. The leather coat was dark chocolate, the chinos and granddad shirt mocha and milk. Tasty.

"Where were you last night?" Bev didn't beat around

bushes. Not when a baby could be hidden there.

"I was with Max," he said.

Bev narrowed her eyes. So Max was telling porkies.

"Till half-eleven."

Had she given Maxine's lie away in her face? Roper's was doing a poker. A diamond stud twinkled in his left earlobe.

"And then?"

He'd gassed the car and picked up a balti on the way home. Bev wrote times and names. "We'll check. Naturally."

It should have taken the wind out of his overblown sails, but he only nodded. "I've probably got receipts in the motor if it'll get me out of the frame."

"Watch *The Bill*, do you?" Bloody cops-on-the-box. Telly addicts knew as much police procedure as some of the uniforms.

"I'm not thick, sergeant. Stands to reason you'll look at anyone who knows the family. But do it quick. 'Cause some bastard out there's got the baby. And if I get to him first, he'll be lucky if he survives." Roper's fists were clenched at his side. The tremor was detectable, as were the tears in his eyes.

Easy words. Byford had heard it all before. "We'll need to talk to you again, Mr Roper."

"You'll find me at Max's. I'm staying here till this thing's sorted."

They watched him walk away, then headed for the motor. As Byford got in, he pointed skywards. A stunning double rainbow overarched the ugly sprawl of the Wordsworth estate.

"Know what, guv?" Bev said. "I'd rather find the baby. You can stick the pot of gold."

8

Bernie Flowers, the head of the police news bureau, had commandeered Highgate's biggest conference room. The vast space only just coped with the numbers. The media turnout here was almost on a par with that of the officers flooding the Wordsworth estate.

A baby-snatch wasn't a filler at the bottom of an inside page. Zoë Beck's tiny face would be splashed across every newspaper and television in the country, posters would soon be going up all over the Midlands and uniform would shortly be swamping the city with thousands of leaflets. Within hours the baby's image would be imprinted on the national psyche in the same way as that of James Bulger, Holly Wells, Jessica Chapman, Sarah Payne... The list was too long. To Bev's way of thinking, one child's name was too many.

She was uncomfortably hot and sweaty under the telly lights and she had to keep screwing her eyes against the glare coming off the table. It was distracting and something was bugging her; she couldn't pin down the errant niggle. She itched to get back to the action. Under the conference table's highly polished mahogany her legs jiggled, desperate to get up and go. Sitting on her butt listening to stupid questions was a complete waste of time. Four hours and counting since that empty cot was found.

She glanced right. Though Byford was in the hot seat, Bernie was taking most of the flak. Not that he couldn't handle it; a passing resemblance to John Major was misleading. Bernie was a grey suit but had one of the brightest brains in the nick, not to mention a technicolor turn of phrase. He'd started in news on Fleet Street and ended up editing a redtop in Docklands. Not a bad background for dealing with the current barrage.

"I'm not dodging the question, mate. I don't have the answer." Bernie poured water into a glass, glanced up and gave a tight smile. "Next." He'd already given them the bare bones of the incident. There was no meat to offer.

The reporters now had a name and timings: when Zoë was last seen, when her absence was discovered. They'd been asked to go big on witness appeals and hot-line numbers for the public to ring. Someone, the cliché goes, must have seen something. Bev reckoned they invariably had and it was usually Elvis galloping round the Bullring on Shergar. Whatever. Experienced officers would vet the calls, ditching the dross and the loony tunes. Other teams were already going through paedo registers and child-porn sites. Still more were checking every crime, cold case or not, anywhere in the country, that bore the slightest resemblance to the taking of Baby Zoë.

None of this satisfied the journos. The pack was after the mother. A harrowing tearful plea for the baby's safe return was *the* story at this early stage. Bev knew the guv had thought long and hard but eventually vetoed all requests. Saturation coverage was a given in the first day or so. When it began to flag, he could whisk Natalie from the wings and inject more impetus.

She also knew – because he'd told her – that he hoped it wouldn't come to that. There was another less palatable reason for not putting Natalie Beck out there for public consumption. A surly sixteen-year-old from a grotty estate on the wrong side of town was a hell of a lot less appealing than a picture of her three-week-old baby.

Being denied the star of the show wasn't the only

reason the press were hacked off. The guv had also quashed requests to be interviewed live on lunchtime news bulletins. Byford didn't give a toss about journalists' deadlines. Not when he had one of his own. Bev knew the big man would happily do a turn – Christ, he'd cartwheel down New Street in the buff – if and when there was something worth saying. She watched him scribbling furiously into a notebook: ideas, reminders, checks, passing notions. He'd carry the pad around, adding more lines as inspiration struck. It was another Byford habit. Not one to which Bev subscribed.

"You're already stretched with the rapes. Will you be getting in reinforcements?"

Byford's pen stopped mid-sentence. Bernie opened his mouth to speak but the guv was already there. "My officers are professionals. They're dedicated men and women who're coping brilliantly. If the situation changes I'll let you know." His glance covered everyone in the room. "Just don't hold your breath."

"Loyalty to the troops. That's nice." Mr Supercilious was on his feet this time. Tall, rake-thin, gold-framed glasses and lank hair scraped back in a tiny ponytail. Bev didn't recognise him. "Do you have teenage daughters, superintendent?" Instantly clear where he was coming from.

"No, I don't, Mr…?"

"Squires. Colin. Sky News. I've been talking to last night's rape victim. She's warning girls and older women to stay off the streets."

"You can't use it," Bernie said. "You know the score on anonymity."

Squires flapped a hand. "She's waived her rights."

"Who put her up to that?" Byford snapped.

"Ask the mother. Not me." The audience was riveted. Squires was enjoying the attention. "Point is, superintendent, are you adding your voice to the victim's warning? Or are you confident you can guarantee the safety of every woman on the streets of Birmingham – when most of your people are currently searching for a missing baby?"

That was catch 22-and-a-half. While the guv worked on an answer that wouldn't land him in it, the women's editor of the *Evening News* threw in another question.

"Are you aware of the mass street protest?"

This time the guv's blank look was genuine. So was Bev's.

Celia Bissell, a tall forty-something redhead, turned a sheet of her spiral-bound notebook. As if she had to. "Yeah, details have just been released. Monday night, a march following the route of the latest attack, then a candlelit vigil. The WAR party's organising it. They're expecting thousands. Could turn nasty."

Nothing to do with Bush or Blair – this was Women Against Rape, formed a few weeks back in response to Operation Street Watch. The news of the demo was a bit of a bombshell. Bev had quite a few contacts among the women but she hadn't heard a whisper.

"We'll be there in force," Byford said, gathering his papers. "The West Midlands Force."

"I've put Mike Powell in charge of Street Watch." Byford kept his glance straight ahead as he pulled out of the car park at Highgate. Bev's partially masticated cheese and onion pasty nearly choked her.

"Watch what you're doing with the crumbs." He brushed crust from a knee.

It was the closest he'd come to fast food since the IBS was diagnosed earlier in the year. He watched his diet like a hungry hawk and drank copious amounts of peppermint tea. Bev ate on the hoof so often she'd almost forgotten how to use cutlery. She'd grabbed crisps and pasty from the canteen and the latter was still slowing her verbal response. Which was lucky, given what she had in mind.

She reckoned Powell was slipping already and not just in the dog-doo. She couldn't say anything to the guv because it'd get Carol Mansfield in the shit as well – tales out of school and all that. But Inspector Clouseau had failed to bring up a couple of potentially significant points during the interview with Laura Kenyon.

They were desperate to discover a link between all three girls. Through careful questioning, Bev had elicited that the first victim, Rebecca Fox, had recently had a butterfly tattoo on her shoulder. Bev even talked to the guy who put it there. Come to think of it, it might be worth having another word in a day or two. Mental note: call Luke Mangold. Sod Powell.

The DI's scepticism was partly down to the fact that when questioned, the second victim, Kate Quinn, said she'd never set foot inside a parlour, let alone been tattooed. So Powell hadn't even bothered raising the subject with Laura.

According to Carol, he'd pooh-poohed the suggestion. After the women had recovered from another fit of the dog-shit giggles, Carol dropped the DI in it further by telling Bev that he'd neglected to ask Laura whether she was a student and, if so, where she studied. Carol had gleaned the information from Laura's mother on the way out. Martha Kemp mentioned a name that had popped up earlier in the inquiry: Queen's College in Edgbaston. It was an obvious lead, and one Bev so wanted to pursue.

Byford broke her train of thought. "I'll still be very much around. But I want you to head up the baby case."

"But, guv…"

"But nothing. I know you've built a rapport with the girls and I know you want to nick the bastard…"

His profile gave nothing away but the silence was telling. "You think the baby's dead, don't you?" Bev asked. And a child murder would take priority over Street Watch.

If he gripped the wheel any tighter it'd come off in his hands. When he spoke, the voice was unutterably sad, didn't even sound like the guv's. "Babies don't get snatched from their cots at home, Bev. Think of the big cases over the years. Babies get taken from maternity wards. Women desperate for a baby of their own sneaking into hospitals and stealing someone else's. Generally speaking, with newborns, it's all over in a day or two. The baby's returned safe and well; woman gets counselling, probation, maybe a suspended slap on the wrist."

"Generally speaking…?" She reckoned there was one case not covered by the norm.

"I only know one instance where a tiny baby was grabbed from her home."

And she was found dead.

"I'll get the Baby Fay case files out when we get back," Bev said.

Byford glanced at her for the first time since they got in the car. "I've already put them on your desk."

"Just fuck off, will you? She ain't talking."

Terry Roper was hurling obscenities through the warped door of number thirteen. If he had the sense he was born with, he'd have realised it wasn't yet another door-stepping journalist after an exclusive with the baby's mother. Though a bunch of snappers was huddled across the road, zoom lenses poised to shoot.

Bev flicked a glance at the guv. It was an exclusive chat with the baby's *father* they were after. And Terry Roper hadn't got a prayer of getting in the way.

"For Christ's sake," she hissed. "It's the police; open up." Bev was hoping Byford's paternal presence might persuade Natalie to open up as well, on the sensitive issue of Zoë's paternity.

Roper, all abject apology and ingratiating smiles, led them into the tiny sitting room. It stank of vinegar and stale smoke. Mother and daughter were still bonding on the settee. Held by an invisible umbilical cord, they looked as if they hadn't budged a centimetre since Bev's first visit, though Natalie's bare legs now bore corned-beef marbling from the gas fire.

"Cuppa tea?" Roper offered.

The coffee table was littered with enough mugs to open a seconds shop. Noting the colour and consistency of the dregs, Bev declined. She almost succumbed to Roper's proffered pack of Marlboro. Three months she'd gone without so much as a puff... But when she went to take one the guv's glare persuaded her it was a bad move.

Social niceties out of the way, Byford got to the point. "I want you to know, Natalie, that we're doing everything in our power to find Zoë." He ran through the current police activity while mother and daughter supped tea and swallowed smoke.

Bev crossed her legs and took out a notebook. Jeez, she'd be glad when Oz was around again. The hard chairs weren't conducive to comfort, which was fine by her; the second-hand oxygen was soporific. She sat back and observed the big man in action. Byford was good at this stuff: open body language, voice pitched right, just enough Brummie accent to make Natalie feel at home. She wasn't exactly putty in his hands, but he was working on it.

The guv wasn't Bev's only focus. She was trying to get her head round the Maxine-Terry Roper thing. His appeal was obvious but Maxine's charms were all but hidden these days. And not just by a shapeless sludge-coloured shell-suit.

Bev looked closer, tried to imagine the woman in decent gear, hair combed, a touch of make-up. It wasn't that hard. There was some decent raw material under the rough exterior. Maxine might carry a few extra kilos but so had Monroe. And though currently puffy and pasty, Maxine's face had the kind of bone structure a lot of women paid through the nose for. It might no longer launch a thousand ships, but it'd have no problem with the odd longboat or two. As for Maxine's intellect, Terry Roper probably wasn't with her for cerebral stimulation.

Right now Mr Blue Moon was eagerly perched on an armchair close by the Beck women. He was all rapt attention, elbows on his knees, fingers steepled under his dimpled chin, switching his gaze to whoever was speaking. Natalie was currently in the spotlight. For the umpteenth time she was saying – in effect – diddlysquat.

"Honest, I'd tell you if I could."

The guv must be feeling the heat; he was running a finger along his collar line. "Natalie, the lad isn't in trouble." It was probably true. "We need to have a word with him, that's all."

With any fellow who'd been in spitting distance, let alone shagging.

The girl was picking a crusty scab on her elbow. "I've said. I can't tell you."

"Can't or won't?" A tad impatient now.

"Leave her alone." Maxine glared. "She's going through hell."

Byford hunched forward, palms up and out. "We need your help on this, Natalie." He lowered his voice to barely a whisper. "So does Zoë."

The silence lasted ten seconds, fifteen... Bev reached twenty-one before it was shattered by Natalie's ear-splitting scream. Muffled by sobs, her words were still distinguishable, though the precise meaning was unclear. "I can't tell you because I don't fucking *know*!"

How many men had she slept with? Two? Twenty-two?

Bev winced as the teenager tore viciously at the scab; fresh blood oozed from raw skin. Roper grabbed a tissue and gently dabbed the weeping site until Maxine snatched it away, took over the nursing. Bev caught a fleeting exchange of glances between Natalie and Roper, but it wasn't easy to read.

"Names, then, Natalie." The guv's voice was neutral. "We're going to need names."

"You'll be lucky." Her eyes flashed, defiant now. "I don't know all the fucking names."

A moue of distaste flickered across Byford's features. Bev doubted anyone else had noticed. "Then you'd better start with those you do." Splinters of ice.

Maxine stubbed a butt into an overworked ashtray. "I'm her mum, Mr Byford, and I'm buggered if I know who's had his leg over."

Byford passed a hand over his face. What could he say? Bev retrieved a cold greasy chip from the floor, tossed it in a mug, then jerked sideways to avoid a backlash of tepid tea. Kids were playing ball in the street; excited shouts and laughter mingled with bursts of static from police radios.

The rasp of a match indicated Maxine was on her next

nicotine hit. Must be catching. Roper lit a Marlboro, tapped Natalie's shoulder and handed her the baccy. Bev caught another furtive exchange. Was something dodgy going on there? Had Terry been keeping it in the family, so to speak? Was Maxine's toy-boy Zoë's dad? It could explain Natalie's adamant refusal to come up with a name.

Bev gave it some more thought. Despite Maxine's slap-dash – to say the least – parenting skills, she didn't doubt Natalie's deep love for her mum. And vice versa. On the other hand, if it turned out Maxine was doting granny to her own lover's baby... The familial knock-on didn't bear thinking about. But its implications were a damn sight more serious. It provided a hell of a motive to get rid of the kid.

SOCOs had taken the house apart and found nothing incriminating. Had they been looking in the wrong place?

Roper broke the silence. "Natalie." He paused, waiting for her to make eye contact. "No point hiding it any more. I think it's time you told them the truth."

The baby was lying on the bed next to the mousy woman. For hours now, she'd been stroking the fine down that feathered the tiny scalp, fascinated by the gentle flicker of a pulse under the translucent skin of the fontanelle. The child was glorious, perfect; the woman thought she could happily gaze forever into those innocent trusting eyes. She could barely drag herself away, but the next bottle wouldn't prepare itself.

She'd hoped to feed the baby herself, but didn't have the milk. It was unfortunate but not a tragedy. Still, it would have been wonderful to feel the baby's cheek on her breast, those gorgeous lips clamped greedily around her nipple, those deep-blue-sea eyes staring adoringly as tiny fingers stroked her flesh. The mousy woman sighed. Surely a bond like that could never be broken?

Gingerly, she eased herself from the bed and gazed down at the tiny wriggling form on the vast mattress. She loved the baby so much it hurt. There was a physical pain in her heart when she thought of all the horrors in the world, the terrible things that could befall the child. Any child. Then she laughed out loud. What rubbish! She'd never allow anything bad to happen to that tiny baby. She'd rather die. Or kill.

The child was sleepy now, white-blue eyelids growing heavy. The mousy woman nuzzled the warm tiny neck, drinking in the precious baby-smell. But if she didn't prepare the bottle soon, it would be too late. The baby would drop off, dead to the world, then wake starving and fractious. Again.

A shadow of a frown appeared briefly on the mousy woman's forehead. The baby did seem to cry a lot.

It wasn't necessary to pass through the nursery to get to the kitchen. The detour and the tapping of the mobile had become a habit, a superstition almost. With the touch of a finger she set it in gentle motion, then stood back smiling as the rainbow swayed and countless sequins glittered in a thin shaft of weak sunlight.

How, she wondered, how could anyone ever harm a single hair on the head of a tiny child?

9

When Terry Roper suggested Natalie tell the truth, it was a close call which of the Beck women was more horrified. Maxine was dumbstruck, slack mouth gaping open, hand clasping her chest. Had she suspected it all along? Had she detected traces of Roper in the baby's features? Roper's face revealed nothing now. Unlike Natalie's. It was wide-eyed, pleading with the man to keep his trap shut.

"Come on, Nats," he cajoled. "It'll be better for everyone if you tell them."

Her bottom lip trembled, panda eyes begging him to stop.

Roper glanced at Bev, shrugged an 'over to you'.

"Let me take a wild guess," Bev said to Natalie, acutely aware the teenager was the only person in the room not looking at her. In an ideal world, Bev would've run her thoughts past the guv first. But this was Balsall Heath. And she knew what she'd seen.

"Zoë's dad's not a million miles away from this room, is he?"

More shifty looks and furtive glances. Bev couldn't keep up with the optical delusions.

"Enough." Byford's patience was paper-thin. "There's no time to piss about playing games," he snapped. "What the fuck's going on?" This from a man who reckoned swearing was the sign of a shit vocabulary.

The Becks and Blue Moon struggled for words. Bev cleared her throat. "The baby's father? My money's on him." She pointed at Roper. "That right, Terry? You the loving dad?"

Raucous laughter from the street broke a stunned silence.

No one in the room was amused, especially Natalie. "You stupid fucking bint." The words dripped vitriol.

Bev shrugged. She didn't expect a round of applause.

"I ain't snogged the bloke," the girl snarled. "Let alone shagged him."

She didn't expect that either. Or believe it. "Yeah, right."

If Natalie had been on her feet, she'd have stamped one. "Tell her, Tel. Tell the silly cow."

"I'm not the baby's father, sergeant." Roper took Natalie's hand, cradled it in his own. "Natalie barely caught a glimpse of him. She got pregnant after being raped."

The Cricketers was a pub best avoided. Big on spit, not hot on sawdust. Its regular clientele were local business-men and traders, which on the Wordsworth meant drug dealers and pimps. The landlord was a fat slap-head whose jukebox blared out pop pap and so-called rock classics. No wonder he had a hearing aid.

"Any more bright ideas?" Byford nursed a bitter lemon; Bev was two-thirds of the way down a large Grouse. They were both near the end of a long day. Just not near enough. This was a pit stop in which to tank up and thrash out a few thoughts. In theory. As it happened, she could barely hear herself think, let alone talk. Probably best. She'd mouthed off enough already.

"Bright ideas?" She raised her voice. "Fresh out."

"Small mercies." A fleeting smile took the sting from the quip.

A massive guy with bad skin and butt-length dreads ambled past, trailing ganja fumes. Bev reached out a hand to steady the table, wondering if he'd knocked it deliberately. She caught the drift of a few words muttered in his wake: pigs, off, fuck summed it up. She'd heard it before; couldn't get exercised. Not when there was so much new stuff swirling round in her head.

It had taken two hours to drag the story from Natalie Beck. Top lines, not small print. According to the girl's account, the rape happened back in January, about one in the morning. She'd been grabbed from behind and dragged into an alleyway only a couple of streets from home. The rapist had a knife and stank of beer but used a condom. She didn't think about pregnancy till the foetus was five months. Not for a nanosecond had she considered getting rid of it. Abortion was dead wrong, wasn't it? Couldn't have coped without Terry. He'd been a rock. No one else knew she'd been attacked. Especially Maxine. Her mum would have been gutted. What irony: Natalie protecting her mum.

Bev reached for the rest of her pork pie, then changed her mind. The pink bits were too reminiscent of the mottled flesh on Natalie's skinny legs. Bev's initial shock-horror-what-a-fucking-mess reaction now included real anger towards the Beck girl. Of course Natalie had suffered a shocking ordeal. But it was infuriating that she hadn't reported it at the time. Because there was an outside chance that Natalie could've been the Street Watch rapist's first victim.

The teenager's attack hadn't featured missing earrings or hacked pubic hair; Natalie had looked blank at both suggestions. But she *was* a young slim blonde, more or less fitting the victim profile. Maybe back then the Beast hadn't yet worked out the sick signature he'd leave in the three later attacks. Bev reached for her drink, scowling. Street Watch connection or not, the Beck girl's silence had let a rapist get away with it.

"Don't be too hard on her, Bev."

The glass stopped halfway to her mouth. How did he do that? The guv could run a stall at the end of Brighton pier: mind-reading.

"I know the horses have already bolted," Byford said. "But she is going to come in."

Natalie said she'd caught a brief glimpse of the rapist. She'd reluctantly agreed to go through the mug shots at Highgate, a none-too-pretty parade of pervs and known offenders. If that failed, she'd work with the E-fit guys, try to compile a likeness. Bev gave an eloquent snort. Eleven months after the event? Just listen to those stable doors.

"I know how you feel," the guv said. "Natalie Beck was selfish and irresponsible." He rubbed a hand over a face etched with exhaustion. "But, my God, she's paying a high price now."

Bev agreed with a sigh. Sixty-five uniforms and almost as many plain-clothes officers had trawled every inch of the Wordsworth estate. All but a couple of dozen householders had been interviewed, more than eighty statements taken. Every empty building had been entered and meticulously searched. Joe and Jo Public had put in more than two hundred calls to the hot-line numbers. The most promising were being acted on first. It was a lot of activity – and nada to show. Nothing had been thrown up that led the inquiry an inch further forward. Not a single hair of the baby's head.

Until now, the disused rail line in Moseley was the only rape scene Bev hadn't attended. This was her second cruise past in the last twenty minutes. It was approaching midnight, bed was calling but the pull of the place was too great. She left the MG on a single yellow line, grabbed a torch to augment pale moonlight, slipped on wellies and headed for the police tape.

After leaving Byford, she'd nipped back to Highgate, preferring to pore over the latest Street Watch reports than prop up the bar at The Prince with Nick Lockwood. The Beeb man had taken her last-minute cancellation in good spirits, sounding like he'd already imbibed a few anyway. As well as the written reports, she'd studied the visuals. But stills, even video, only went so far. Bev had to feel a crime scene. The smells and touch, the atmosphere, the *being there* was vital. A good cop had a sixth sense, sometimes more.

Not that she had any right to be here. Powell was in charge of the inquiry. She was on the missing-baby case. Professionally, she'd rarely been so torn. Talk about a rock and a slab of steel. Zoë's image was constantly in her head. Bev would go the extra mile and then some to get the baby back. But she owed the rape victims as well. She'd forged a bond with the first two girls. They phoned her now and again to find out if there'd been any developments, sometimes staying on the line to chat about films or frocks. Teenage things, normal things.

She didn't want to let them down, so she'd come up with a working compromise. She just hadn't told anyone at work. She'd decided to give her all to finding the baby, a hundred per cent. Then pull out more, on her own time, for the big girls: Rebecca Fox, Kate Quinn and Laura Kenyon. Though the guv had taken her off Street Watch, there was nothing to say she couldn't cast the odd glance down the road.

Carefully she started edging down the embankment to the track. The slope was drier now but she didn't want to do a Powell. What with the moonlight casting sinister shadows and the gnarled branches and twisted roots, it looked like a location from *Lord of the Rings*.

She gasped when a rat the size of an Alsatian darted for cover. There'd be colonies of the buggers round here. Imagine poor Laura lying scared and alone in the dark and rain, dehumanised, dumped like rubbish. Bev hadn't met the girl yet but hell... How do you get over something like that? She shivered, though it wasn't cold.

Another minute or so and she'd seen enough. She wasn't here to search. There was no point, not when the SOCO A-team had covered every inch. She turned to head back to the Midget and stopped so suddenly she had to shoot out a hand to keep her balance.

The crime boys hadn't been here in moonlight. Or torch-light.

It was probably a ring-pull or a shard of glass, but something near the track had definitely glinted in the light. She backed fractionally, slowly moving her head, adjusting her eye-line, trying to reproduce the exact angle at which she'd spotted it. No good. Probably a rat's eye. One more go. Carefully, she inched forward, shining the torch in the direction of whatever she'd seen. Yes: a definite glitter. Now she had a firmer fix, it was worth a closer look.

Inching and sliding, she homed in on one of the rotting sleepers. Down on her haunches, she spotted it at close quarters, reached a fingernail into the cracked timber and pulled out a tiny earring. It was silver and the diamond looked real. Bev closed her eyes, tried to call up the interview notes she'd read that evening. She was certain Laura Kenyon had told Powell she'd not been wearing earrings. Was the girl lying? And if she'd lost an earring during the attack, what had happened to the other? Was it down here as well? Or had the rapist added it to his trophy collection?

Bev held the earring between thumb and forefinger,

twirling it to catch the moon's silvery light. Deep in thought, she was unaware of a figure in the shadows, barely twenty feet away.

He was taking great pains not to be seen. Not yet. The time would come soon enough.

Gondolas, gondolas, more fucking gondolas. The Monty Python sketch popped into Bev's head every time she set foot in her new home. Only it wasn't gondolas, it was packing cases. Six months she'd been here and still hadn't located the microwave, two library books and a particularly fetching pair of French knickers. She was sick of it: bits of her life crammed into crates and cardboard boxes. Towering stacks of the stuff.

Was it lack of time? Or inclination? The Baldwin Street terrace didn't feel like home, but if she didn't do the unpacking and have her things around her it never would. Maybe she needed a housemate. Or a wife. How good would it be to come home to dinner in the oven and slippers by the fire?

She slammed a piece of granary in the toaster and checked the answer-phone. Frankie. Shit. Bev had forgotten to call that morning to put off their fun for another day. Seemed like a lifetime ago.

"Thanks a bunch, sister." Not a trace of Frankie's Italian accent. Not good, then. Bev closed her eyes. Her mate, Frankie Perlagio, was closer than a sister. And she'd let her down. Again. It was too late to call now.

Her mum's voice was next: Emmy. "Can you make lunch tomorrow, love? Roast beef and Worcesters. I'll even do you a treacle pud." The pause was deliberate. And the lowered voice. "Sadie misses you, Bev. She'd love to see you."

Bev clenched her fists. Another stick to beat herself

with. Sadie, her gran, was scared of her own shadow since a vicious battering nine months back. An intruder connected to a case Bev was working had broken into the family home. The bastard smacked Sadie round the face before hacking off her lovely long hair. Bev doubted her gran would ever fully recover.

She sighed. The chances of making lunch – even Emmy's signature Worcester puds – were as good as Bin Laden doing Big Brother. The bread popped up, burned to a crisp. She slung it in the swing bin and headed for bed. Ten minutes later she was sprawled fully dressed on top of the duvet, snoring for Europe.

The Baby Fay case files lay open across the pillow next to her.

It was twenty-two hours since Baby Zoë had last been seen alive.

Bill Byford was gazing at the sprawl of city lights glittering like diamonds and ice in the indigo distance. Sleep was a long way off too. He'd got up, made tea, brought it back to the bedroom. He'd been looking out for twenty minutes, looking back nearly twenty years.

The superintendent didn't need the case files to remember Baby Fay. He'd been a uniformed sergeant when she'd been snatched in '88. He and another officer had found the body. Byford had come close to a career change. Only the thought of watching a sick pervert go down for the rest of his life had kept him going. And the loving support of his wife. Margaret had died six years ago. Byford still missed her like a limb.

An anonymous letter had told the police to search a building site over in Chelmsley Wood where the foundations for a new school were being laid. Without the tip-off they'd probably never have found the baby. The tiny body had been stuffed into filthy sacking; covered in concrete dust, she'd resembled a miniature mummy. The pathologist recorded twenty-three broken bones, eleven cigarette burns and indications of sexual abuse. Fay lived in Byford's head now. Always would.

The baby had been snatched from her cot in the middle of the night from a white, middle-class family in Northfield. Fay was six months old and the parents' only child. Within a year of burying her, they'd separated. The father took off to America, if Byford remembered right. The mother took an overdose. She died three weeks later without regaining consciousness.

He pressed his head against the window, welcoming the cool on his clammy skin. It took three long weeks to find Fay. After eighteen years, they still hadn't caught the evil monster who'd killed her.

10

"Brought you a stick of rock."

Bev looked up from a desk that was in imminent danger of collapse from paper-fatigue. Oz's smiling face was the last thing she expected to see poking round the incident-room door. She hoped, very much, that the rest of DC Khan was present in the corridor. It was. He strolled in, looking considerably tastier than the proffered stick of sugar and E-numbers. Man in black, today: fitted linen trousers, torso-hugging t-shirt. Lucky t-shirt. It was easy to forget how staggeringly fit Oz was in the flesh: classic bone structure, big brown eyes and first-degree brain. What more could a girl want? A peck on the cheek would be good. No one else was around. Not this early on a Sunday.

Bev had been in since 6am. Apart from a quick no-can-do-lunch call to her mum, the time had been spent going through the Baby Fay case files. Oz was a sight for extremely sore eyes. She was glad she'd made more of a sartorial effort herself this morning. As usual, Bev was woman in blue; her entire working gear was blue, blue and a touch of blue. But the skirt was new, fitted and knee-length. When she was on her feet.

She casually crossed her legs and, just to show willing, tugged at the rock's sticky wrapping before taking a lick. "Thought you weren't back till tomorrow?"

"Pining for you, sarge." So why was he riffling paper-work? "Couldn't sleep, couldn't eat, wasting away I was."

"Yeah, yeah." I wish. A year ago, maybe…

He grabbed a chair, turned it and straddled. "I saw the story on the news about the missing baby. Hands-on-deck job, isn't it? Thought I'd get up to speed on the reports."

She bit off a chunk of rock. "How'd the wedding go? Did the bride blush? Did you lose the ring?"

"Did I what?" Oz winced as she crunched and swallowed.

"Best man always loses the ring." She flashed a grin. "Traditional, that is. Like the groom's hangover and the mothers bawling their socks off and…"

He was studying her closely. "What've you been up to, Bev?"

"Nothing!" How come he could see right through her?

"You've got that glint in your eye. And you're babbling like a brook. In flood."

Apart from a word in DC Carol Mansfield's ear, Bev had intended keeping it quiet. But Oz soon had edited chapter and verse of her midnight recce at the crime scene.

"What's the guv's take on it?"

"Ah. That's a long story, Oz." She walked round the desk, slipped an arm through his. "Come on, I'll fill you in. Breakfast's on me."

"It's not the only thing, Sergeant Morriss." His smile was heart-stopping. "Come here."

Stay mean, keep 'em keen. "Best not, mate." She went for coy. "The others'll be in any time."

He handed her a virgin-white cotton handkerchief. "Wipe your mouth, sarge. It's covered in pink gunge."

They nipped to a greasy spoon just round the corner from the nick. Oz was getting the full works: a verbal update from Bev on both inquiries. It was littered with one-liners and caustic comments but as an up-sum it was fast, professional and incisive. She did a mean wheat-from-chaff and it beat written reports into a cocked helmet. Oz was digesting details and ingesting eggs: two, soft-boiled.

It was sixteen minutes before the guv's brief and Bev was ploughing her way through a full English. If an army marched on its stomach, she'd be well ready to join up.

And judging by the WAR posters that had appeared overnight in the streets of south Birmingham, maybe the whole force should consider enlisting. Women Against Rape had plastered almost as many notices as those pasted up by uniform about the missing baby. Every other lamppost carried signs about the mass protest and candlelit vigil. Those that didn't showed Zoë Beck's picture and a plea for information from the public.

Oz broke a yolk with a soldier. "If the baby's not found soon, the guv'll have to re-organise the squads, won't he?"

Bev nodded, took a slurp of tea. "I'm already off Street Watch." Registering his wide-mouthed surprise, she waved a reassuring fork. "I'm cool with it now. He's made me SIO on the search." She dabbed at a cluster of beans soaking into her shirt. "Anyway…"

"Hold on. If you're off the case, what were you doing at the scene last night?"

She thought she'd slipped that in but it snagged on Oz's radar. No point in diversionary tactics now. She leaned in, lowered her voice. "I needed to see it, Oz. I'm off the case but…I can't just drop it. I want the bastard behind bars."

He could barely hear her but was in no doubt how strongly she felt. "We all do, Bev." He took her hand. "You have to let it go. DI Powell's…"

"A plonker." She snatched her hand back.

"…a good officer," Oz persisted. "Have you told him? About finding the earring?"

She sighed, shook her head. "That's something else I'm really looking forward to."

Oz opened his mouth to speak but changed his mind.

He knew when to leave it. Bev hoped the guv'd leave her and Oz as a team as well. They knew each other's ways, didn't always see eye to eye but in a tight corner... Oz had covered her back more times than a duvet. He was the only man in the entire universe who knew it sported a tiny rose tattoo. Though they hadn't shared the bottom sheet much recently. Not since she'd beaten the shit out of the psycho-killer who'd attacked Sadie. It hadn't been a pretty sight – and Oz had seen it. Now, apart from on shift, he saw a lot less of Bev.

"There's a limit to what the guv can do." Oz was back on safer ground. "He can switch people round, but it's all a bit Peter and Paul."

Bev nodded. Oz was spot on. Whatever Byford said to the media in the public domain, privately he'd told Bev that West Mercia police were already on standby, should he have to call in more bodies. It went against the grain, implying an inadequacy, an inability to cope. But two high-profile on-going operations, constant high-alert security status and normal run-of-the-nick crime were enough to stretch any force to its limit. Maybe beyond.

Sunday, 8am, day two of the search and it was standing room only. Huge blow-up photographs of the missing baby dominated the briefing room where more than eighty men and women gathered, many – like Oz – turning up on a day off. About a third had been temporarily re-assigned from Street Watch, which explained Mike Powell's presence – a sort of two-briefings-with-one-stone scenario.

Bev was seated next to the DI behind a metal desk up at the front. She'd attended hundreds of similar meetings, couldn't recall an atmosphere remotely like this. It could power the national grid, no problem. Every officer was focused; many were grim-faced. There was no slouching posture, no irreverent asides, no black humour. Most of these people had kids. All were acutely aware that the first twenty-four hours following a crime were important; in the case of a missing child they were crucial. Baby Zoë hadn't been seen for twenty-nine.

"We're extending the search parameters." Byford was on his feet, centre stage, an impatient hand jiggling keys in a trouser pocket. An enlarged street plan of Balsall Heath and surrounding suburbs had been pinned to one of the incident boards. The map was dotted with coloured markers showing the places teams had already covered. The guv waved a pointer over the areas to be added, plus special-interest sites such as wasteland, derelict buildings, allotments and a recreation ground. Sniffer dogs and handlers were already out there; divers would shortly be dragging further stretches of the canal.

"Back here," Byford said, "we'll continue phone-bashing and putting in the checks. As of now, Jack's control room co-ordinator."

Inspector Jack Hainsworth lifted an arm like a leg of pork. Early forties, thinning ginger hair, he was admired and respected by everyone in the building, not necessarily liked. He was chunky, bull-necked and had the look of a night-club bouncer wearing uniform for a bet. A Yorkshireman who loathed cricket, he'd read classics at Cambridge and was into campanology. He suffered neither fools nor fuck-ups gladly; in fact, not at all. Hainsworth's sharp beady eyes would scan every sheet of paper, assess every piece of data; he'd then prioritise and point the inquiry in the right direction. He had a brain like a computer and a mouth like an open sewer. It was currently running through state of play and future activity.

Notes were taken, questions posed. It was donkeys-at-desks stuff, methodical and tedious. Bev wasn't big on routine plod-work but appreciated that just one call, one follow-up, could give them the breakthrough. And she reckoned it was more likely to come via the backroom players than anyone on the ground.

Widening the hunt, though logical, was an almost certainly futile step. They all knew, even if no one would say, that without a steer locating the baby was virtually impossible. It made a needle in a haystack look like a piece of piss. If Zoë was still alive, she and the abductor could be holed up anywhere. If it was a body they were looking for, the list of places it could be buried or dumped was endless.

Point was, they had to be seen to be doing something; a big police presence was vital. They had to keep Zoë uppermost in the public's mind. If they were out there in strength, the media would be out there in force. A powerful weapon, if a two-edged sword.

In an apparently motiveless crime, with no forensic evidence and a lack of quality witness reports, the police were almost entirely dependent on the community's help. Tip-offs leading to arrest were the top end of the informants' market. More commonly people saw stuff but didn't realise its significance, others forgot what they'd seen, still more were reluctant to come forward and needed a shove. Emotionally powerful footage could even prompt confessions. A kidnapper's not likely to pick up the phone but his wife/daughter/mother might cough on his behalf. It had happened before. Look at Michael Sams and *Crimewatch*. Although, Bev conceded, there was still any number of upstanding citizens who wouldn't piss on a copper in flames.

She glanced at Mike Powell, reckoned she'd need to be desperate for a wee. Powell's appraising gaze was directed downwards. Sitting cross-legged on the floor, clipboard in lap, hand tentatively waving in the air, was DC Sumitra Gosh. She'd only been in CID a month and Bev still wasn't used to seeing her out of uniform. Not that Goshie didn't look equally stunning in mufti. Every inch of her was elegant, and at nearly six feet tall, that was a lot of elegance. She had a river of blue-black hair and eyes like toasted almonds. There was nothing remotely plain about Ms Gosh. And neither was she just a pretty face.

"What about the baby's mother, sir?" Gosh asked. "Is she prepared to do an appeal?"

"Good point," Byford acknowledged. "Time's not right yet. We'll almost certainly get round to it."

"I could mention it to her," Powell offered, gaze still fixed on the rookie. "I'm arranging for her to come in later to go through mug shots."

Bev knew the guv's thinking, could see he was torn.

"Hang fire, Mike," he said. "Let's give it twenty-four hours."

Bev tended to agree. Natalie Beck was a ladette who aspired to chavdom. In the punter-appeal stakes, she was running on empty. Anyway, in one more day, one way or the other, the waiting could be over. She closed her eyes, mouthed a silent prayer.

"Do you want to say a few words, Bev?" the guv asked.

As senior investigating officer, Bev knew she'd have to take the floor. Didn't make the ordeal any easier. It wasn't her first case as SIO but it was the biggest. And some of the Highgate hard men would shed few tears if she failed to close it. She rose and took a deep breath, hoping her skirt wasn't stuck up her bum and her voice would carry to the back.

She assigned actions, answered queries, then: "I've not got a lot more to say."

"Thank Christ for that," Powell muttered behind her back.

"Crime involving a kid's a shit job. You don't need me telling you how to do it. I'll be around the Wordsworth most of the day and I'm on the end of a phone 24/7. All I ask is keep me informed. I need to know every development, however small, before it happens." Heads nodded, ties were straightened, fingers combed hair. She sensed they were chomping at the bit. She knew she was. "And that shit job?" She tried to include everyone in her glance. "You're doing it brilliantly."

"I second that," Byford said. "Ignore the rubbish in the media. They're stirring. It's what they do best."

He was referring to that morning's coverage in the *Sunday Post*. The banner headline read 'POLICE IN CRISIS'. Despite the journalistic device of sticking quotation marks around the words, it came across as hard fact, not what it was: predictable prejudice from a rent-a-mouth Midlands MP.

Josephine Kramer was third-hand cant on legs. The media loved her. Christ, she wasn't even Natalie Beck's honourable member, nor as far as Bev recalled did she represent any of the rape victims. Informed opinion was a concept Kramer had yet to discover; 'outraged of Edgbaston' was more her mindset. The popular sport of cop-bashing was on the rise, and Kramer was in training for an Olympic gold.

Fuck the impact on morale.

"Talking about stirring." DC Darren New took up the guv's point. "Anyone hear the radio this morning?" Dazza listening to the wireless? Bet it wasn't Radio Four.

"Birmingham Sound. They were trailing a Martha Kemp special: WAR on the streets of Birmingham."

"The protest tomorrow?" Bev asked.

Dazza nodded. "Kramer's gonna be at the rape scene with the organisers and there'll be a bunch of studio guests."

"Like who?"

He ran through the usual pundits and pondlifes. "Kemp promised a special guest as well: a young rape victim. She teased it as 'the most moving interview I've ever conducted, the most moving you'll ever hear.'"

Laura Kenyon? Would The Mouth use her own daughter to boost ratings and take a pop at the police?

Talk about the stage and Mrs Worthington.

Powell's limp-wristed round of applause was presumably meant to be ironic. "Nice one, Morriss. Your patronising little pep talk in there?" He jabbed a thumb in the direction of the incident room. "Pass me the sick bag."

The DI was lounging casually against a corridor wall, ankles crossed, condescension incarnate. It hadn't been her finest hour; neither had it been the shit he was making out. And if it came to that, his troop address hadn't exactly inspired any martyrs. She laid a concerned hand on his by-now-furrowed brow. "Must say, sir, you do look a bit peaky." She peered closer. "Maybe you should stay in more."

Powell's lips were so tight they looked glued.

She leaned her head to the side, enquired politely, "Perhaps you could give me a few tips before you go?" He hadn't a clue till she enlightened him. "People skills? Do share."

Powell sprang forward, invaded her space. "Just one tip, Morriss." An admonitory finger headed her way but an industrial-strength glare forced it off course. "Don't stick your nose in." A pause. "If you have Street Watch input, it's me you talk to. Savvy?"

How the fuck did he know about last night?

"Carol Mansfield has the makings of a decent copper. I wouldn't want her picking anything up off you. Back off."

Bev gave a huge mental sigh of relief. The DI was still in the dark about last night. Though he'd obviously cottoned on to the fact she and Carol had discussed lines of questioning both before and after the Laura Kenyon interview.

"You're not even on the case, Morriss. You'll not undermine my authority again."

An evidence bag rustling against her skin begged to differ. She took it from a shirt pocket, handed it to Powell. He screwed his eyes as he held it to the light.

"It's an earring," Bev said. "I found it last night at the Moseley rape scene. Nothing to do with me, of course, but I suggest you speak to Laura Kenyon again."

She turned at the end of the corridor. Powell was still standing open-mouthed.

"As for undermining your *authority*." She gave a mock salute. "I'd have to find it first."

"Don't let him wind you up, sarge. It's not worth it." Oz was more interested in trying to find a space to slot the motor than Bev's blow-by-blow account of her latest run-in with Powell. The Wordsworth estate resembled a police car park, with some vehicles straddling pavements and others cluttering grass verges. Officers were everywhere, knocking on doors, stopping passers-by, leaning in talking to motorists. Hearing the questions wasn't necessary; the blank faces were answer enough.

Bev pointed out a gap further down, then ransacked her

bag on the off chance there'd be something edible at the bottom. The spat with Powell had left a nasty taste in her mouth. Dissing him gave her an instant high but did no good in the long run. And right now it was taking the edge off her pleasure over the guv's 'if it ain't broke, don't fix it' policy on the make-up of the squads.

"You're right, Oz. The DI's an arsehole." She located a mental backburner marked arseholes, left Powell simmering. "Want a bit?" Oz looked askance at the half-bar of chocolate she was wielding. It had a coating of fluff and a couple of hairs.

He shook his head as he locked the motor. "You've not long had breakfast."

"Think of it as pudding."

Their arrival at number thirteen provoked a barrage of clicking lenses and flashing lights from a bank of cameras still camped opposite. If anything, numbers had grown since the day before. Bev spotted at least two TV crews as well as a shed-load of stills men. The opening of the door unleashed a second photographic volley.

Mandy Forsyth's strained face appeared and Bev and Oz squeezed through a narrow gap in the door; any wider and zooms would be homing in. God knew what they'd pick up chez Beck.

"How's it going?" Bev asked.

The family liaison officer grimaced. Mandy had been a flo for more than a decade, seen it all. She was Mrs Twin-Set, with a face you wouldn't glance at in an empty room, but her voice was the warmest Bev had ever heard. She'd watched Mandy in action, reckoned she'd prise a word or two out of a concrete clam.

"Mrs Beck hasn't moved off the settee. Natalie won't come out of the baby's room. They're not eating, barely talking. Living on tea and cigarettes."

"Where's Roper?"

"Nipped to the shop. They've run out of fags."

"You gonna answer that?" Bev could never ignore a ringing phone.

Mandy shrugged. "I'm in no hurry. They'll ring again."

"Who will?"

"Whoever's getting off on it."

Bev listened incredulously as Mandy explained. A number of malicious calls had been made, accusing the Becks of doing away with the baby. The voice was muffled, maybe deliberately disguised, could be male or female. The sad sack was well informed, knew about the Becks' dysfunctional past: Maxine's flight to the sun and Natalie's subsequent acquaintance with hospital food.

"How come this is news to me?" Bev asked.

Mandy frowned. "I called it in first thing."

There was no point having a go at Mandy. "Check it out, Oz. If they're not already organising a trace and 24/7 protection, put the wheels in motion." She turned back to Mandy. "What's the gist?" As if she couldn't guess.

"Nasty. Mean. Spiteful. Talk about kicking someone when they're down."

And both women were as low as it gets. Maxine Beck was slumped in front of the gas fire. There was no reaction when Bev looked in briefly.

Oz was in the hallway still trying to sort crossed wires. Bev asked him to sit in with Maxine when he'd finished. "I want to know if the other pics have turned up. I'll be upstairs with the girl."

Natalie was sitting on the floor at the side of the empty cot, staring into space. The sight was so unexpected, so shocking, that Bev clung to the doorframe to steady herself, taking a deep calming breath.

The girl was cradling a baby in her arms.

"Shush." Natalie put a finger to her lips. "You'll wake her."

The teenager's rocking motion was calm and measured. She was singing now. It sounded like lines from *Angels* but the voice was barely audible.

There were tears in Bev's eyes as she moved slowly across the room. Natalie was clearly on a knife-edge. Bev brushed at the dampness on her cheeks before kneeling. Natalie was still now, silently weeping. Bev took her into a tender embrace, then gently removed the doll from her arms.

11

Helen Carver dabbed a starched linen napkin at the stray croissant crumbs caught in her expertly applied Subtle Plum lip-gloss. Flecks of pastry fell on to Zoë Beck's face, which covered most of the *Mail on Sunday* front page. "I see that baby's still missing, darling."

Her husband didn't respond. She glanced across. "Is there a problem?"

David Carver was still standing, cradling the phone, a pensive expression on his brooding features. He appeared to be gazing at the waterscape through the window of their apartment, but if the pope had sailed past on a narrow boat Carver wouldn't have noticed. Neither was he listening. "Mmmm?"

"The call?" Helen sipped espresso. "Anything wrong?" It was probably the college, she thought, or a pushy parent wanting extra tuition for little Johnnie or Joanna.

Carver pushed a hand through thick black hair that was a shade too dark and a tad too long for a man clinging to middle age by short fingernails. "No. Just the police."

Helen's hand jerked, sloshing coffee over the side of the porcelain cup. "Damn." She dabbed her napkin at a spreading stain on the white damask. "Cloth's ruined."

David either didn't notice or didn't care. He resumed his seat at the table and continued reading *The Observer*.

Her hand was steadier now, if not her voice. "What's it about this time?"

"Oh, the usual… Blair's-a-lying-bastard rubbish."

She exhaled sharply. "Don't try to be funny. What do the police want?"

"They want to talk to me. They'll be here in an hour." He shook the paper: end of subject.

Not for Helen. "About the girl who was…?" She hated the very word. It contaminated her carefully created world where the garden was full of prize-winning roses, babies didn't get snatched from their cots and teenage girls could walk the streets unharmed.

"A different one. There was another rape on Friday, apparently." He reached a hand from behind the paper, drew it back clutching toast.

Helen seethed. It was too bad. The police had a job to do, but… She treasured their Sunday breakfasts. On other days David was usually out of the apartment before she was out of the bedroom. Even with the baby, Helen rarely rose early – no need with Veronica fussing around like a mother hen. Grandmother and child were out now, feeding the ducks. Helen's dream of a peaceful idyll was shattered by the prospect of the police arriving, flat-footed and heavy-handed.

She slung the napkin on the table. "I must say you're taking it very calmly."

He lifted his glance from the newspaper. "There's little point in us both having hysterics."

"But, David… We're having people over. Why can't it wait until tomorrow? I don't see why they need to interrogate you anyway."

"*Talk*, Helen." He folded the paper precisely, lined it up with the edge of the table. "They want to talk to me. She's a student of mine. They think I might be able to help."

"Help how?" She tugged compulsively at a sleeve.

He shrugged. "Like before, I suppose, with the Quinn girl. They spoke to everyone in college who knows Kate. It'll be the same this time with Laura Kenyon. And quite honestly, Helen, if something I say helps catch the sick bastard who's violating these poor girls, it'll be a pleasure."

"Don't swear. You know I hate it." She shook the crumbs off her newspaper, the baby's face now splotchy with grease. Helen used it to hide behind while she sneaked glances at her husband. She watched as he brushed a floppy fringe from his eyes. It was a habitual gesture, like the way he flicked his tongue across his top lip, hated Stilton and sang *Satisfaction* in the shower. She knew him intimately. So why, occasionally, did she feel she didn't know him at all?

She sighed, rose and started clearing the table.

"Helen." He reached out, stroked her arm. She'd cut it recently, winced as his ring touched the wound. "Don't get upset. I hardly know the girl. They're only going to ask a few questions."

There are only so many ways a question can be asked. DI Mike Powell was no Jeremy Paxman, but even so the DI had already voiced his sixty-four-thousand-dollar poser five times. And rape victim Laura Kenyon had responded in similar vein: no, no way, never, non, nay. She had not, she insisted, worn earrings the night she was attacked. She'd never in her life seen the earring DC Carol Mansfield was holding. As for wearing diamonds? Over her dead body.

They were seated in the drawing room of Martha Kemp's Moseley home, a sanctuary of sage green and soft vanillas. Its plush surroundings were doing nothing to draw out Laura, who lolled opposite, examining her nails. Watching the pose, the DI slowly tapped his fingers against his thigh. Laura Kenyon appeared less vulnerable than he remembered, and less regal. The little-princess look had been replaced by street Goth. Most of her lower half was encompassed in skin-tight Levis with strategic rips flashing glimpses of flesh. The denims were teamed with a black hoodie; across the chest in lettering like dripping blood was a general invite to 'Suck My Punk'. The girl dangled an ostensibly casual leg over the arm of her chair.

"See, Miss Kenyon." Powell traced a finger along his chin. "I have absolutely no idea how else it could have got there."

She shrugged. "Best get on and find out, then, hadn't you?" She sipped full-fat Coke; hadn't offered drinks.

DC Mansfield was note-taking and taking note. Why was the girl so lippy all of a sudden? Was she deliberately trying to piss them off? And why keep checking the time? And the door? Laura had readily invited them in, even though her mother was out. Did Laura now want momma Kemp in on the action?

The crunch of scattering gravel outside the room's stained-glass windows suggested her minder was home. Behind leaded panes, a gleaming black people-carrier hove into view. Carol watched closely, expecting Laura to relax a little. Whatever emotion flitted across the teenager's face, it wasn't relief.

Laura sat up, straight-backed. Her voice was too loud and too high. "I'm tired now. I want you to leave."

The clack of heels on marble preceded the crash of door on wall. Martha Kemp briefly assessed the tableau, then storm-trooped her way across polished floorboards. Shiny black boots and an ankle-length leather coat underlined the SS effect.

She stamped into Powell's comfort zone. "How dare you? How dare you come in to *my* house and talk to *my* daughter without *my* permission?"

The DI looked as if he'd been caught smoking behind the bike sheds. Carol Mansfield rallied faster. She rose to take advantage of her five-ten height. "Laura isn't a child. She's eighteen. We were invited in. She's been under no pressure to speak."

Three reasonable points, calmly delivered. Kemp paused, briefly. "I don't want you in my home when I'm not here."

"Why?" Carol asked. "We're trying to catch the man who raped your daughter. Isn't that what you want?"

Kemp ran a hand over her face. Of course it was; she just loathed not being number-one controller. She had the grace and sense to cede. "Sorry. Please, sit down."

Carol resumed her seat next to Powell.

"So, Laura…" he started.

"Mum, I don't feel too good." The teenager paused, then pushed the point. "Like I'm about to faint, you know?"

Kemp crossed to Laura, laid a hand on her daughter's forehead, then turned to Powell. "I'm sorry. She's burning up. Tomorrow, perhaps?"

The DI was on his feet. "No problem."

Carol was thinking on hers.

Kemp held the door open and Carol, as she passed, shoved the earring in front of the other woman's face. "This yours, by any chance?"

Kemp's eyes lit up. "Wonderful. Where did you find it?"

"Ask your daughter." Carol glanced back at Laura, who was keeping her head down in more than one way. Her earlier twitchiness hadn't been due to her mother's absence. Quite the reverse.

"I don't understand," Kemp said.

Carol did – and its implications. "When did you lose it?"

"Them, actually. I lost them both about a month ago. They were insured, of course, but it's the sentimental value, isn't it…?"

Carol nodded. Emotional cost in this case was going to

be shattering.

"Where did you find it?" Kemp repeated. "Any sign of the other one?"

Carol paused, letting Kemp work it out. Maybe she couldn't. After an increasingly uneasy few seconds, the detective told her it had been discovered at the railway embankment in Moseley, embedded in a sleeper. Martha Kemp wasn't stupid. Carol didn't need to spell it out further.

Kemp glanced back at Laura, curled foetus-like on the sofa, softly crying and visibly shaking. "But that means…"

Carol nodded. Either the rapist was also a jewel thief who'd just happened to nick Martha Kemp's earrings or Laura had a penchant for diamonds and was lying through her teeth.

Carol didn't put it quite like that. Neither did she mention immediately that she'd glimpsed a tattoo under Laura's left buttock. One rip in the jeans had momentarily revealed a tiny black heart.

The wires and wherefores were in place to trace future malicious calls to the Becks, should the obnoxious little shit have further faeces to dump. Patrols would keep an eye on the property but 24/7 surveillance was too costly. Bev's considered opinion was that the caller was a sad sack rather than a psycho. And family liaison and Terry Roper were both in residence for the foreseeable.

"I reckon it's covered," Bev said. "I'm gonna head off."

Mandy Forsyth was making tea. "Drink before you go?"

"Mandy, after this morning my blood group's PG. I'll just pop my head in to say 'bye. Catch you later."

Mother and daughter Beck were ensconced in the small, cluttered sitting room again, mute and immobile. Bev had noticed it before. When anxious relatives wait for news, their world often shrinks to the same four walls, shattered lives go on hold as if to stave off further damage. Bev lifted a hand in farewell.

"Give us a bell any time, Nat. Day or night. But you'll be seeing me again. Regular Arnie, me."

Maxine hadn't a clue. "You what, love?"

"Arl bee beck." Natalie's Schwarzenegger impression was spot on but Maxine was still perplexed. Natalie gave Bev a knowing look. "Don't worry, mum. Everything'll be OK."

The transformation was stunning, given how she had lost it earlier. Two hours Bev had sat with her, held her, talked to her. Two hours desperate to connect, using everything from inconsequential chitchat to life-and-death stuff. Flake by flake, she'd chipped a way through Natalie's brittle carapace. Tiny step by tiny step, Natalie had come back from empty-eyed zombie to teenager stable as any in her appalling circumstances.

The breakthrough, Bev discovered, was tapping into the daughter's love for her mother. Bev convinced Natalie that Maxine needed her even more now, that her mum'd never survive the next few days without Natalie's support. It was touch and go but the need to be needed, combined with the teenager's caring nature, gradually won whatever battle her mental demons were waging. Bev had no doubt there'd be wobbles ahead, but for now Natalie had a reason to carry on apart from her missing baby. She had to look out for her mother.

Bev was at the front door when Natalie placed a hand on her shoulder.

"Thanks for all that. Appreciate it."

Bev made eye contact, held it. "I'm here for you, Natalie. I'll help anyway I can."

Natalie's eyes brimmed. "Find Zoë, Bev. That's all."

12

Fading light and falling hopes.

Bev called off the search at four that afternoon. It'd be resumed first thing but as of now it was thirty-nine hours since Zoë Beck was last seen. The search paraphernalia had been packed away, the personnel headed for home or back to base. Bev was taking a final solitary pass round the Wordsworth before hitting Highgate and a stack of paperwork. The estate was like a ghost town after the day's frenetic activity. A feral cat rooted in an upturned bin. A mangy dog defecated in the gutter. An elderly dosser was kipping on a bench under a cardboard duvet.

The old codger was missing the fireworks. They'd actually been going off all day. Now that it was dark, at least the kids could see their pocket money going up in smoke. Multi-coloured showers and starbursts flashed intermittently against a swathe of sable velvet. Bev scowled. It'd been the same for weeks. It was November 15th, not the fifth, but bonfire night these days went through to Christmas and New Year.

Christmas. And what of Baby Zoë?

It was a train of thought Bev refused to board. She slipped Aretha Franklin into the CD player and took a left. All the houses in Blake Way looked the same: dingy little boxes, so normal, so ordinary. Number thirteen should be weeping and wailing and wiping its windows. God, she wished she had better news for the Becks.

The search teams had covered the area like nappy rash and not come up with so much as a sniff of the kid. She smiled wryly, recalling some of the items they *had* found stashed around the place: pirate DVDs, counterfeit designer labels, a warehouse full of hot white goods. Fact was, an unofficial amnesty was operating along the lines of 'you scratch my back'… If a local villain came up with a tip-off, they wouldn't nick him for giving Curry's a run for its money.

Meanwhile, every cop with a snout had put feelers out. A few informants had come forward anyway. Not with decent dope but promises to keep their eyes peeled. Crimes against kids were the most despicable in the book. Normal rules of engagement didn't apply.

"OK," she told herself. "Once more around the block, dear friend, then hit the nearest chippy." Food. Fuck. Frankie. The thought association stemmed from the fact that Frankie's dad, Giovanni, ran an Italian restaurant. Bev still hadn't phoned Frankie to apologise for failing to show yesterday. She made a mental note: ring Interflora. And grovel.

Then joined Aretha Franklin, who was saying a little prayer.

"You look like you need this more than me, Bev." Vince Hanlon was on the front desk. Highgate's longest-serving sergeant drank more tea than Tony Benn, and he'd just brewed. Big Vince raised a Charles and Camilla wedding mug in one hand and half a Wagon Wheel in the other.

"You're a star, Vincie. Anyone ever told you that?"

Vince parked brawny forearms across an impressive paunch and looked set to launch into the latest gossip. She loved the man but he could talk the hind legs off a donkey sanctuary.

Scooping up both offerings, she blew him a kiss and hit the stairs. A call in the car from Carol Mansfield had put a spring or two in Bev's step. Not only did Laura Kenyon have a tattoo, but she'd blatantly lied when she first said she hadn't been wearing earrings during the attack. Not surprising, given she'd nicked the studs from her mother. Laura had eventually admitted 'borrowing' other items of jewellery from Kemp over a period of some months, mostly selling them to eke out her allowance, but she'd taken a shine to the diamond studs. She'd lied because her mother scared the shit out of her.

The file Bev needed to check was in the Street Watch incident room. If Laura had lied about an earring, it raised several questions about mothers and daughters, especially their lines of communication. It was just possible, for similar reasons, that Kate Quinn had been less than frank on the tattoo front.

Carol had informed DI Powell about Laura's tattoo, but Bev knew he hadn't yet instigated any action. Question now was whether she should follow the lead herself? She jotted down a couple of numbers but a decision was deferred in favour of answering a phone. "Bev Morriss."

"What are you doing there?" The guv, who'd sounded happier.

"Answering the phone." Whoops, wrong reply. The quality of silence at the other end was severely strained. "Sorry, sir. Didn't mean to be flip. I'm the only one around at the mo."

"I want DI Powell."

Someone had to. "Can't help you, guv. He's not here."

"Have you seen the TV news?"

Yeah, in between painting my toenails and licking Haagen Dazs from Johnny Depp's every orifice. "Nope."

"I've just watched footage of Natalie Beck in the back of a police motor being driven into Highgate."

"What?" Unbelievable. It had to be connected with the Beck girl's rape. Powell must have got her in to go through albums of known offenders. It was a bit hot off the mark, considering what the poor kid was going through.

"Precisely," Byford said. "I told him to hang fire."

Casting her mind back, Bev caught a loophole in the guv's argument. As she recalled his conversation with the DI, Byford had been referring to a different issue entirely – that of putting Natalie Beck in front of the TV cameras. "You were talking tearful appeal, guv, not mug shots."

There was an audible groan from the guv's end. Either way, Bev couldn't see how Natalie's premature public appearance could jeopardise the baby inquiry. Given the complete lack of progress, the young mother's time in the wings had been coming to an end anyway. An emotional plea from Natalie via the nation's media was the next logical step.

"May as well fix an appeal, then?" Bev asked.

"Tomorrow morning. 11.30."

She snatched the receiver from her still ringing ear. And a good night to you too, guv.

It wasn't a good night. Bev was pissed off returning to an empty house and an empty bed. Oz hadn't even left a message on the answer-phone. Come to that, no one had. It was little wonder she couldn't sleep. Her stomach churned and her head was spinning with a zillion thoughts, fears, hopes and ideas. The missing baby was foremost but the Street Watch girls were going round in there as well. The tattoo question still bugged her. Powell had done sod all so far. Surely it couldn't hurt if she put in a few quick calls, had another little chat with Tattoo Man, Luke Mangold?

She'd scanned the rape latest before leaving Highgate.

The team had been out all day interviewing. It was routine stuff: no new leads or fresh lines. One name rang a bell with Bev: David Carver, the English lecturer at Queen's. She'd interviewed him herself after Kate Quinn's attack. He'd seemed straight, apart from fancying himself rotten. She smiled, recalling his nickname with the students: Heathcliff. Not that his missus bore the slightest resemblance to Cathy. Helen Carver was so determinedly upbeat she made Pollyanna look like a manic-depressive. Powell's interview notes were a bit sparse; maybe she'd have another word with Carol Mansfield.

The mug-shots session had been a no-no. Bev discovered this when she'd phoned Natalie to tell her the arrangements for the telly appeal and make sure the teenager was up for the ordeal. No problem: she'd do anything if it helped get Zoë back. As it turned out, Natalie could kill two birds with the proverbial; she was due back in Highgate anyway, to help put together an E-fit of her attacker.

The alarm was set for 6am. It was almost midnight. Tomorrow would be the third day in the hunt for Baby Zoë. Bev reached out a hand – best make that 5am.

A dark shape was barely perceptible in the shadows, watching, waiting. He'd been there two hours, biding his time, making sure. He'd seen a rat scuttle into the alleyway opposite; a tabby had brushed against his trousers then slunk away; the last piss-heads had staggered past ages ago. Apart from the occasional firework, the place was dead.

The man didn't want to be here tonight. The pictures on the news had forced his hand. He lifted his gaze as a cascade of colours burst across the night sky. It put him in mind of the Beatles' *Lucy in the Sky with Diamonds*. The man was still smiling as he checked the time. He'd already checked his pocket to make sure the matches were there. Humming softly, he adjusted the rucksack, headed for the house.

The baby was fractious, the now-frazzled woman in-experienced, unable to contact the only person she could ask for help. The little one couldn't be hungry; she'd refused the bottle again. And her nappy was dry. The mousy woman checked it anyway. She took the naked child into her arms, gently tucked the tiny head under her chin and stroked the smooth perfect skin. The baby wriggled and squirmed, hot, flushed, crabby.

The woman tried to recall what the books said. Some recommended soothing motion to calm a crying child. A drive in the car often helped. No, she decided, too many people around. On edge anyway, she jumped at what sounded like distant shots, quickly realised it was only fire-works. The booms and bangs had spooked her a couple of times already that night. Maybe the sudden noises were unsettling the baby.

The nursery would be quieter. Supporting the baby's head, she cradled the tiny form gently in her arms and stole up the stairs. A soft tap set the rainbow swaying. The baby seemed to follow the motion with her eyes. The books said babies couldn't focus before six weeks old, but this baby was clearly special. The woman smiled proudly as she gazed at the tiny face, her incipient panic replaced by renewed confidence.

After all, it was early days. It would get easier in time. Everything would get so much easier.

13

Scarlet flames licked at the agonised face, jagged fire-fingers stretched towards the skull, the tiny body was already charred black. Thirty or more firefighters stood round helplessly, beaten back by intense heat, choking smoke. Bev, restrained by Oz in a powerful grip, kicked and fought, desperate to free herself, desperate to save the baby, knowing it was too late. Scalding tears streamed down her cheeks as she watched the baby's head become a ball of fire.

Bev screamed then, a lung-bursting, ear-piercing scream that shattered her sleep, jarred her awake. Heart racing, pulse pounding in her throat, she could barely catch her breath. Only vaguely aware of its ring, her hand reached automatically for the phone.

Something big was going off on the Wordsworth estate. A control-room operator at Highgate said they'd received five triple-nines. "It's being treated as a major incident, sergeant. Thought you'd want to know."

"Cheers." She squinted at the clock: half-one. "What's happening?"

"Fire. Domestic. Blake Way. Still patchy but four occupants unaccounted for."

With a foot on the floor it took five minutes. She ran six reds and nearly mowed down a drunk who was doing a big Fred Astaire number in the middle of the Moseley Road. Emergency vehicles nose-to-tail blocked Blake Way. Nearest access was round the corner. She ditched the MG, legged it the rest of the way. A cacophony of sound: engines, pumps, generators, radio transmissions, shouted instructions. Eyes closed, it was the noise of a fairground. No eau de candy-floss, only smoke. Cloying clinging suffocating fumes.

It was impossible at first to see past the vast bulk of the fire engines. Their revolving lights cast sickly blue-grey hues on the faces of the crowd. It looked as if the entire neighbourhood had turned out: women smoking, men with pyjama bottoms flapping under their coats, kids feigning indifference, even a couple of toddlers. It wasn't *Towering Inferno* but it was live action.

Please God. Let it be live action.

Smoke stung her eyes, caught in her throat as she assessed the situation. The blaze looked under control; crews trained hoses at what appeared to be the seat of the fire, the front sitting room. Damping down was in operation elsewhere. Anything not destroyed by flames or smoke was under four inches of water. Bev grimaced; the Becks hadn't had much to begin with.

She glanced round, recognised a few of the firefighters from previous incidents. It was the main man she needed. A uniformed cop pointed her in the right direction. As she approached the house, though there were no flames, a huge pall of smoke hung in the air. More drifted or billowed from blackened blistered window frames.

Bev picked her way through pools of filthy water and charred debris. Household items chucked out during the search of the property lay soaked and smoke-damaged. Heartbreaking. Nothing compared with the junked toys and baby clothes.

Then she saw the side wall. Daubed in red paint, letters a foot high, was a chilling message.

BURN IN HELL BABY KILLERS

Her fists were tight balls. The threat laid to rest any

doubt about the fire's origins. But questions clamoured for answers. She searched for a familiar face in the crowd. John Preston, the chief fire officer, was easy to spot – a six-foot Geordie with a voice like an amplified foghorn.

"What's the score, John?" Apart from Becks nil.

"One occupant out by the time we arrived. Crews in breathing apparatus brought out two more. Both women. The paramedics are working on them."

Ambulances were parked across the street. She'd check it out soon as.

"I was told four occupants," Bev said.

He nodded, grim-faced. "We think there's still someone inside."

It wasn't Mandy Forsyth. The family liaison officer was heading over, a blanket across her shoulders. Bev grabbed the woman's hands. "Mandy. Thank God. How are you?"

"I got out before the smoke got too bad. I'll be OK. " She shivered. "Best start paying me danger money."

"You up to telling me what happened?"

She nodded, but drew the blanket tightly round her chest, shaking, clearly in shock. Bev grabbed the nearest uniform, told him to take Mandy to a squad car. "I'll be with you in five minutes, Mandy, OK?"

She turned to the CFO. "So…if there is anyone in there." She nodded at what was left of number thirteen. "What are the chances?"

He shook his head. "Smoke, sergeant. It's a killer."

She closed her eyes. Terry Roper. It had to be. He'd moved in with the Becks to do his knight-in-shining-armour routine. What was that going to do to Maxine?

"We'll know soon enough." Preston tipped his head towards the house. Another breathing apparatus crew was preparing to enter.

"Any idea how it started?" The writing on the wall couldn't make it clearer but Preston was the expert.

"Place was torched, petrol bomb most likely. You can still smell it."

Bev bowed to the fire officer's refined olfactory powers. The only thing she could smell was smoke coming off her clothes, hair, skin, everywhere. Yet she craved a ciggy. How did that work?

"Should have something more solid after the fire investigation team's been in." Preston took off his helmet, wiped the back of his hand across a soot-streaked forehead. "It could've been a lot worse."

Looked pretty shit to her. She raised an eyebrow.

"A couple of minutes later and we'd be looking for more than one body."

He promised to give her a shout as soon as he heard anything, then rejoined his men. Bev scanned the street as she hit fast-dial on her mobile. No hacks or video vultures in sight. Amazing that the media hadn't heard a whisper. The guv answered after five rings. It took a couple of minutes to bring him up to speed. Byford was happy for Bev to continue calling the shots. There was no sense him turning out as well. They agreed he'd take the early brief while she caught missed zeds.

The temperature had fallen a couple of degrees. She was pacing so she wouldn't seize up. Mandy was in the back of a police motor a couple of doors down. Bev slipped in. "Sure you're up for this?"

Black flakes fell from the liaison officer's hair as she nodded. "Let's get it over with. I want to get home."

"Sure. Soon as you like, Mandy."

"Natalie went to bed about eleven. I followed soon after. I was out like a light, woke up a couple hours later with a pounding headache. I got up to fetch a glass of water to take a painkiller. Soon as I opened the door I smelled smoke. You know what it's like when you're half asleep. For a second or two I wondered why someone was lighting a fire that time of the morning. Then I saw the smoke, drifting up from below." She paused, pinched the bridge of her nose. "I've never moved so fast in my life, Bev. I shouted, screamed, banged doors. Natalie'd taken a couple of sleeping tablets, was well out of it. I shook her, called her name, then ran to the bathroom thinking I'd get some water to chuck over her. I looked into Maxine's room, saw the bed empty, assumed she and Terry had gone down and out the back." Her bottom lip trembled and there was a tremor in the hand clutching the blanket.

"You did brill, Mandy. What happened then?"

"I got Natalie on her feet. She seemed OK, told me to go on ahead. I was scared, Bev. I didn't need telling twice. I didn't know till later that Maxine hadn't been to bed at all. She was in the sitting room when the fire started. Natalie went to get her out."

The Beck women were still in the ambulance undergoing initial medical treatment. Bev stood a few yards away chatting to a couple of uniforms. She was waiting for a green light from the paramedics before grabbing a word with Natalie. Maxine wouldn't be talking to anyone any time soon. She was on oxygen and intravenous drips, still unconscious.

"Give us a baccy, Simon." Three months Bev'd been off the weed. One of the cops handed her a Marlboro. "Ta, mate." She sneaked another. "I owe you."

"Take the pack, sarge. I've got more."

She slipped it into her bag. What the hell, she could fall

under a bus tomorrow. Or have a baby snatched. Or see her life go up in shit. She took a deep drag, savouring the nicotine hit. The thought that the arson attack was down to the Becks' malicious caller, seriously upping his sick game, was tearing her to shreds. She'd dismissed the poisonous shit behind the calls as deranged, not dangerous. If he or she had taken to fire-raising, she'd badly miscalculated, could've got four people killed.

She inhaled again, creased her eyes as the smoke drifted from her nostrils. There was another possibility. The arsonist could be some sort of self-styled vigilante: a wacko who'd seen pictures of Natalie Beck being driven away in a police car, put two and two together and come up with infanticide. In which scenario, Powell was in the shit. He'd authorised and arranged the girl's session at the nick.

The thought gave Bev no pleasure. Whichever way it panned out, the Becks had been badly let down by the people whose job description majored on protection.

She lit another baccy from the butt.

PC Simon Wells, her supplier, looked on. "What now, sarge?"

Jack Daniels? Southern Comfort? "Watching brief for you pair."

Most of the other squads had been released or diverted to other calls. Simon and his partner had been questioning the street gawpers: Balsall Heath's equivalent of Neighbourhood Watch. But the locals had been as much use as eyeless needles. Simon reckoned the Yorkshire Ripper could move in and no one'd notice. Either way, by now the audience had drifted home for its Horlicks.

"We'll talk to them again in a few hours," Bev said. "And everyone else on the estate. I can't believe we won't get a steer."

It had taken more than the few seconds needed to lob a Molotov or whatever. The arsonist had left a wall painting. Early teams would get cracking on door-to-doors, grab people before they left for work. Come to think of it, that wouldn't be a major consideration: Wordsworth wasn't big on gainful employment.

"As for now." A drag, then she ground the butt under a damp Doc Marten. "Keep your eye on the house. It's our crime scene but it's Preston's turf till he pulls his men out."

"Sarge." Simon tilted his head, pointed behind her.

The CFO was striding towards them. It wasn't good news. The look was sober even through a face blackened with smut and smoke. "Waste of fucking time. I could have lost men in there."

The breathing apparatus crew had been through every room in the house. Hadn't found a skin cell. Alive or dead.

Bev frowned. "So Roper got out. Or was never in there…"

The fire chief shrugged. Not interested. "Duff info happens. But in this case, every call reported four trapped."

And there'd been five calls. Bev thought it through. It was less than forty-eight hours since Roper had taken up residence. It was doubtful five people beyond the family even knew he'd moved in. So who'd raised the alert, upping the head count? And why? And where the fuck was Roper now?

"Thank God it's not a fatal," Preston said. "But my blokes…"

Risked their lives, having potentially been fed a five-pack of lies. Bev made mental notes: not back burner.

"Sarge." Simon was pointing again.

She turned to see a paramedic on the steps of the ambulance. Hoisting her bag, she headed for the harassed man in green scrubs.

"I'm sorry, love. She doesn't want to talk."

Bev's heart sank; she lifted a finger. "One minute, mate. Just one."

"The girl's in shock." He rubbed a hand over non-designer stubble. "She ain't making a lot of sense anyway."

"How bad…"

"She's had plenty of oxygen. I reckon she'll be OK. Physically."

Bev cleared her throat. "And the mother?"

The paramedic turned his mouth down. "She swallowed a hell of a lot of smoke. They're getting a bed ready at the General. ICU."

Bev closed her eyes. Intensive care.

The paramedic was already closing the doors. As Bev opened her eyes she caught a glimpse of Maxine flat out on a stretcher and Natalie kneeling, her head burrowed into her mother's side. Maxine looked like death. Not even warmed.

14

"Fucking hell." The rude awakening was down to an alarm still set for a 5am start. A fruitless hour hanging around the General Hospital meant Bev had slept all of ninety minutes. She reset the call time, turned over, tossed a bit. And crawled out. Sod it. She'd have an early night. After a shampoo and shower involving myriad fruits and essences, she reckoned she still reeked of smoke. How did Mrs Fire Officer Preston cope? A sado-erotic vision of the pyro-pair coupling underwater in rubber gear and masks flashed before her bloodshot eyes. Sleep deprivation'll do that. She hoped.

Bev settled on a Cambridge-blue trouser suit and her old DMs. Her favourite pair was curling on the radiator in the hall. She refused to look at the crates and boxes. Christ, the place was more of a tip than usual. After last night's action, she was starving, headed for the kitchen in search of a horse. It was equine-free. Best hit the canteen.

En route to Highgate, traffic was light and stars still glistened in a navy sky. She ran a mental check of calls and actions. The guv was taking the brief on the missing baby, which left her free to track loose threads from the fire. Locating Terry Roper was high on the agenda. Had Mr Blue Moon done a moonlight flit? As for the five emergency calls, she'd already requested recordings and transcripts. It was enough to keep her going but if she could fit in a quick meet with Tattoo Man she'd definitely go for it. The morning's priority, however, was Natalie Beck.

After breakfast.

Forty minutes and a canteen fry-up later, Bev was contemplating a third coffee when DI Mike Powell pulled up a chair.

"God, you look rough, Morriss. Late night?"

"You old charmer, you." She flashed a bright smile.

"Very droll." He picked at a bowl of mouse-droppings that might've been muesli.

She cast a covert glance or two, not able to read his expression but sure there was a hidden agenda. The canteen was deserted. Why choose her table? Of all the breakfast bars in all the world...

Her spiky relationship with The Blond had been going on so long, she barely recalled how it started. His promotion to DI over her, four years ago, no longer miffed. Much. They'd both gone for the post but Powell was a yes-man and the force already had its token little lady. Whatever. He was often out of his depth and Bev was sick of throwing life-belts. He saw her as a threat. If she went platinum, had a boob job and zipped her lip they'd get on dandy. Like that was going to happen.

Bev sucked a biro, blew imaginary smoke. She glanced at Powell again. She didn't want an escalation. It was unpleasant as well as unprofessional. And in a way she felt sorry for him. Rumour had it his wife left him for a toy girl. He lived alone and, given his solitary nature, was probably a right Billy No-Mates. She'd make an effort. Proffer, if not the branch, a couple of olives.

"What's new?" She balked at adding 'sir'. He'd stopped insisting.

"That you don't know?" A derisory snort, maybe a sniff. "Been sticking your nose in again, haven't you, Morriss?"

Stuff the olives.

"If you're gonna go through my files," he mumbled

through a mouthful of oats, "for God's sake don't leave footprints."

"Sorry?" And that third coffee was right out the window.

"You left Vince's mug." Charles and Camilla, what a give-away. "And chuck your sweet wrappers away next time."

"Right." The wayward Wagon Wheel. "Nothing new, then." She watched, waited, keen to hear his take on Laura Kenyon's tattoo.

"You putting in a guest appearance at the WAR thing tonight?"

Either the tattoo lead had slipped his mind or he didn't rate it. Far as she was concerned, that gave her carte blanche to have a sniff. As for the Women Against Rape march, she'd barely given it a thought.

"Not my baby, is it?" she said. "Street Watch territory." Bland delivery. Blank look. Total bollocks. She was getting good at this.

"Screaming harpies banging on about men? All blokes are rapists? Right up your street, that."

The genesis of her anti-Powell attitude was coming back to her now. She loathed him because he was an arsehole.

"Practising again?" she asked.

He was picking foreign objects from his teeth with a fingernail. "What?"

"Charm school."

He smirked. Probably thought she meant it. "How's lover boy?" The DI's tone was so casual, it had to be carefully calculated.

Bev stiffened. Oz Khan was off-limits. She definitely wouldn't rise; well, maybe, an eyebrow.

"I didn't realise Genghis was into polygamy?" Powell's idea of a cutting remark.

Thank God Lil had cleared the table. And taken the cutlery.

"Just bumped into him and Goshie in the car park. Like this they were." The DI held two fingers in front of her face before slowly twisting them together.

Stirring. Had to be. She sat on her hands, mentally chose a larger spoon than Powell's. "Seen the guv this morning?"

He sniffed, shook his head.

"Figures." She smiled sweetly. "Be walking with a limp else."

"Fuck you on about?"

"Wants you to explain why Natalie Beck was all over the news. Shots of the house, cops driving her away."

"So?" His indifference was probably feigned.

She added a pinch of spin to the pot. "Some mad fucker thought we were taking her in for questioning."

"Your point being?"

"The house was firebombed last night. 'Burn in hell baby killers' sprayed on the wall." She popped her phone into her bag and rose, looking down at him. "I was there most of the night. It's why I look so rough." She gave his stricken features an ostentatious once-over. "What's your excuse?"

The tape and transcripts were on Bev's desk. The same person had made all five emergency calls. A man's voice, young-ish, accent-less. It didn't ring a bell. The content was short and simple: fire at a house in Blake Way, four people trapped. She'd already despatched door-to-door teams.

"The Becks'll have to hear it." Byford nodded at the player.

"Could be a problem there. Maxine's still unconscious. And Natalie's not talking to me."

The silence in the office underlined the dilemma.

"What a mess, Bev." The guv slouched on a wall, stared at the floor. The posture said it all.

It wasn't personal. She knew that. Byford spoke more in sorrow than in censure. He'd just taken an early brief without a single development in the hunt for the missing baby. The squads weren't losing interest, just hope. The operation was forty-eight hours old. After today, they'd be going over the same ground again. The trail wasn't just cold, it was invisible.

"Why take a baby from her cot?" she asked. "That's the big one, guv. What's the motive?"

They'd already hashed and re-hashed the point. Hadn't come up with an answer.

"What?" Byford had detected a glint in those bloodshot-blues.

She was trying a different approach. She rose, started pacing, hands gesturing. "Why take that particular baby?"

"Go on."

"We're talking Becks, not Beckhams."

Byford pulled his feet out of the way. "We've ruled out kidnapping."

"Exactly. So if not a ransom, what are they after?"

"Not with you."

She wasn't there yet, still feeling her way. "Suppose Zoë's value's not in cash? Suppose she's special in some other way?"

"Like…?"

She halted in front of him. "How about medical?"

"Rare blood group? Bone marrow?"

She spread her hands. "I don't know yet, guv. Something like that. It makes sense. Got to be worth a check."

Nothing else had panned out. "Careful how you tread, Bev. Anything along the lines you're thinking implies inside knowledge, collusion from a doctor, nurse, staff at the hospital where Natalie gave birth, ante-natal clinic, even the girl's GP."

"I'll get Oz on it. He's good at that sort of thing."

Byford nodded, headed for the door. "You'll give me a bell from the General?"

"Soon as."

The guv was hoping she could persuade Natalie to appear before the cameras that afternoon. He'd rescheduled the media appeal for four. Bev wasn't convinced the girl would see her, let alone talk to her.

15

The last person Bev expected to run into at the hospital was Mr Blue Moon, sprawled on a plastic bench in a shabby waiting area off intensive care. The laid-back Terry Roper looked as if he'd taken excellent care of himself. His soft leather jacket smelt expensive and competed with tangy aftershave she knew was pricey. Oz wore it. Both odours held their own against the smorgasbord of medicinal aromas that invariably made Bev want to throw up.

"Well, well, well. The wanderer returns." Amiable smile.

He flashed one back. "Hi, sarge." *HELLO!* magazine was obviously more interesting.

She dreaded to think what Roper's attitude was doing to her blood pressure. She moved in on him; unless they exchanged body fluids, she'd not get any closer. "It's sergeant to you. And where the hell have you been?"

He glanced up, a slight frown marring the fine features. "Here. Since the early hours."

"Not that early. I didn't leave till gone four." Pushing it a bit.

"I got here soon as I could." He licked an index finger, turned the page. Bev had never understood Kate Moss's appeal. She grabbed the magazine and Roper's full, if belated, attention.

"Not soon enough." The blue eyes blazed. "You were supposed to be looking out for Maxine and Natalie. Where were you when they needed you?" She knew it was a pot-kettle-black call but she'd already given herself a hard time. It was Roper's turn.

"Get over it. Nobody's dead." She'd kill Roper if he didn't

104

stop checking his reflection in the glass opposite. "Maxine's off the ventilator. Natalie can leave any time."

"Thanks, doc. But you haven't answered the question."

Neither had he forgotten it. He shrugged indifference. "Max and me had a row. She was doing my head in. I needed to chill, went back to my pad."

"What time?"

He twisted his mouth. "Must've left about midnight, half-twelve."

"And you went straight home?"

"Yeah. Then I felt guilty. I mean, it's not Max's fault, is it? I slipped back about five. Had a word with your people and came down here."

"Liar." A squad car had checked Roper's place in Selly Oak. Several times. "You didn't go anywhere near home."

He held his palms out. "True as I'm sitting here."

"That's it." She turned her back. "I'm taking you in."

"You can't do that."

"Watch me." She put the mobile to her ear. Not that it was switched on.

"OK, OK." Roper raised a placatory palm as he watched her lower the phone. "Look, sergeant. I was hoping this wouldn't have to come out…"

She wasn't prompting. The lines were predictable.

"I was…" He cleared his throat. "With a woman."

Bev's lips couldn't get any tighter.

"I don't want Maxine to know." Pinching the bridge of his nose was so over the top. "I'd like to spare her that."

"Spare me an' all," Bev muttered. "Name. Address. Give. Now."

She wrote down details, then hit buttons on the phone.

"What are you doing?" It was almost a shriek.

"Organising wheels. Your lift to the nick."

105

"But Maxine needs me," he pleaded. "And Natalie. Why do I have to go to a police station?"

"So you can help our enquiries."

"Into what?" He looked even more attractive when he wasn't putting on an act.

"Zoë's disappearance. Arson. Wasting police time. Where shall I stop?"

"But I haven't done anything."

Far as she knew, he was right. They didn't have a scrap of evidence against him. Being a cocky toe-rag and ham actor weren't crimes, last time she looked. "Firemen repeatedly risked their lives for you last night, Roper. They entered a blazing building looking for the sodding invisible man."

"You're right. I'm sorry." They were probably the first words he hadn't rehearsed. "But it doesn't make me a criminal."

"I want the clothes you were wearing last night."

The shock was definitely genuine. "You can take my entire wardrobe if it'll get you off my back."

"And I want a search of your place."

"Anything. I swear I've done nothing wrong."

"I caught you out in one lie, Roper." She practised hard stares in her bathroom. She was fixing him with the concrete-piercing one.

"I was only protecting Maxine."

"Your arse is what you were protecting."

"You're wrong, sergeant. I'd do anything to help Max, Nats. Anything at all."

Eureka. Music to her ears. "When you say *anything*…?"

The checks would be run, including criminal background, but she didn't really think Roper's hands were dirty. She did suspect pretty boy could wrap Natalie round his little finger. And get her to talk.

"I'd rather eat shit."

"That a no?" The question was superfluous. Not a pore on Natalie Beck's face was open to appeal. Bev had been giving it her best shot for the better part of thirty minutes. Natalie, stringy arms tight across her chest, legs clamped round the legs of a chair at her mother's bedside, hissed through clenched teeth, "Look at her! Look what those bastards have done."

Maxine Beck looked like a stiff. Heavy sedation and grey skin reinforced the deathly aspect. She was off the ventilator but by no means off the sick list.

Natalie was scared; scared to death she'd lose her mother. As well as her baby. Bev reached out a hand. The girl recoiled.

"Fuck off. Leave me alone."

Neither noticed God and his band of angels hovering at the end of the bed. God was in subtle pinstripe and shiny brogues with stethoscope accessory. The band was in white. The voice accustomed to being obeyed.

"I want to examine the patient."

They weren't asked to leave; the consultant's request was implicit.

In the corridor Natalie asked, "Got a smoke?"

"Sure. Outside?" Thank you, PC Wells.

They sat puffing on a low wall opposite the main entrance. An azure sky and bright sun contrasted sharply with the teenager's black mood. Natalie's first deep drag sparked a coughing fit. She'd probably swallowed enough smoke last night to last a lifetime. No point mentioning it.

Bev delved in her bag and proffered a bottle of Evian. "I know you're angry, Natalie."

"You got that right."

Bev sniffed. It was gone eleven. Charm and sweet talk hadn't done it and she had a stack of other stuff to get through. "I didn't take your baby, Natalie. And I didn't set fire to your house."

The teenager bit her lip.

"I want to nail the bad guys. I can't do it on my own."

"Some mad fucker almost killed me. I'm not laying myself open to a load of crazies."

"You won't be. My governor's sorting that as we speak." Byford had called a news conference to issue a warning on the potential impact of irresponsible coverage. There was no proof the TV pictures had led to the arson attack, so it would be a subtle slap on the wrist combined with an appeal for common sense and restraint. Like, yeah. Either way, if the rollicking was the guv's big stick, the fat juicy carrot was alongside Bev, still stonewalling.

"You lot have done sod all." She took another cigarette without asking.

Bev's patience was on its way out. She recalled the strained expressions on the search teams' exhausted faces, firefighters selflessly putting their lives on the line, contrasted it with the girl's monosyllabic grunts. Natalie had contributed nothing. Not a single thought on who might have lied to the emergency services, let alone torched the place. A media appeal for Zoë didn't seem a lot to ask.

"Managed a damn sight more than you, love." Bev flicked the dog-end away and briskly rose. "Tell you this. If my kid was taken I'd swallow razor blades and shit glass if it got her back. Sitting in front of a couple of cameras is a piece of piss, Natalie. And it just might work." She made a move to leave, then turned, chucked the pack at the girl. "Have another fag, Nat. Don't put yourself out, will you?"

Back in the motor, Bev pounded the steering wheel with

both hands. It drowned the first rap on the window. At the next, she turned her head. Natalie Beck did not look like Little Miss Happy but at least she was there.

An hour later, Bev was in Mac's café opposite Luke Mangold's tattoo parlour – Pain and Ink – in Digbeth. She'd shoehorned a brief encounter into a day already bursting at the seams. And the man was running late. When she at last spotted him striding across the road, her sigh of relief was audible.

Before their first meeting, Bev had envisaged a hairy biker, all chains and leathers, running to fat and crawling in tattoos. Early forties, Mangold was more lace cuffs and paisley cravats, a cross between a camp hairdresser and a men's tailor, a sort of suits-you-sir with scissors.

As he approached the table, Mangold removed his elegant panama and gave a mock bow. His hair was mole-grey action-man crop. Except for a bald spot the size of a ten-pence piece. "Sergeant Morriss." He gave a conspiratorial wink, the tone mildly flirtatious. "We can't go on meeting like this. People will talk."

She forced a weak laugh. "Good of you to see me again, sir. Appreciate it." Given the distance from his workplace, it wasn't exactly putting him out. He'd suggested meeting here the first time as well. Probably just didn't want police on the premises. Bad for business and all that.

"Have you ordered?" Mangold asked.

"Just coffee." She lifted the mug. "You go ahead." The Highgate fry-up was still lining her stomach. Anyway, she was pushed for time. Not to mention a tad on edge. This little chat was off the record. And her own bat.

A blonde waitress called from behind the counter, asking Mangold if he wanted the usual. Mangold gave a thumbs-up,

109

then fixed his gaze on Bev. "So what can I do for you this time, sergeant?"

No point prevaricating. "Another girl's been raped."

"And?" Was that a slight edge in the voice?

She tipped sugar into her mug, slowly stirred. She should've thought this through a little better. "As you know, we're still trying to establish a link between the victims."

"And?"

"We know one of the girls got a tattoo…"

Mangold leaned in close, too close for her comfort; the eye contact was positively claustrophobic. "Let's get things clear. Am I a suspect? Because if I am, stop pissing around and come straight out with it."

She would if she could. Fact was, there was no evidence against Luke Mangold. Gut instinct and making her skin creep didn't count. "We're talking to everyone who's come into contact with the girls."

"Girl," he snapped. "I've only come into contact with Rebecca Fox. Like I told you before. When, as you'll remember, I bent over backwards to help."

She nodded. Interesting. Hundreds, thousands of people must pass through the man's hands. "Do you remember the name of everyone you tattoo?"

Mangold's stare was unnerving. "Only when they've been raped." He paused. "And the cops come sniffing round."

No more Mr Nice Guy then? On the other hand, if he was innocent maybe the attitude was justified.

"Here you go, Luke." The girl plonked a plate of egg and chips in front of him.

"Cheers, Will."

Bev did a double-take. Will was no waitress. The dark-blond hair had now been pulled back into a neat ponytail, revealing fine though definitely not female features. Tres fit, in fact.

"Get to the match Saturday, Luke?" The waiter's knowing smile showcased perfect teeth and suggested he didn't need Mangold's answer.

Bev observed as the tattooist sighed theatrically and reached reluctantly for his wallet. "The ref was blind, my son."

Will winked at Bev as he tucked Mangold's tenner into a back pocket. "Yeah, yeah. And Villa were rubbish."

For Bev skin setting on custard had more going for it than football, but even she knew Blues had thrashed Aston Villa. Half Highgate had policed the game.

"Five-nil, wasn't it?" she asked. "Two penalties?"

Will inclined his head, impressed. "Sure I can't get you anything, lady?"

She could think of a few things but none involved food. The salacious fantasy prompted a quick smile. "No, thanks, mate."

"Shame."

His eyes held hers a second longer than strictly necessary. Or was that wishful thinking? She watched as he executed a playful salute, then headed back to the counter.

Mangold was scrutinising her. "You're not his type, sergeant." The man's smile was more of a smirk.

She ignored it, kept her voice casual, conversational. "Kate Quinn. Ever come across her?"

"Nope."

"Laura Kenyon?"

"Nope." Another unwavering stare as he bit into a thick chip. "Far as I know."

"Far as you know?"

"They can say they're Madonna if they want to. I don't ask for ID." He sighed, made a beckoning motion with his hand. "Let's have a look at the pictures. I never forget a face."

She stiffened. Photographs. Fuck.

"You've not brought any?" A patronising Mangold shook his head in contempt.

She could kick herself. Seeing Mangold was a last-minute, spur-of-the-moment arrangement but that was no excuse. Maybe she was taking on too much. "I'll get them to you, soon as."

He took a biro from an inside pocket, jotted a number. "My solicitor. Go through him next time, love." Egg yolk glistened on a chipped front tooth. She saw it when he smiled. "Better still... send a senior officer, eh?"

16

Back at Highgate, Bev raced across the car park, head down against a heavy shower.

"Whoa, where's the fire, Morriss?"

Powell. Great. She'd almost slammed into him; he was holding her at arm's length. Could life get any sweeter?

She pulled away. The Beck girl's media appeal needed a final touch or two and Bev was well late. The sodding MG had let her down in Digbeth. Still smarting from Mangold's verbal mauling, she'd had to borrow jump leads from some old bloke who'd told her at great length that little ladies shouldn't have to worry their pretty heads about what goes on under the bonnet. Bev knew full well what was going on under hers: the starter motor was on its way out. The Midget had been on the blink for a fortnight, was booked in for the work.

"Making up for lost time, are we?" Powell asked.

There was a point in there somewhere. "Look, mate, it's pissing down and I'm in a hurry."

He tapped the side of his nose. "Little tip, Morriss. Stop telling lies and stirring."

"You what?"

"All that crap in the canteen? Taking a pop at me?"

Must mean her implication that the arson attack was down to the TV pictures of Natalie being driven into Highgate. The visit Powell arranged. She shrugged.

The DI jabbed a finger. "You'd not be running round like a blue-arsed fly if you focused on the job and quit shit-bagging."

"Can you get a move on? Natalie Beck's waiting for me."

"You think you know it all, don't you, Morriss? Well, you don't. One more step out of line…"

She didn't hang round to find out. The lecture was superfluous anyway. Her crass handling of the Mangold interview had been lesson enough. She'd got up his nose and put him on his guard. Far from advancing the Street Watch inquiry, it could have jeopardised it. If it went tits up, it would be her fault and it wasn't even her case.

Frail and fragile, dwarfed by the mahogany table's vast expanse, Natalie Beck faced a bank of cameras and media hard men. The backdrop was a huge photograph of her missing baby. Apart from Natalie's breathy voice, pleading and at breaking point, Highgate's conference room was hushed and still. The teenager was a natural. But it didn't come across as a performance. Natalie's honesty, concern and love shone like sunlight on water.

"My heart's hurting really bad. She's my little angel. And I'm her mum. We need each other." The baby was in her mind's eye; the ghost of a smile played on the girl's lips. "She's such a tiny little thing." Natalie shook away the image, stared straight into the lens. "I'll do anything to get my baby back. Anything. If you can help me, please call the police. Please let me know where she is and that she's safe and well."

Bev exchanged an abashed glance with Byford. They'd done her a disservice. With her pierced eyebrows and pebble-dash skin Natalie might look like an extra from Little Britain, but the sixteen-year-old spoke eloquently and movingly from an open heart the size of a planet. Would the viewing public see beyond the sink-estate schoolgirl-mum image?

"I brought her this." Natalie produced a tiny teddy bear,

set it on the table in all its pink-furred cock-eyed glory. "She loves it. Can you give it to her? I'll leave it so you can pick it up. Anywhere you like." She dropped her head. "Just till you give me my baby back."

The teddy bear was Natalie's idea. There wasn't a dry eye in the house. No one shouted pointless questions, no one urged the girl to look up. The silence told its own story. The tear-stained polished wood surface added a poignant postscript. Bev put her arms round the weeping girl, helped her stand and led her from the room.

Within minutes of the Natalie Beck Show hitting the airwaves, the control room switchboard resembled a light display. The missing baby had been sighted in Cardiff and Cannock, Derby and Dorset. One caller reckoned he'd seen her take off from Birmingham International Airport – in a spaceship. Other information was less promising.

By seven pm Bev was in the incident room listening to the latest update from the control co-ordinator, Jack Hainsworth. She just held back from taking out her frustration on the phone. "Loony tunes and fruitcakes." Instead, the bin took the full force of a size seven.

Oz knelt, gathered the load of litter and empty coffee cups. "It's early days, sarge. Break could come any time."

Break as in through or crack? Natalie Beck's fragile veneer couldn't stand much more. The third day's search had just been called off. It would not resume on the Wordsworth estate. The teenager was back at her mother's bedside.

Oz shucked into his jacket. "If there's nothing else, I'm off."

"Sure." The sigh came from her boots. She was still in the foothills of the latest paper mountain. So much for an early night.

Oz picked up on her mood, came over, took a perch. "It was a good thought, sarge. A medical link."

She snorted. Good thought. Crap result. Oz's report was on the desk in front of her. He'd contacted every medico who'd so much as laid eyes, let alone hands, on the baby. Not so much as a hint of surgical skulduggery. Short straw wasn't in it. It was brick wall after brick wall.

"Fancy a drink, Ozzie?" They could job-talk, bounce ideas. She missed that. She missed him.

"Not tonight, Josephine." Making light of it didn't work. He saw her face. In a normal voice he said he had something on.

Something or someone? She'd brushed off the DI's poisonous dart about Oz and Sumitra Gosh. Maybe it had left a flesh wound.

Pointedly, she turned her back, picked up a file. "G'night."

Nothing beat a couple of hours' ploughing through the tangled prose of police witness reports. Well, maybe feeding your head through a mangle. Bev leaned back, rubbed the taut tendons in her neck. Her running commentary of notes included a few thoughts for tomorrow. She rang control one last time before hitting the road. Loads of callers had expressed sympathy, a handful was beyond abusive. One nutter claimed slags like Natalie Beck sold babies for cash; it'd be best all round if she was sterilised. Bev sighed. At least there were no more little green men.

She grabbed her jacket and bag, mouth watering at the prospect of an Indian. She'd pick up a takeaway, then nip into Threshers for a cheeky little number from the chill cabinet. With a following wind, she'd still be in bed by ten.

And then the phone rang.

"If you ask me, there's more to that story than meets the eye." Helen Carver was multi-tasking: applying a fresh coat of lipstick and watching the ten o'clock news. She paused, jabbed the tube at the TV. "The girl's revelling in the attention, look at her." David Carver, who was marking course-work, glanced at the screen: Natalie Beck flanked by police officers against a huge blow-up photograph of her baby.

Carver shrugged disinterest and returned to another startlingly original take on Jane Austen.

"Well?" There were times Helen sounded more like the lecturer. "What do you think?"

Had Helen not been finishing the paint job, she'd have seen his fingers tighten round the pen. "Seems genuine enough to me. Poor girl's probably in shock."

"Poor girl?" Helen sneered. "Poor baby, more like." In Helen's opinion sluts like Natalie Beck shouldn't have children. She frowned, eyes creased. The shot now showed Bev shepherding the teenage mother out of the conference room. "Isn't she one of the officers who talked to you after your student was…" She couldn't bring herself to use the word.

"Raped?" Carver said. "Yes, it is. Her name's Morriss. Sergeant, I think."

Helen mentally filed that but hadn't finished with the baby yet. "Do you think the baby's dead?"

Carver sighed, resigned to a discussion he didn't want. "I think it's strange she's not been seen. My understanding is if a new baby turns up somewhere out of the blue, a neighbour or someone tips off the police."

Helen adopted a pensive pose. "Maybe the kidnapper's not some deranged woman. Maybe it's more sinister than that." She glanced round as her mother-in-law walked in cradling Jessica. The baby smelt divine after her bath. Helen barely paused the conversation. "So what do you think is really going on?"

Carver strolled to the sideboard, poured a scotch, held the bottle aloft. "Drink, mother?"

Subject closed, then. Helen scowled, tugged angrily at the long sleeves of her cashmere sweater before reaching to take Jessica. The old woman turned and smiled at her son, then settled into the recliner opposite her daughter-in-law. "Just a small one, Davy."

The nightly exchange had become a ritual. Not one in which Helen participated. Or approved.

She had little time for David's widowed mother. It was pathetic, the way she doted on him. He'd suggested Veronica move in with them and initially Helen had welcomed the arrangement. Domestic challenges held no appeal, and she'd come to regard Veronica as little more than unpaid housekeeper. Given the old woman's tight bun and strait-laced wardrobe, it wasn't surprising. But though Veronica had never uttered a word against her daughter-in-law, Helen sensed her disapproval.

Irritated, she half-listened as mother and son chatted cosily. Their family history was a subject Helen neither shared nor cared about. She snatched at the remote control and increased the volume. The baby coverage on the regional news was virtually the same but showing now was an item on the street protest that night in Moseley: Women Against Rape. Which reminded her…

"Is that business over yet, David?"

Heavy dark eyebrows knotted as Carver wondered what Helen was getting at. He followed her gaze, caught a line of women wielding placards.

"The police haven't caught anyone, if that's what you mean."

"I mean are you likely to be questioned again?" The tone was peremptory.

"I don't see your problem, Helen."

Uneasily she looked down as the baby shifted slightly in her sleep; mauve eyelids fluttered, then stilled. Helen lowered her voice. "Unless you've done something wrong, it's police harassment."

She hadn't meant it to come out like that. It sounded like an accusation. An apology was probably in order but before she'd framed it, he was almost at the door.

"Where…"

"Out."

The slam startled Jessica who started bawling. Helen glared. Veronica rose, loomed over her daughter-in-law.

"I'll take the baby, shall I, dear?"

17

Bev's sides ached. So did the middle bit, currently awash with mussels, lasagne and tiramisu in a chianti suspension. Frankie Perlagio was laughing gas on tap. Given that her poppa ran an Italian restaurant, eating at Little Italy in Moseley was a bit chips-to-Silicon-Valley, but it was Frankie's call. When she'd phoned, Bev had almost turned her down, was so glad now she'd said yes. Though it took a while to recognise the feeling, she was almost laid back.

She'd met Frankie on their first day at primary school and, as a mate, she was better than a pack of Prozac. She was a semi-pro session singer and had she been offered as many recording contracts as she'd turned down modelling deals, she'd be filling the Albert Hall by now. Think Nina Simone with a killer accent and tumbling raven locks.

Frankie had only phoned to say thanks for the flowers: Bev's Interflora grovelfest. Frankie's emotional radar being sharper than NASA's, she'd said, "You sound shit. You're coming out to play, my friend."

No had not been an option.

Anyway, Little Italy was in staggering distance of Baldwin Street. Luckily, as Bev was making inroads into a second bottle. Frankie was in full Italian flow with a waiter who bore a passing resemblance to Pacino. Mind, in lighting this subtle Bev could pass for Keira Knightley. She clocked the ambience while Frankie flirted shamelessly. There were chipped busts and flaky statues in every candle-lit alcove and the owner had a thing about water features. Bev had been to the loo three times.

"Are you back on the weed, Beverley?" Frankie's Roman nose could sniff out cigarette smoke on Bonfire Night.

"Might be."

"Sucker."

She took a drag on a breadstick. Frankie rolled her eyes. "Patches, gum, cold turkey. You've tried everything. What about Drumsticks?"

"How's that work? You play Ginger Baker solos till the craving passes?"

Frankie, who'd been rummaging in her bag, pulled out a kid's lollipop. "This, my friend, is a Drumstick. Mate of mine swears by them. Every time he fancies a ciggie, he sticks one of these in his mouth."

"So why've you got one?"

She cocked an eyebrow. "I don't wish to go there."

"Pass it over, then. I'll put it behind my ear for later."

Pacino hovered, handing them grappas on the house. Frankie's flirting always paid off; Bev generally had a share of the proceeds. They covered more of the usual ground: blokes, books, the blues (music and Bev's gear). Then Frankie mentioned the big b-word.

"If you want to talk about the baby, Bev…"

They discussed cases from time to time. Frankie was solid, wouldn't breathe a letter, let alone a word. Bev held nothing back: the Becks' chequered history, Natalie's rape, the arson attack, Roper's dubious role in the women's lives, the decision to call off the search. Talking it through, she felt fear for the first time. Fear they'd never find Zoë, or her body. She didn't share the thought.

Frankie put a hand over Bev's. "She might still be alive, my friend."

Bev swallowed, looked away.

"You've checked women with a history?"

"One of the first things we did." Every baby-snatch on file. "Thing is, there's only one record of a baby being snatched from its *home*. Maternity wards, sure. Off the street? Def. But…" She shrugged.

"What happened in that case?"

Baby Fay. Burned, abused and buried. The evidence had been checked and triple-checked in the last forty-eight hours. Witnesses had been re-interviewed. They were trying to track down Fay's father in the States.

"The baby was murdered. We never discovered who took her, or why."

They finished the grappa in silent sync.

"What happens to the women?" Frankie asked. "Are they jailed?"

Bev shook her head. "Probation. Psychiatric treatment. They rarely harm the babies – damage themselves more, in the long run."

"How?"

"They're all over the media. The public hates them. They're pointed out wherever they go." So might they change their identity? She made a mental note.

"What you thinking?" Frankie asked.

"Not sure yet. Fancy another drink?"

Pacino brought the bottle. When he'd gone Frankie asked about Natalie.

Bev sighed. "When she's not at the General with her mum, she's at Terry Roper's place. Natalie's only got the clothes on her back. The blaze destroyed everything. She'll get a handout from Social Services, and the council will re-house them. Eventually."

"Poor kid." Frankie stared into space. "Imagine your baby being snatched… It doesn't get much worse than that."

But it does. Bev felt a tingle. She sat up straight, focusing.

What about babies who died? At birth? Grief could push people over the edge. She'd assigned a team to run checks on women who'd snatched a baby. Not on women who'd lost a baby. It was conceivable a desperate woman would try to replace the child she'd lost. Bev had no idea what the figures for stillbirths were. And what about miscarriages? And how far back should they go? It could be mega – had to be worth it.

"Frankie." Her blue eyes shone. "I've said it before, I'll say it again."

"Yeah, yeah, yeah." She flapped a hand. "Born genius, that's me."

"Nah, mate. Smart-arse."

So smart, Bev had to explain why. They were nearly back at Baldwin Street before Frankie was on the same page. That could have been down to the grappa.

Half a mile away a more sober scene was being played. The Women Against Rape march was approaching the railway embankment where Laura Kenyon had been attacked. The organisers' claims that the protest would attract hundreds of followers were not realised. The concept of a midnight vigil perhaps losing its attraction with the reality of freezing your ass off on the streets of Moseley.

Spearheading about sixty placard-carrying participants were The MP and The Mouth. The Tory member, Josephine Kramer, linked arms and joined voices with Martha Kemp. They led a chant that barely rhymed and made little reason.

"Safer streets…cage the beast…safer streets…cage the beast…safer streets… cage the beast…"

"Catchy little number." DI Powell cast a disparaging look through the side window of an unmarked car. "Wonder how long it took to come up with that."

DC Carol Mansfield cast a surreptitious glance at her watch.

"Keen to get off, are we?" The smirk was not subtle.

Having been stuck in a confined space with The Blond for over an hour, she'd jump at a Mexican wax. And fears that the demonstration could turn nasty appeared exaggerated. Uniforms accompanying the route weren't so much peacekeeping as preventing asbo louts taking the piss. Unlike the foot soldiers, Powell and Mansfield were keeping a watching brief from a slow-moving motor.

"It's hardly the Battle of Little Big Horn," Carol observed.

Powell's yawn revealed a couple of fillings. "Nah, all mouth and knicker elastic. Still, you never know. We'll stick around till they light the candles. Reckon there'll be a cake?"

The crack didn't merit comment. The chant continued.

"Safer streets, cage the beast, safer streets…"

"Look at them, Caz. What d'they reckon this'll achieve? What's the bloody point?"

Carol tilted her head. "That." Across the street, a TV reporter was doing a piece to camera with the motley crowd as a moving canvas. "Public awareness," Carol said. "And it puts the heat on us, doesn't it?" She pointed a gloved finger. "Look at the placards."

'Police crisis? What police crisis?' The irony was supposed to echo an insensitive comment on the economy by a seventies Labour PM, who was subsequently kicked out by an underwhelmed electorate.

Powell was clearly not impressed. "Yeah. And who's gonna catch the bastard? It'll be us, not this bunch of tarts." He added a mutter.

"What did you say?" She'd caught the odd word: dyke,

dungarees, mouthy, bints.

"Nothing."

The march had arrived at its destination; the women were beginning to gather alongside the wire fencing.

"Safer streets, cage the beast…"

Powell pulled over, parked. "It's bloody true, though. Comes down to solid police-work and shoe leather. Not shouting your mouth off and getting your mug on the telly."

"When you doing *Crimewatch*?" It was a childish but irresistible dig. Powell had been poncing around ever since the call from the programme's producer. She'd been forced to drop an item at the last moment and wanted Powell on that week's show. The DI had been hustling for a spot for months. He was like a kid in Toys 'r' Us.

"Great, isn't it? Couldn't have timed it better if I'd tried." Powell would have a nationwide audience for an E-fit that Natalie Beck had finally produced. He'd grabbed her that afternoon after her appeal at Highgate.

Carol had seen it and was surprised at the detail. Still, as he was in a comparatively decent mood…

"Laura Kenyon's tattoo? When are we following it up?"

The smile vanished. "Just 'cause Morriss bangs on about something doesn't mean it's kosher."

"Are you pissed because you don't rate it as a lead or because of whose lead it is?"

"Are you questioning me?"

Does shit stink? She shrugged.

"Look, Carol. One thing you need to learn in this job is when to let go. I had a sniff at the tattoo line. I don't think…"

Whatever he thought was lost. Martha Kemp was mouthing off and the megaphone was superfluous. Even with the windows closed, they could hear every word. The gist boiled down to: women should fight for freedom; rapists should get jailed for life. And the crowd went wild.

Powell sniffed. "What's Kemp doing here, anyway? I thought she was supposed to be talking bollocks in the studio."

"They decided not to go ahead with that." Carol shook her head as she recalled the fraught scene at the Kemp house when Laura admitted stealing from her mother. "I guess the star attraction lost its shine. Either Martha dropped the interview or Laura pulled out."

"Got a new best buddy now." Powell nodded in Kemp's direction. She was hugging Josephine Kramer. The MP then gave the gathering the benefit of her take on capital punishment and concluded with a call for the establishment of a national police body along FBI lines. That was new. Yawn.

Powell checked his hair in the mirror. "Not mentioned castration? There's a surprise."

Carol perked up as the first candles were lit. Guidelines had been established showing where and how the candles were to be placed. Within minutes flickering flames spelt the letter W.

Powell's face creased in puzzlement. "Women? War?"

"Could be wanker." The merest hint of a lip-twitch.

"Are you…?"

"We calling it a night, then?"

He wavered, not sure. Sixty-odd females bursting into the first bars of *You'll Never Walk Alone* tipped the balance.

He turned the engine on. "Where d'you want dropping?"

The man in the shadows rather liked his pet name. The Beast of Birmingham had a certain ring to it. He smiled.

The women's chanting had given him a hard-on.

"Cage the beast…cage the beast…"

He'd masturbated along to it. Shame he couldn't come in their faces. Couldn't risk being seen, though. Not when he had so much work to do. He'd selected his next prey already. Given the pigs were out in force tonight, he'd half-expected to see her here. Like last time. He reached in a pocket for the silk French knickers he'd taken from her house. The semen was already stiffening. Shame. They didn't smell of her any more.

"Cage the beast…cage the beast…cage the beast…"

18

Tuesday. Eight am. Highgate. Cappuccino in one hand, a stack of printouts in the other, Bev bummed the office door shut and headed for her desk. A picture of a geek from a boy band was propped on the keyboard. Why? Her frown deepened as realisation sank in. The pretty boy with smouldering looks wasn't some pop-star wannabe. It was an artist's impression of the man who raped Natalie Beck. Underneath was an E-fit. Ditto.

A hand-scrawled post-it note fluttered to the floor. It wasn't signed but Powell's name was all over it.

Morriss, these are hot off the press via your mate Natalie Beck. They'll also be on network telly Thursday night. Thought I'd keep you posted – save you poking your nose in again.

Why couldn't the berk just say *Crimewatch?* Bev sipped coffee, deep in thought. Cosying up to Fiona Bruce would be the fulfilment of a lifetime's ambition for Powell. Good for him – if it got them any nearer a collar.

She parked the cup on a beer mat and picked up the visuals again. Something wasn't right. E-fits were often one-size-fits-all. Christ, some of them were so general they could be your mother. This picture had a fair bit of detail: a mole above the top lip, a tiny white scar on a dark eyebrow, a crucifix dangling from an earlobe. Bev drummed the desk with her fingers. It was impressive, given that Natalie claimed she'd only caught a brief glimpse of the attacker almost a year ago.

Whatever. She had to back off; it wasn't her case. She laid them to one side, unwrapped a lollipop and got stuck into her own. Phone-bashing the hospitals was a big job. She'd make a start but it would have to be dished out. The thought led to Frankie. The girlie night had been great. All being well, Ms Perlagio was coming round on Saturday to lend a hand getting Baldwin Street straight. She'd taken one look at the place and told Bev to call the cops, she'd been burgled. Bev shook her head and smiled. Mind, not being able to lay her hands on things was getting to be a pain.

On that thought, she rang the General to get the latest on Maxine Beck's condition. Sounded promising: if the X-rays looked good she'd be moved from IC later that morning.

The letter, marked Personal, was on Byford's desk when he arrived at Highgate that morning. There was no postmark. Inside, three words typed on a sheet of A4. His hand shook as he read and re-read the contents.

REMEMBER BABY FAY?

Every day. Every night. He'd never forget that tiny burned broken body.

"Everything OK?" An admin assistant breezed in with a handful of post. Rachel habitually dressed in black but her nickname was Ray, as in sunshine.

"When did this arrive?" The voice was sharper than he'd intended.

She glanced at the envelope, her smile wavering. "No idea. Obviously not with this lot." She dropped the mail in his in-tray. "Sure you're OK? Can I get you anything? Tea? Coffee? Bacon roll?"

He almost gagged at the thought. "Don't fuss, woman." He'd known her ten years, never spoken to her so harshly, nowhere near. It wasn't her fault she had a walk-on part in his personal nightmare.

The early brief was tense and tetchy. It was the fourth day of the search for the missing baby. They were seventy-two hours down the line, not a step further forward.

Determination was now tinged with depression. To many, it was no longer a question of finding the baby alive, but when they'd find the body.

As Jack Hainsworth ran through overnight reports, Bev glanced at the guv. He'd not opened his mouth; with a jaw so clamped, maybe he couldn't. When Hainsworth finished, Bev took over. She moved to the front and outlined the calls that needed follow-ups: the less outlandish sightings and dubious steers from a public that seemed desperate to help but didn't have a lot to offer.

By contrast, a sadistic sleaze-ball had reported finding a baby's body in a dustbin at the back of a butcher's in Aston. Squad cars were there within minutes. Officers discovered a doll dumped on top of a load of stinking bones and putrid meat. The sleaze-ball's IQ barely equalled his hat size. Wasting police time was the charge. He'd be wasting magistrates' in a couple of hours.

"Sick bastard." Darren New's up-sum was universally shared.

"There's a new line on the arson attack." Bev hoped for a show of enthusiasm but bodies slouched and faces were mostly down-turned. "As you know, we traced the phone boxes where the calls were made." Both in Balsall Heath. "A youth was seen – right place, right time – by three separate witnesses."

"So?" DC Ricky Shephard: young, brash, bordering on bolshie.

Thanks, mate. It wasn't earth-shattering but it was a development. If they tracked the kid down, it could open a new line of inquiries. She put Shephard on the trail, then assigned the rest of the actions.

A glance at Byford invited him to chip in. A barely perceptible shake of his head declined. She outlined her embryonic theory that the snatch was down to a woman whose baby had died either ante- or shortly after birth. Given the expressions, people were thinking it over. Dazza voiced his.

"Hell of a haystack, isn't it, sarge?"

"It is and it isn't." She'd thought it through a bit more. "Zoë wasn't snatched at random. Whoever took her didn't hit the Beck house on the off chance a new-born just happened to be lying around."

"They had to know Natalie was pregnant. Had to know she'd given birth."

Bev knew the voice, looked round for the speaker. DC Gosh was at the back. Next to Oz. Bev filed a thought, expounded her idea. "So we're looking for someone who was maybe in hospital at the same time as Natalie, someone on the same GP list, maybe a woman who attended ante-natal classes. Anyone with that level of contact."

"I'll give you a hand, sarge," Oz said. "I already contacted some of the likely places on the earlier medical line."

She nodded thanks, then threw the brief open. Discussion was desultory. It was as though everyone knew the ending. And that there'd be tears.

"I've no idea. You tell me." Byford's head was in his hands. Bev was floundering. She'd been summoned to his office immediately after the briefing. She'd never heard the guv sound so… diminished? Defeated? And why hadn't he mentioned the anonymous letter to the troops? Was he doing a Morriss? Getting personally involved? She placed the paper on the desk between them.

"Could be anyone, guv. It was a big inquiry at the time."

"Bull." He strode to the window, perched on the sill, nearly dislodged the cactus. "Whoever sent it knows something. That letter's a taunt." He tucked hands under armpits. "And it's personal."

She didn't read it that way. "It's hardly Sutcliffe territory, guv." Coppers' blood still ran cold at the mocking tapes and letters sent by the hoaxer purporting to be the Yorkshire Ripper. It had taken nearly thirty years to track the sicko down. "It's just three words. Sounds innocuous enough to me."

"You weren't around at the time, sergeant."

She shrugged. "So what's behind it?"

"How the devil should I know?"

Least he wasn't swearing. "What do you want to do about it?"

"What the fuck *can* I do about it?"

"Start by finding out how it got here." Highgate wasn't exactly access all areas. Someone in the building must have dropped it off.

Her sharp tone seemed to galvanise him. Back at his desk, he opened the Baby Fay file. "Then we track down the father."

Bev frowned. There wasn't so much as a thin hint at the time that Fay's father had anything to do with his daughter's murder. "How does that work?"

Byford shook his head. "Unfinished business, Bev."

"What d'you mean?"

"I'm not sure myself." He took out a picture: the father holding Fay in his arms. Uncertain smile, curly perm, gold stud. "I never took to the man," Byford said. "Don't get me wrong. We couldn't have checked him out more. His alibi was sound. He seemed mad with grief. But there was something not quite right. Call it a copper's gut feeling."

"That the same as a woman's intuition?"

He didn't return the half-smile. "And I'll tell you this, Bev. If that letter isn't a taunt, it sounds to me very much like a threat."

"If this is down to you, Morriss, you'll be on traffic in the morning." Powell flung the late edition of the *Evening News* on her desk. "M6. Fast lane. Rush hour."

Powell's missile sent paperwork flying. Bev had spent the better part of six hours poring over or writing reports. The DI was making another bad day worse. "Fuck's sake. What's your problem?"

He jabbed a finger. "Bottom of page five."

EARRING CLUE IN HUNT FOR BEAST

The story had Matt Snow's by-line, the paper's crime correspondent. Bev frowned. She'd leaked the news gem to Nick Lockwood, her man at the Beeb. It had been in the way of a sop for pulling out of their session at The Prince. Had Lockwood then fed it to Snowie? She knew the hacks did a bit of horse-trading from time to time.

"Sod all to do with me, mate." She'd not said a word to Snow.

"How'd it get out, then?"

"I'm a cop. Try Mystic Meg." She picked up the fallen papers, turned her back.

"Don't fuck with me, Morriss."

"Like that's gonna happen."

She hadn't released it to piss Powell off. She hoped it might rattle the Beast's cage. According to the papers and the news, the Street Watch cops had lost the plot. The

Beast, like everyone else, probably imagined they didn't have a clue, let alone a lead. Bev reckoned a line about the Beast's trophy-taking compulsion might at least capture a few airwaves and column inches, if not goad the Beast. The fact the rapist was still out there irked her almost beyond reason.

"You sure you're not behind this?" Powell's arms were tight across his chest, his back ramrod-straight. There were times he put her in mind of some anally retentive house-master in a poncy prep school.

"Read my lips." She mouthed a fuck-off-arsehole.

"Can't handle it, can you, Morriss?" He was doing heavy-breather sound effects.

"What's that?"

"The fact I'll be the one bringing in him, seeing him sent down."

"Soon as you like, mate." She raised the coffee in mock salute. "I'm behind you all the way."

He glared. "You surely are."

"Can't stand chrysanths, make me sneeze." Maxine Beck sniffed. "Drop of Gordons'd go down a treat."

The hospital visit was on Bev's way home. She bit back a line about beggars and choosers. "Not sure how that'd go down with the doctor, Mrs B." She took the hard chair next to Natalie. Terry Roper sat on the bed, admiring his nails.

"Medicinal, innit?" Maxine croaked. Her throat had taken a battering from the smoke inhalation. Though she'd been moved from intensive care to a chintzy cheerful side ward, Bev reckoned it would take more than a gin and tonic to restore Maxine to her pre-fire self. The woman's eyes were lifeless, her skin dull, her attitude jaded.

"Brought you this as well." Bev ferreted in her bag. Since

she'd scoffed most of the grapes on the drive over, her fingers bypassed what remained of the bunch. A family-sized bar of fruit and nut was at the bottom. "There you go."

Maxine curled a lip. "Got any fags in that thing?"

Yeah. Twenty Drumsticks. "Sorry, love. I've stopped." Bev was still rummaging. "Brought you something as well, Natalie."

The teenager perked up but her face fell when she saw the newspaper. Her artwork was splashed across the front page. Bev watched like a hawk with binoculars, eager to pounce on any reaction. Her suspicious mind had been in overdrive on the way to the General. What if Natalie had come up with a likeness purely to keep the police off her back? No problem – till it hit the press. Of course, the idea could be a complete no-no. A flash of emotion momentarily ousted Natalie's sulk but Bev was hard pushed to define it. Excitement? Pleasure? Semi-smirk? Either way, a jaw-breaking yawn followed as the teenager dumped the paper in the bin. "Seen it already."

Bev took the wrapper off a Drumstick, sucked it a few times. "Couple of punters've already called in." A whopper but it wiped the scowl off the girl's face.

"You what?"

"Yeah. We've got a name to go on as well now."

Natalie tightened an already taut ponytail. "So?"

Bev opened her mouth to speak but Roper butted in. "Come to apologise, have you?" He reached casually for the Cadbury's.

She almost choked. "What?"

"Accusing me of every crime in the book." Chocolate melted on his teeth. "Waste of time, weren't it?" Roper was clean. Maybe he just hadn't been caught. "Time you should've been out there searching for the baby."

She buttoned her mouth. The words on the tip of her tongue should probably stay there. Three pairs of eyes were waiting for a response. "I can assure you we're do…"

Roper pointed a finger. "You're not. Doing enough. Tell her, Natalie."

"I'm talking to the papers and the telly and that."

Bev frowned. "You've done an appeal, love."

"They want more than that," Roper sneered. "They're after interviews."

"Paying, are they?" Bev asked.

"No!" Natalie was Little Miss Indignant. Not Roper. Bev reckoned he was already counting the cheques. "It's not about money. I'll do anything to get her back." There were tears in Natalie's eyes. Bev didn't doubt the girl's sincerity. She rose, flicked the lollipop stick in the bin.

"So will I, Natalie." She lifted a hand. "Catch you later."

She turned when the girl called. "What name did they give you? The punters who phoned?"

She made great play of racking her brains. "Nope. Sorry, love. It's gone."

19

Helen Carver gazed into the huge gilt mirror that dominated the apartment's hallway. Her make-up was immaculate, of course, but it would take cosmetic surgery to lift those tired lines. She widened her eyes and attempted a bright smile that failed. Maybe she could still get away with botox.

She listened at the nursery door. Veronica, stupid woman, was reading a story to a baby barely a month old. Helen slipped the key from the pocket of her jade silk kimono and unlocked the study door. David was so precious about his personal space. She never locked her studio. Anyone could go in and look at her work.

Not that she'd done any recently. The landscape series was only half-finished. She sighed. Would she ever paint again? She was exhausted all the time and it seemed to be getting worse. David assured her it would get easier as the baby got older. Was that another lie? Like tonight. He said he was going out with a male colleague – but the colleague had just phoned to have a chat with David.

She stood with her back against the door, wondering where to begin, seeking peace of mind as much as anything. Her palms were damp and she felt sweat trickle down her spine as she slid open a desk drawer. It was David's fault. She hated snooping like this. He knew it upset her.

"Damn." The nail was broken. Badly. She sucked at a few drops of blood as she glanced round. Theatre posters covered the wall, David's college productions alongside the classics. Carver and company. Helen raised an over-plucked eyebrow. Delusions of adequacy.

The décor was not to her taste. The dark greens and darker woods were so macho, so obvious. She wrinkled her nose, lips pressed in disapproval. He still smoked in here. Another lie. Then a nostril flared as she caught the faintest trace of an unfamiliar perfume. The next drawer was flung open. And the next. She searched filing cabinets, riffled books and magazines, ran a hand along and under shelves. Nothing incriminating. She sighed her relief. White lies she could handle. What had she been expecting, after all? David didn't have time to be unfaithful.

Her glance fell on the small black velvet pouch as she was leaving the room. It was on top of a speaker, not even hidden. She opened the drawstrings and tipped the contents into the palm of her hand.

Three earrings. Different designs. None hers. Blood drained from her face as she slapped a hand over her mouth and gagged. She'd read about earrings in that night's newspaper. Only the reporter used another name to describe them: trophies. Snatched from young rape victims.

She barely made it to the bathroom before throwing up.

Veronica Carver watched from the door of the nursery, hoping the drama-queen hysteria wouldn't wake the baby.

As each day passed, the mousy woman felt more at ease. Maybe her increasing confidence conveyed itself to the baby. Or maybe the little one sensed the bond between them as it grew, strengthened. Either way, the child was less fractious, slept more deeply and for longer periods. The woman gazed down, an adoring smile transforming her plain features.

She brightened further at the prospect of tomorrow. Supplies were due to arrive: more nappies for the baby, food for them both, a few basics. She'd already prepared the next list. She sighed, then banished faint stirrings of a dark mood. She could cope with another few months. For Angel, she'd endure anything. Anything at all.

Angel. It sounded wonderful. As soon as the woman had heard it, she'd known it was the perfect name. She leaned over the cot and tenderly stroked the baby's head. Angel. Angel. Running a finger along the curve of a delicate cheek, she whispered it softly.

"Sleep tight, my darling Angel."

Bev laid the phone down pensively. She'd been picking Nick Lockwood's journalistic brain. Now she grabbed a pen, worked figures on a lined pad. On a rough calculation, Terry Roper stood to net around twenty grand in interview fees. Made thirty pieces of silver look like small change. She creased her eyes, sucked on the day's third Drumstick. Unwittingly her cheeks were going like bellows.

"You shaving your head next, sarge?" DC Darren New ran a hand over his pate as if she needed sign language to follow the drift.

Kojak jokes were going round like circles. She tapped a beat with her fingers. "Next clown's gonna get a stick shoved where the sun don't shine."

Dazza's "Promise?" prompted a chorus of snickers.

It was a rare moment of levity in an incident room heavy with disappointment and near-despair. Twenty-plus detectives made phone calls, ran computer checks, input data or chased paper. When any one of them glanced up, the baby's image stared back from the walls and picture boards. Many felt it was the only connection with her they'd ever make.

The early brief had thrown out a load of negatives: nothing on the hospital front, nothing on the latest sightings, nothing on the hoax calls. It went with the territory; police work was often a process of elimination. But nothing was filling the gaps. Now they were treading the same ground: re-interviewing witnesses, checking reports and records. Uniforms were out on the streets with clipboards and questions. It was plod-work and it was inevitable, given the state of play. Didn't make it appealing.

Bev pursued thoughts following on from the Lockwood call. Nick reckoned each media outlet would cough up two to three grand for an exclusive one-to-one with the mother of the missing baby. Roper had already tried negotiating a deal with the Beeb's London operation. If the slimy toad timed it right, he could flog any number of exclusives. If all the material came out on the same day, who'd argue? Wall-to-wall scoops. Everyone happy.

"Except Natalie." Unless she knew cash was part of the equation. "Friggin' blood money, if you ask me."

Oz's fingers hovered over a keyboard. "Say something, sarge?"

She gave a half-smile. "Talking to myself." She watched as he continued tapping out whatever lack-of-progress report he was writing. Her smile grew when a tiny pink tip appeared between his lips. Always happened when he was concentrating. He'd not been aware of the tongue thing till she pointed it out ages ago. When a lock of hair fell across his forehead, she itched to stroke it away. She glanced at the time. "Lunchin', Oz?" She was already on her feet, bag hoisted.

"Love to, sarge." She sensed an unspoken but. "I'm meeting someone in town. Maybe tom…"

"No prob." The incident room had fallen silent. Or was that her imagination? She dropped half-a-dozen lollipop sticks in the bin on the way out. Who loves ya, baby?

The crystal glass held three fingers of single malt. Helen Carver, who hated the taste of alcohol, drained it in two gulps. The liquid burnt her throat, set fire to her belly. For a woman who desperately needed to feel in control, Helen's thoughts were spiralling. And the mental turmoil was David's fault. The earrings could mean only one thing: she was married to a rapist. A man who'd attacked three teenage girls. The Beast of Birmingham.

She threw her head back and laughed out loud. It was ridiculous. There could be any number of reasons why the earrings were in his study. So why not ask? And why act the lush? She half-filled the heavy tumbler this time, caught her reflection in the glass: beauty and the beast. She laughed again, neither loud nor convincingly. She looked like a dog. She'd barely slept and well past midday was neither showered nor dressed.

What should she do?

Her gut reaction had been to call the police. That lasted the two minutes it took for her head to react. Helen knew only what she could *not* do.

Already swaying a little, she stepped carefully across the deep ivory carpet. The lounge was her favourite room: every item handpicked, exquisite, expensive. She pressed her forehead against the picture window, gazed across Brindley Place bustling as usual with businessmen, bright young things, loud tourists. She could not give this up. Would not.

A key turned in the door. Veronica, the old hag, back with the baby. Helen stumbled on the way to the bathroom. She locked herself in and stared at her ravaged features in the mirror. She loathed imperfection, hated ugliness. In that instant, Helen knew what she would do. It was David's fault. He'd pay for his sins. He'd brought it on himself.

A lunchtime mooch round Moseley had done sod all to boost the Morriss morale. She'd nipped into her usual retail therapists: patchouli-scented shops full of arty-farty flimflam and ethnic mood music, the odd singing whale or chanting monk. She loved it all. But its magic hadn't worked. Bev had spotted Oz folding his long legs into Sumitra Gosh's low-slung two-seater in the car park at Highgate. A threesome with Johnny Depp and Joseph Fiennes wasn't going to erase that particular image.

She shifted the bag on to her other shoulder. Its awesome capacity was nearly breached. It now contained a birth-day present for her mum and a few bits to cheer up Sadie. She'd try to get there tonight. The Sicilian pizza she'd been munching on her solitary travels was already making its own alimentary journey. She popped in the last mouthful as she passed the front desk. Vince Hanlon was spooning sugar into a mug. She waggled her fingers and headed for the stairs.

"Not out celebrating?" Big Vince had a broad grin. Think Cheshire cat. On happy pills.

Lottery? Promotion? Gold handcuffs? Bev waited patiently. Vince was clearly dying to share, rubbing his hands together. It put her in mind of copulating sausages.

"Uniform brought the rapist in. Half-hour back. He's banged up downstairs. Powell wants the bastard to sweat before he gives him a grilling."

20

DI Powell was in the pub with the lads. Bev raised Carol Mansfield on the phone for the detail. Apparently three punters had called the Street Watch incident room in response to the visuals compiled by Natalie. All supplied the same identification – a twenty-eight-year-old man named Callum Gould. A squad car had picked him up in Balsall Heath.

Bev ended the call and gave a low whistle. Her whopping great porkie to Natalie in the hospital last night had turned out eerily prescient. She took the stairs two at a time and got an eyeful through the cell's spy-hole.

There was no crucifix dangling from an ear. Apart from that, Bev reckoned the guy could have posed for the E-fit. There was a minuscule white nick in the right eyebrow and an ink-spot mole over the top lip. Callum Gould was the Beck girl's rapist made flesh.

He sat straight-backed on the bed. His mop of black hair looked limp and greasy but that was probably down to the constant raking of his long tapering fingers. Nut-brown needle-cord strides and an open-neck check shirt gave him the look of a trendy geography teacher. Which he was.

"Having a nose, Morriss?" The DI's stealthy approach was presumably meant to startle her.

She refused to jump. "You charging him?"

Powell leaned against the wall, arms folded. "Natch."

"With?"

"The Beck girl's rape, for starters."

Bev rose on her toes, took another butcher's. No doubt about it: he was a dead ringer for the E-fit. Natalie either had perfect recall, or she'd lied about only catching a glimpse of her attacker. "What's he saying?"

"What they all say. She asked for it."

"For Christ's sake," Bev hissed. "These are real people. Not stock baddies from some naff B-movie. What's Gould *actually* saying, as opposed to the crap script you've given him?"

"Natalie Beck was gagging for a shag. Clearer?"

As mud. They'd had sex. But was it consensual? Or was Gould a lying two-faced bastard? He'd hardly admit the offence; on the other hand Natalie wouldn't be the first girl to cry rape. But why so long after the event? And why the sudden clarity of vision? And had any of it got a flea's thighbone to do with the Street Watch attacks?

"Let's face it, Morriss, Gould's hardly going to put a hand up to raping an ex-pupil."

"Gould was her teacher?" She sounded as if she'd been at the helium. But if Gould had taught Natalie, why hadn't she blown the whistle before?

"I know what you're thinking. Took her frigging time, didn't she? Scared shitless, that's why. He threatened to kill her. 'Course," he drawled "That was the first time."

What? She rarely spluttered; she did now. "First time?"

"Back in January. Gets the horn, comes back for more. Raped her again. Friday night."

Her thoughts swirled. A million questions tumbled round. Was Callum Gould Zoë's father? Had Natalie told Gould about the baby during Friday's alleged attack? Paternity could be proved with DNA samples: DNA from a baby who went missing within hours of the alleged rape and five days later still hadn't been found.

It could be kosher. On the other hand, Natalie could be away with the fairies. The wicked fairies, if she was

144

stitching up some innocent sod out of spite. Bev shook her head. It boiled down to the same old same old: his word against hers, Callum Gould v Natalie Beck.

Natalie Beck had gone to ground. It was early evening. Bev and the guv were having a jar in The Prince of Wales.

"I called the General six times and paid Terry Roper a home visit." The house dry white tasted like paint stripper, so she'd eschewed her preferred poison for tonic water. A tentative sip produced a sour grimace. "It's not like the girl's got that many places to hang."

Byford shrugged. "Probably holed up in some five-star hotel, courtesy of the *Sun* or the *Mail*."

Lucky girl. But Bev was still desperate to have a word or several with Natalie. Slinging accusations around the place didn't marry with what Bev knew of her. But then, what did she know? Maybe Natalie had a chameleon gene. Or maybe the accusations weren't so outlandish.

Gould's image as trendy geography master wasn't the whole picture. Colleagues and neighbours had painted other aspects. The guy's marriage had fallen apart and his career looked set to go the same way. He was on a second official warning for bad timekeeping and absenteeism. Three strikes and he'd be out. His wife had already gone, fed up with Gould's drinking and skirt-chasing.

"What d'you reckon, guv? Is he in the frame?"

The superintendent had sat in on Callum Gould's questioning that afternoon. Now he leaned back, hands behind head, and gave it some thought. "Hard to say. He's admitted having sex with the girl on Friday. They met by chance, apparently in a club on Broad Street. Claims she was all over him. He was off his face."

"Yeah, yeah." She flapped a hand; heard it all before.

"What about back in January?"

Byford shook his head. "Denied it absolutely. Refused to answer any more questions. He was pretty open till that point, then he clammed up, demanded his brief."

The lawyer was defending in a big murder trial at the Crown Court. Gould's interview had been terminated. It wasn't the only premature action, in Bev's opinion. There'd been no chance to question him about Street Watch or the missing baby.

She unwrapped a Drumstick, sucked pensively. "He doesn't teach her any more and Natalie's not under-age. It's not Romeo and Juliet but it's not wrong."

Byford lowered his voice. "In January the girl was fifteen. And if she was raped, her age is irrelevant."

"If." She sniffed. The barman had lit up. She took a surrogate drag as smoke drifted by.

"You think she's lying?"

"Who knows?" What she did know was that Natalie had been through more blokes than hot baltis. She'd told Bev as much that day in the baby's nursery. Casual sex was no big thing for street-wise cookies like Natalie. Especially given a role model like Maxine. Natalie saw sex as a sticky handshake. Until Gould's arrest, Bev had seen her as an insecure kid looking for love. Natalie didn't just kiss frogs – she fucked them. She'd not yet come across a prince. But the girl's say-so on its own didn't make Gould a pervert.

"'Who knows', as you put it, sergeant, isn't good enough." Bev flinched as Byford slammed his glass on the table. "There are too many unknowns at the moment. And no one's coming up with any answers."

Bev parked the MG, slammed the door and kicked ass out of the drive. Byford's outburst rankled at a time when she felt bad enough already. She'd tried putting herself in his size tens. The big man's attack was almost certainly prompted by tortured thoughts of Baby Fay. He wasn't the only one affected. The dead baby was a shadow in Bev's soul. As for the baby she prayed was still alive? She was doing everything she could.

There was only one antidote to blues this big.

Emmy Morriss was in the hall when Bev unlocked the front door. "Sweetheart, lovely to see you." Soothing words, a verbal massage. And the house smelt of beeswax and basil. Not a packing case in sight. Bliss.

"You should've called," Emmy said. "We're off out."

Bev's shoulders sagged along with her face.

Her mum winked a Bev-blue eye. "Only joking. Come on. I'll pop the kettle on."

A golden fur-ball with teeth and tail bounded out of the kitchen and hurled itself at Bev's thighs. She picked it up before it wet itself. "Glad the training's going well."

"He's pleased to see you, Bev," Emmy gently admonished.

The retriever puppy was a recent acquisition in the wake of the attack on her gran. Gnipper had yet to get his teeth into the guard-dog role. Anything else lying round, no problem. He'd been to the vet's three times to have his stomach pumped.

"How's gran?"

"Fine." Sadie had slipped in behind Bev. She didn't look it. What hair had grown back looked like off-white candyfloss. Dark circles under the old lady's eyes were now a permanent feature. "You're looking a bit peaky, our Bev."

"Dandy, me mate." She hugged her gran's tiny frame.

"Here you go." Emmy laid out a comfort-food combo: camomile tea, cinnamon toast and chocolate layer cake three storeys high.

Bev demolished a good half of it as they sat around chatting. The kitchen was the cosiest room she knew: warm lighting, pink gingham, polished pine. She sat back, forced herself to switch off. Otherwise what was the point being here? She watched her mum and gran grinning like school-girls, listened as they finished each other's sentences. They were warm loving people. The dysfunctional fuckwits she came across in the job were light-years away. For an hour or so, anyway.

"What's Gnipper doing?" Emmy asked.

The puppy's nose was in Bev's bag. She dragged him away and caught a glimpse of the goodies she'd bought Sadie at lunchtime. "Almost forgot. Here you go, gran."

The old lady perked up at the sight of the latest Reg Hill, a Sudoku book and a tin of Roses. They did serious damage to the chocolates during a few rounds of Cluedo.

"Thought you'd be dead good at it, our Bev." Sadie winked at Emmy.

Bev gave a weak smile as she packed the box. "Obviously I was holding back there."

"What, every game?" they chorused.

The guffaws nearly woke the puppy. Mind, on the available evidence he was too stuffed to move. Chocolate coated a lolling tongue and pink flecks of toffee were caught between his teeth. As for the location of the stick, Bev really didn't want to go there.

21

Natalie lifted her sleepy head, strained her ears. Crocks rattled outside the door. Someone tunelessly whistled *My Way* as they passed along the corridor. The teenager sat up, glanced round, took a few seconds to remember where she was. She'd only been to London once, never stayed in a hotel before. Bed and breakfasts didn't count. The girl shuddered at a montage of flashbacks: stained sheets, stinking bogs, peeling walls, black mould, cockroaches big as rats…

She banished the bad times with a shake of her head, threw back the heavy white satin bedcover and headed for the shower. Tel had done them proud, twisting that stuck-up reporter's arm to fork out for this place. It screamed posh with polished knobs on. She lingered under a jet of water, not too hot, not too cold. Bring on the porridge and call me Goldilocks.

Sod that for a game of soldiers. They'd scoffed the full monty on room service. Tel had shovelled it down his neck, then took off on a bit of business. She'd been knackered, gone back to bed for a bit. Now she was running late for the meet. She stowed the bath freebies in a Morrisons' carrier, pulled on denims, pink pixie boots, navy fleece, then moved to the dressing table. Sitting on a plush velvet stool, she struck poses in the mirror. She'd look fitter with a bit of slap but Tel said she'd come across better without. He was probably right. He usually was.

Dead generous an' all. He knew it took it out of her, talking about Zoë and that. She'd gab 24/7 if it got the baby back, but she kept blarting, breaking down. Tel had slipped her fifty quid for spends, something to cheer herself up a bit.

Callum Gould would probably need a bit of cheering now – if someone had fingered him on the strength of her E-fit. Served the bastard right. She'd not seen it till Tel'd said. Gould was a teacher, supposed to look out for his kids, not get off with them. If Gouldie hadn't turned nasty and told her to fuck off she might not have gone along with it. It was Tel's idea. Supposed to get the cops off her back. She snorted. Like that'd worked. Bev Morriss had texted her more times than she could count.

Her face fell. She felt really bad about Maxine. Resting her chin in her hands, she gazed at her reflection. What a freakin' mess. If the cops hadn't come on heavy wanting to know who Zoë's dad was, she wouldn't've lied about the rape back in January. But she'd no choice. If Maxine knew she'd been screwing Tel it would kill her. Terry *could* be the father. Natalie had told him he was. Fact was, she didn't know. It could've been any Dick or Harry.

She lifted her hair, turned her head this way and that, pouting. Dropping Gouldie in it had seemed like a good idea at the time. Not only would it throw Mr Plod off the scent, but Tel reckoned Gould would be good for a bob or two: hush money. Smart or what? Tel made her look dense.

The teenager reached for a cigarette, watched herself light it, blew smoke through her nostrils. Still, she was a quick learner. If she fitted up Gould for one rape, she reckoned he might as well take the rap for both. He'd lied about wearing a condom when they had it off on Friday, so the bastard had it coming to him.

Anyway, teachers were easy targets. It'd be his word against hers. Anyone who read the papers knew what that meant. She'd come clean, put him out of his misery, before he was in the dock. Blame it on that post-traumatic stuff. Probably.

Right now she didn't give a toss about anything except getting Zoë back.

"Fuck's sake." She retrieved her mobile from the bedside table. The message was the same: *call me NOW bev morriss*. The girl scowled: the cop's needle was *so* stuck.

She hit a few numbers, waited while an operator put her through to the ward. "Can you give my mum a message?"

Five minutes late, Natalie and her meagre belongings vacated the room. People to see, places to go, and fifty quid burning a hole in her back pocket.

"You'll bust that if you're not careful." DC New indicated the cell phone that had just crash-landed on Bev's desk. It was mid-morning on the sixth day of the search for Baby Zoë and all sixteen detectives working in the incident room were desperate for something besides a phone to break. Over six hundred calls on the hot-line numbers, three hundred and twenty-seven statements taken, thousands of hours invested, incalculable effort expended. It was as though the baby had never existed.

Bev retrieved the phone, relieved it was still intact. "Wonders of sodding communication." She'd called or texted the number a dozen times in two hours. Her ensuing sigh ruffled papers.

Oz glanced up from a screen. "The Beck girl?"

Bev nodded. She wasn't the only frustrated bunny. Natalie Beck's mystery tour had taken up a good deal of discussion at the early brief. It was incomprehensible to most squad members that the girl had taken off while her baby was still missing. There were one or two vague mutterings, speculation as to whether she was involved in the child's disappearance. Bev didn't think anyone took the idea seriously; but as every cop knew, absolutely nothing could or should be ruled out till the fat lady read the jury verdict.

A boot shot off a desk and a few spines straightened as the guv popped his head round the door. "Lydia Pope's in reception, Bev. Five minutes, OK?"

"Sure." Pope was Gould's lawyer, finally arrived. Let me at her. Powell's loss was Bev's gain. Though the guv would take the lead, Bev was sitting in on what by rights was the DI's baby. It was one reason she'd made repeated efforts to contact Natalie. Further input from the Beck girl could help determine a line or lines of questioning. Given what they had, they'd be flying not quite blind but partially sighted.

"Wonder how the DI's getting on?" Oz tapped a pen against his teeth. There wasn't an officer in the nick who wouldn't be glued to *Crimewatch* that night. Ratings'd go through the skylight.

"Creaming his jeans if he's on the sofa with La Bruce," Darren leered.

Oz nodded. "He'll think he's died and gone to heaven."

Bev lifted an eyebrow. "Down, boys."

"Nah." Darren corrected his earlier comment. "Nick and Fiona don't have sofas. That's Richard and Judy."

"It'll be Punch and Judy in a minute." Compared with Bev's delivery the Sahara was damp.

Dazza started singing, "Hit me baby one more time," before being forced to duck a flying stapler. "Sexual harassment." He was all mock outrage. "I could have you for that, sarge."

Pad under elbow, pen behind ear, Bev turned at the door and winked. "You wouldn't know where to start, Dazza."

Lydia Pope was almost as tall as the guv and thin as a rake on a diet. Garbed entirely in shiny black from skull-hugging cloche to scuffed court shoes, Bev reckoned the brief looked like a well-groomed exclamation mark – from the back. Face-on, she could have been a man in drag. The nose was made to hang coats on, not enough teeth took what looked like temporary residence in too much gum and either a pair of anorexic caterpillars had died on her face or the eyebrows had been pencilled in by a piss-head. With those looks, Bev reckoned Pope must be a shit-hot lawyer. A mental wrist-slap swiftly followed. She was catching macho habits from Highgate's cavemen.

Interview Three was a tad cave-like: no windows, with fresh air and space at a premium. Pope swept in like it was the Supreme Court. She gave a metal chair an ostentatious wipe with a grubby tissue, seat and back, and was waiting, pen poised over yellow pad, before Bev closed the door. Gould was already in situ behind a metal desk with a bashed tin ashtray as centrepiece. His five o'clock shadow was impressive; a week and he'd be combing a beard. The uniform who'd been keeping watch asked Byford if they wanted tea, coffee.

"That won't be necessary," the lawyer drawled without bothering to turn. "We won't be here that long."

Bev exchanged an ooh-la-la glance with the guv, then crossed the room, ran through the spiel for the tape and took a pew next to Byford, opposite La Pope and Gould.

The woman's business voice made Bev's bum prickle. Think Anne Robinson on a menstrual-meets-migraine sort of day. Forget the weakest link; the brief went straight for the carotid.

"Help me out here. My client admits having sex. The girl's not a minor." She riffled a lined pad that even Bev saw had zilch written in it. "Last time I checked, that wasn't an offence." Pope looked up quizzically. Though given the lie of the eyebrows, facial expression was severely restricted.

Byford raised a more articulate arch. "If Natalie Beck was drawing her pension, it'd still be rape if she didn't want it."

Pope scratched the back of her neck, relieving an itch clearly more of a priority than giving a response. The hand inadvertently dislodged the cloche. The slightly comic angle was the only vaguely amusing aspect in Lydia Pope's entire attitude.

"And the evidence?" She looked expectant, held the pen ready.

Byford revealed that, as well as Natalie Beck's statement, five people had now phoned a hotline naming Gould as the suspect depicted in the E-fit.

Her scorn was predictable. "And that proves?" She offered her own suggestion. "That Ms Beck's imagination is as active as her sex life?"

Given what Bev knew, there was no answer to that. Anyway, Pope didn't hang round for comment. Tapping her pen, she hammered home points. "My client has gone out of his way to co-operate. You've had access to his home, car, bank account. Charge him or release him."

Byford ignored her. "Where were you, Mr Gould, in the early hours of January 12?"

Gould briefly closed his eyes, took a deep breath. "I have absolutely no idea. Could you recall where you were?"

"According to Nat…"

He surged forward, slammed his palms on the table. "The only thing I know is I wasn't within spitting distance of Natalie Beck!" He slumped back, leaving damp handprints on the aluminium. "I wish I'd never laid eyes on the bloody girl."

"Bit more than eyes," Bev said.

CCTV footage had captured Gould and Natalie staggering out of Jollies nightclub on Broad Street. Looked like they were giving each other mouth-to-mouth.

"She was giving it away. No man's going to say no."

"You're wrong there." The guv's opinion wasn't open to argument.

"Charge him or let him go." The lawyer sounded as if it was her call.

Byford turned to Bev. "Ask one of the lads to bring in tea, please."

Bev collared a passing uniform and crossed back to the desk. En route she shot a loaded question. "The baby's not yours, then?"

She was after a snap reaction. The words elicited a range of emotion. She couldn't isolate the real from what might have been rehearsed. Had a nerve been touched? If so, where? And why?

"What baby?" He had to be joking.

"What planet are you on, Mr Gould?" Only the tape recorder prevented a Morriss snort. "The baby that's been missing nearly a week. The one all over the telly and the papers." Christ, the man lived in Balsall Heath; the place was smothered in Have You Seen posters.

Gould's face was going like an emotional windsock. Shame she wasn't a mind reader, or meteorologist. "I know nothing about a baby. Missing or otherwise." He fiddled with an earlobe.

"Zoë Beck," Bev supplied. "Nearly four weeks old now. Natalie says she's the result of the January rape."

"Alleged rape." Pope raised a hand.

Ignoring her, Bev took a photograph from her bag, slid

it across the table.

Gould's hand shook as he lifted it for a closer look.

"Only a day old there," Bev said. "Prob'ly changed quite a bit by now. Assuming she isn't dead."

Even Lydia Pope looked aghast as Gould clutched the picture to his heart. Silent tears flowed down his cheeks, diverted only by day-old stubble. "I'd like to talk to Natalie."

Pope whispered in Gould's ear, then addressed Byford. "My client is under duress. He has nothing further to add at this time."

Bev would have cracked on but it wasn't her call. She glanced at the guv, who nodded. "Interview terminated at 12.07," she said, switching off the tape, then looked at Gould. He wasn't the only one who wanted a word with Natalie Beck.

22

"I doubt she'll talk to you, detective. But you're welcome to try."

The junior doctor was a dish. Bev refrained from licking her lips. They were closeted in a cluttered side-office, all bulging files and bowing shelves. Zachary Caine's six-two frame leaned casually against a wall-chart promoting healthy living. Given the guy's drop-dead looks, Bev reckoned he could induce cardiac arrest, never mind care for it.

"May as well give it a whirl." She flashed a smile, toyed with the idea of clutching her chest, rolling her eyes and executing a quick swoon. Caine, who was making notes on a clipboard, was oblivious to her imminent demise.

Her current heart rate was actually the result of a mad dash across town. She'd hotfooted it to the General on the off-chance Natalie Beck had put in an appearance. It was a no-show. The only thing Natalie had put in were a couple of phone calls checking her mum was still in the land of the living. Bev was praying that Maxine could point her in Natalie's direction.

It was increasingly urgent that she speak to the Beck girl. The search team at Gould's house had sent word back to Control. Two uniformed officers had entered a room on the top floor that was kitted out as a nursery. Brand-new gear, pristine baby clothes, boxes of nappies, bottles, bedding – you name it, Gould had it. Only one thing he didn't have. And never had. A baby.

Caine was following a different train of thought. Not an easy ride, the beginnings of a frown suggested. "It's as if

Mrs Beck's given up."

"Oh?" Bev'd seen Maxine Tuesday evening, reckoned she was on the mend.

The doctor squeezed fingertips into pockets of uncommonly tight moleskin trousers. Bev forced herself to maintain eye contact.

"It happens, detec…" He inclined his head. "May I call you Bev?"

Call me any time. "Sure."

"I've seen it in patients before," Caine continued. "There's no physical reason why they don't respond. In Mrs Beck's case, the X-rays are more or less clear, her oxygen levels are as normal as they're going to get, given she's a heavy smoker. But…" He gave a one-shoulder shrug.

"Delayed shock?" Bev speculated.

He pushed himself off the wall and indicated the door. "It's more than that. It's like she's shut down."

They were outside Maxine's ward when he tried to explain further. "Are you familiar with the expression 'turning your face to the wall'?"

Yeah. And banging your head against it. She nodded.

"As a way of coping with trauma, it's not uncommon," Caine said. "She lost everything in the fire, didn't she?"

"And her granddaughter went missing before it."

"The baby on the posters?" His eyebrows disappeared under a thick blond fringe. "I should have realised."

Bev gave a grim nod. "Now her daughter's buggered off."

"Know what?" He took a chest-expanding breath. "If I was Maxine Beck, I'd switch off too."

"Yeah." She rested a hand on the door. "But for how long?"

Corporation Street was stuffed with flashing lights, fake snow and nauseatingly jolly blow-up Santas. Christmas, lock stock and flying reindeer, appeared to have hit town. Bev gave a silent groan: it wasn't even December, for Christ's sake. She'd come straight from the General and hit Caffè Nero from force of habit. It was just about the only coffee shop in town where you could still smoke. She settled into a chunky leather armchair, rested her bag on her lap and delved. Delved again. Of course she hadn't got any. She'd given up. "Bugger."

The profanity provoked a puckered tut from a nearby mauve rinse. The old woman's creased sepia cheeks caved in as she sucked furiously on a king-size. Bev, who'd even run out of Drumsticks, nearly snatched it out of her mouth. She sighed, sipped on a double espresso, then took a bite-sized chunk from a Mexican chicken wrap. A bit of sustenance was called for, before breaking the good news.

She hit a number, then quickly brought the guv up to speed on Maxine Beck's ultra-stable condition. He asked the same question Bev had posed to Caine. She answered through a mouthful of pepper and breast. "It's a piece-of-string job, guv." Basically no one knew what was going on in the Beck brain, or how long the near-catatonic state would last. "Think of it as psychological meltdown."

The thought was almost enough to put her off the late lunch. She hoped Byford wasn't sharing the mental picture of a mushroom cloud spewing steaming grey matter. The guv appeared lost for words. She pricked her ears, heard a rasp on the line again. He was using his hand as a razor. The image brought to mind their hirsute reluctant interviewee.

"What's the latest on Callum Gould?"

Byford snorted. "He's pulling a Maxine. Refusing to open

his mouth. Pope wants him released."

"Pushing it, isn't it? What about the baby-free nursery?"

"We're trying to trace the erstwhile Mrs Gould. Pope says she left because they can't have kids. The perfect nursery was premature pie in the sky. They tried everything, including three rounds of IVF. When it became clear it wasn't going to happen, she took off. Spain, apparently."

"*They* couldn't have kids?" Bev asked. "Or *he* couldn't?" If Gould was shooting blanks, there was no way he was Zoë's father.

"It's one of the questions we need answered. Fast."

Bev reran the scene in Interview Three, recalled Gould's emotions when he saw the baby's photograph. Were the tears for the babies he'd never have? Or the one he'd lost? Or worse?

"Is he implicated, guv?"

"The baby's disappearance?" Byford must've been thinking along similar lines. "SOCOs are still out there but we'd've heard by now if they'd found anything. As it stands we've no evidence, no witnesses. Nothing tying Gould to the snatch. You know as well as me, he wouldn't be where he is now without the Beck girl's allegations."

And where the hell was she?

Bev frowned, recalling the hospital bedside scene. "You said Gould was pulling a Maxine. I don't reckon she's faking it, guv."

The woman could've come straight from the set of *Land of the Dead*: hollow-eyed, grey clammy skin. Bev shuddered. Mind, she'd hedged her bets and given Maxine an earful. If she was actually more compos mentis than comatose, Momma Beck could be in no doubt now how vital it was that Natalie contact the police generally, Bev specifically. Whether a single word had filtered through what appeared to be a self-imposed mental safety net was anyone's guess.

She could hear the guv's sigh in his voice. "Either way, it's no use to us, is it?"

Couldn't argue with that. Still… "Something'll give soon, guv. Bound to."

"You sound amazingly chirpy under the circumstances."

"Gotta look on the bright side, guv." She smoothed out a scrap of paper she'd been clutching in a sweaty palm. Doctor Caine's phone number. Personal. He'd winked an extraordinarily beautiful grey eye and urged her not to wait for an emergency. With humour that cutting-edge, she obviously wouldn't die laughing. But then, given Zach Caine's amazing anatomy, the main attraction was never going to be his funny bone.

Oz ended the call, cradled the mobile in his hands. Was he doing the right thing? It was the third time in as many days he'd as good as told Bev to get lost. He tightened the bath-towel round his waist, lay on the bed, hands behind his head. Watching a bit of TV at Baldwin Street was no big deal. Except it would almost certainly lead to bed, maybe breakfast.

He wasn't sure he wanted either, any more.

Wasn't sure what he wanted.

He gazed at familiar surroundings, favourite possessions. Failed to feel the normal cosy glow. He was twenty-five years old and still lived with his parents. His bedroom was more like a teenager's with its Freddie Flintoff posters, school cricket trophies, shelf of Wisdens, CD stack of Stones. He sighed. He loved his family deeply, of course he did. His mother and sisters were downstairs now, laughing and chatting as they fixed dinner. Cumin and cardamom wafted from the kitchen. The Khan women doted on him. Even his father had started to consult, occasionally defer to, First-Born Son.

It was no longer enough. He wanted a life with Bev. He snorted. If only it were that simple. He reached for her photograph by the bedside: low-cut red dress, high heels, lots of make-up; so not Bev. His smile was unwitting, mirroring hers. The bloody woman had a chip-shop on her shoulder and a stable of high horses, but on the odd occasion he didn't want to kill her, he'd die for her.

She wouldn't even live with him.

He knew it was wrong always to get what you want, but with Bev he wasn't even close to it. She wouldn't let him near. Paranoid about being hurt. Sex was OK, but not secrets. She wanted a bedmate; he needed a soul-mate. He was in way too deep and it hurt like shit. Yet Bev was pissed because he was putting distance between them. Ironic or what? Not that she'd said anything; she never opened up about anything personal. He heard it in the silence.

The bedroom was too quiet. He hit the remote: Dylan's times were a-changin' as well.

Oz sighed. He'd asked Summi for advice. She was in the stay-mean-keep-them-keen school. But he wasn't into mind games. He'd rather not play at all.

He strolled to a desk under the window, opened the top drawer. The paperwork had been there since February. He'd not been ready when the guv suggested it. He was now. And with a first in Law he didn't think the exams would be too taxing. He looked in the mirror. Sergeant Khan? It had a definite ring to it.

Then he'd ask for a transfer.

He took a small blue heart-shaped box from the next drawer. Best find something more fitting for Bev's Christmas stocking.

Bev looked like a cat locked in a salmon farm. She was already working out what to wear. A mound of rejects on the bedroom floor suggested her current wardrobe wasn't up to scratch. The slinky purple silk shift held against her body got the thumbs down and joined the pile on the carpet.

She ran a hand along the rail. Black velvet? Too dressy. Oyster cotton? Too cold. Tartan kilt? Get a life. It was no good; she'd have to find time to flash the plastic before Tuesday. She'd just fixed a date with the delicious Doctor Caine. She reckoned Zach was more Armani than Man at Next. She'd best hit Morgan.

Oz could go fuck himself.

It was his fault. She'd never have called Zach if Oz hadn't given her the bum's rush. Again. Christ, she'd only offered a take-the-piss-out-of-Powell-on-the-box session. It was hardly a bodily fluids exchange.

She scooped up the discarded clothes and shoved them into the bottom of the wardrobe. She'd sort everything properly on Saturday when Frankie came round. Take a stack of stuff to Oxfam. Maybe she'd come across those French knickers. They'd cost an arm and a leg, considering they barely covered her bum. She gave her butt a seductive wiggle in the mirror. And was still laughing when she hit the kitchen.

23

Incident-room clowns held a line of scorecards aloft when DI Powell made his post-*Crimewatch* entrance next morning. The DI's marks weren't perfect but he'd pulled off a creditable performance. Even Bev had been impressed with presentation, if not content. She lifted her head from a paper mound as he strode past.

"Well done."

He halted mid-stride. "You taking the piss?"

"Straight up. The phones haven't stopped ringing." It was true. According to Jack Hainsworth, they'd taken eighty-plus calls. A few even sounded promising.

Bev had ploughed her way through a pack of Doritos and a half-bottle of pinot watching Powell in action on the programme. ID issues restricted filmed inserts to general views of the crime scenes and a few shots, ostensibly from the girls' view point, walking the routes where the three attacks took place. This generally meant great product placement for Nike and the like.

Back in the studio, the feline Fiona had drawn Powell out on the trophy angle. There were close-ups of identical earrings and vapid speculation on what compelled serial offenders to steal from victims. As expected, there was no allusion to the macabre cutting of the girls' pubic hair. It finished with a solicitous Ms Bruce appealing for anyone with information to get in touch with the police, and thirty seconds later that nice Nick Ross imploring viewers not to have nightmares.

Bev glanced up to see Powell standing by the whiteboard surrounded by fans. Filthy laughs suggested the DI was milking his three minutes of fame. Good for him. He'd done a decent turn: got the facts across and came over as an intelligent and sensitive bloke.

"Hey, Morriss. Has that Beck bint shown up yet?"

Yeah, well…

Natalie Beck was on a Virgin train en route from Euston to New Street. Terry Roper was sprawled opposite. He'd settled for the Sundays, eventually: *People, News of the Screws, Mirror, Express*. Sixteen grand, cash in hand. Well, in back pocket.

"What's up, doll? Look like you're chewing a lemon."

Roper was getting on her tits. "What you think's up?"

He sat forward, tried to take her hand. "Come on, babe. If this don't get Zo back…" He didn't have the balls to finish the sentence. Natalie did.

"Nothing will. Go on – say it."

Roper glanced round. "Keep your voice down, doll."

"And her name's Zo-ee, case you forgot."

Natalie leaned back, closed her eyes. If he thought she was asleep chances were he'd button it, before she decked him. She was beginning to think Tel was all talk. She'd pissed off to London on his say-so. It was all well and good staying in a swanky hotel on a nice little earner but at the end of the day the baby was still missing. What difference were a few poxy newspapers gonna make? Mr Big Gob Roper, the man who had an answer for everything, had kept pretty shtum on that lately. As for getting the police off their back, no chance. She was surprised Bev Morriss hadn't melted the bloody mobile.

And now Max had taken a turn for the worse. How'd that posh cow on the ward put it? "Your mother's condition is giving cause for concern." What the freaking hell was that supposed to mean? She cocked an ear. According to Darth Vader on the speakers, they were approaching Coventry. Wouldn't be long before she found out. Found out what'd happened to Callum Gould, too. Not so much time to face the music as the full sodding orchestra.

The letter lying on Byford's desk was identical. He'd received its twin four days earlier.

REMEMBER BABY FAY?

Bev looked up eagerly. This could be the break they badly needed. So why the guv's grim face? Realisation dawned and Bev's question was rhetorical. "The drop's not on camera?"

The pre-emptive measures, taken within hours of the first missive's arrival, had clearly failed. Byford had established quickly that the envelope had been hand-delivered to Highgate reception. It was sod's law that the desk sergeant hadn't noticed whose hand. Byford had authorised extra CCTV to cover the entire area. The writer could easily have slipped a few bob to a passing kid, but whoever dropped it off might, after police persuasion, also deliver a steer.

Bev was damn glad it wasn't her neck on the block. "Duff tape? Or did it just run out?"

"Neither." He indicated the letter. "That was on the door-mat when I got home last night."

"Shit."

"That's one way of putting it."

There was a carafe of water on a low table. She rose, filled a cup and moved to the window, deep in thought. There was no doubt now. It was personal. The guv had been right since the word go. Distracted, she poured water into the drying cactus. Was the message a malevolent taunt or a veiled threat? But who from? And why?

The guv was drumming his fingers on the desk, staring into the middle distance, probably asking the same questions.

"Could be someone pulling your strings, guv."

The beat stopped. "I don't do puppet, sergeant."

"Who was around back then?" She returned to her seat. "Did you cross anyone? Rattle a few cages?"

He'd given it thought, passed a list across the desk. Names and parts played. She turned her mouth down. Sex offenders, by and large. The register was the first port of call in cases involving kids. Paedophiles were checked as a matter of course. They took offence. Tough. One name stood out.

"This a cop?" Bev glanced up at the guv.

"Gallimore. Inspector. He was uniform. A right bastard."

"Must be if he's on here."

"Hated my guts. Don't know why. Took against me from day one and that was it."

Sounded like someone she knew.

The guv did that mind-reading thing again. "Pete Gallimore makes Powell look like Mr Softie."

Hard to believe. She shrugged, gave him the benefit of the doubt. "Would a cop really stoop to something like that?" She nodded at the letter.

"I'm ruling nothing out." He flicked a mangled paper clip into the bin. "Check, check and check again."

"The baby's dad's not on here." Baby Fay's errant father. "You had a problem with him."

"He's not giving anyone trouble any more ." He pushed a fax across the desk. According to the New York Police Department, the man had died in a road smash three months ago.

"Give the airport a call, shall I?" She was already on her feet. "Get us on a flight first thing?"

"What?" His hand halted mid-air. It held a ball of paper that was about to follow the paper clip's flight path.

"You said it, guv." A grin ruined the deadpan delivery. "Check, check, ch…"

The missile hit the door. She was already through it.

The mousy woman raced to the door. She'd been out of her mind with worry. The delivery hadn't shown up on Wednesday. It was now Friday. She'd cut back on her food intake, of course, but she couldn't deprive a growing baby like Angel. One more day and there'd be no more milk. She'd already had to use towels for the last three nappy changes. It really was too bad.

She looked through the spy hole. No one there. Oh God. She clutched trembling fingers. What was she to do? Now the baby was crying. Damn. Why did these things have to happen to her?

She opened the door an inch or two, peered out and breathed a huge sigh of relief. The bags had been left in the porch. Quickly, efficiently, she moved everything into the house. She searched for a note, an explanation perhaps, some indication when the next delivery would arrive. She looked through every bag. Looked again. Nothing. Not a word. Not even a receipt.

Still, there was enough here to last at least a fortnight. She'd hear before then. She was a little calmer now, more in control. So was Angel; the darling little girl had fallen fast asleep.

The woman took another deep breath, slowly exhaled and smiled. There was no need to panic. Everything would be all right this time.

It was the dog end of a dead-end week. Friday evening, and

the seventh day of the search for Baby Zoë was drawing to a close. It was pitch-black outside and the incident room was replicated in reflections on the windows.

Bev perched on a desk, tapped a biro against her teeth. Hainsworth had just run through the latest statistics: more than seven hundred calls, four hundred statements. There wasn't a lot to show, considering the thousands of people-hours and endless checks. Maintaining motivation could become a problem if the inquiry continued to drag. Every man, woman and rookie wanted the bastard behind bars, but the atmosphere after those first frenzied days was undoubtedly more subdued. The squad had already been scaled down and the guv would cut numbers further if nothing broke over the weekend. Crime in the city hadn't conveniently come to a halt just because the cops were having a hard time.

"Haven't you got a home to go to, our Bev?"

She glanced round. "Vincie. What's new?"

Vince Hanlon, on a rare foray from front desk. "Christmas raffle. Dig deep in that thing you call a bag."

She scrabbled in the depths for her purse. "What am I going to win, then?"

"Murder-mystery weekend." The stage wink was a dead giveaway. "Nah. Tickets for a West End show and a couple of nights at Claridges." He winked again, added a nudge. "For two."

"You've twisted my arm, Vincie. Give us a book."

The call came in as she handed over the cash.

"Sarge."

Bev turned. The young cop looked shit-scared, the voice deadly serious.

"They've found a baby. On the Wordsworth. In a phone box. Dead."

169

24

Bev was hooking up with Oz at the scene. He'd been closest to the Wordsworth estate when the call came in. She drove like a learner on a test. Speeding would only get her there more quickly, the last place she wanted to go. Not to a body. Not to a life snuffed out almost before it began. This wasn't how it should end.

She hit the wipers as squally rain slapped the windscreen. The scrape of the blades, the night's foul conditions, were like special effects. Except this wasn't a movie. Posters showing the baby's face were still plastered on every other lamp post along the Moseley Road. Bev couldn't look, consciously averted her eyes. Couldn't censor the mental pictures.

Keats Way was next left. She pulled over, parked the MG just past the junction with Coleridge Drive, grabbed a battered black umbrella from the back. It was textbook crime scene: squad cars, ambulance, flashing lights, uniforms keeping back a growing crowd. She sensed a difference, too. Couldn't put her finger on it initially, then realised it was eerily quiet. No one spoke. Maybe no one knew the words.

Oz stood in the rain under the soft orange glow of a streetlight. His hair dripped ink spots on to the shoulders of his leather jacket. He jumped when she tapped his elbow, said nothing, just nodded his head and pointed. The tears in his eyes and the continuing stillness should have prepared her.

Nothing could.

It was the saddest sight she'd ever seen. A tiny naked body, barely covered by a crumpled sheet of newspaper, dumped on the filthy floor of a public call box. As her emotions reeled at the pathos, the futility, her brain registered facts.

It wasn't Zoë Beck.

This tiny scrap of humanity had three or so inches of umbilical cord still attached. More than that, the baby was male and almost certainly Asian.

The stench of blood was unmistakeable among all the competing odours. She knelt on the grimy piss-stinking concrete, itched to take the tiny body into the warmth of her arms. A tender touch of posthumous love. Surely nothing could be so little or so late.

"Poor little sod." She hadn't meant anyone to hear.

"The poor little sod's beyond help."

The casual delivery of the callous remark punched a button. Sod anger management. Bev sprang up, ready to lash out at the unknown speaker. The middle-aged woman in what looked like a man's suit either didn't notice or didn't care. Her eyes, creased in concentration, were scanning the cramped interior.

"And if you don't find her fast, the mother'll be beyond it as well."

"Doctor Overdale?" It had to be Gillian Overdale, the new police pathologist. It was Bev's first face-to-face with Harry Gough's replacement; best not turn it into a head-to-head. She offered a hand. "Bev Morriss, Detective Sergeant."

The pathologist's round face was pitted with acne scars. "I've heard a lot about you."

"Not all bad, I hope?"

"No." She paused. "About half." A twinkle in the pale blue eyes took out any sting.

Bev stood to one side to give Overdale access to the interior, watching as the pathologist peeled on latex gloves. The talk going round Highgate was spot on. Gillian

Overdale was Harry Gough in drag: same Cockney drawl, same ravaged skin, same well-cut wardrobe. And if the Neanderthals weren't talking through their hairy bums, fancying women was something else Overdale shared with Harry.

Bev missed the old goat. Harry had taken early retirement and a laptop and buggered off to Bermuda or Barbados, somewhere hot and steamy beginning with B. His plan was to write crime novels. At last month's leaving do he'd outlined half-a-dozen plots. They were variations on a theme: brilliant pathologist thwarts kinky killer. Nothing new there, then.

"I'm worried, Beverley." The words reinforced the concern etched on the pathologist's face. "All this blood says the mother's haemorrhaging badly. She needs urgent hospital treatment."

Bev nodded, already calling Control. Given the mother's condition, it was unlikely she'd gone far. Bev ordered increased patrols in the immediate area.

"Get them to keep an eye on hospitals, GP surgeries as well," Overdale suggested. "If she has any sense she'll seek medical help."

And a minder. Bev briefly closed her eyes. The knock-on didn't bear thinking about if the mother was a young unmarried Muslim. Family honour was the bottom line, top line, every line.

Oz appeared as Overdale was preparing to leave. Bev did the intro thing but it was neither time nor place for small talk. She watched as the pathologist climbed into a sleek two-seater Jag, then turned to Oz. "Anything doing?"

He'd been knocking on doors in the hope someone had seen something. He shook his head. "Zilch."

Bev sighed. "Can you get on to the news bureau?" If

Bernie or whoever was on called a press conference within the hour, the story should make the late news on the telly. It was too late to save the baby but with luck they might trace the mother in time.

Her own phone rang as she was stowing it in her bag. The guv. He listened as she ran the scene, went through what she'd set in motion. No response.

"Still with me, guv?"

The silence lasted a few seconds more. "A baby's dead out there. Know what I felt when you said it wasn't Zoë Beck?" He paused. "I felt relieved. How sick is that?"

Pretty sick. She was a few feet from the tiniest body she'd ever seen. But she knew where he was coming from. Wanting Zoë alive didn't mean he wanted another baby dead.

Before she could offer her thoughts he changed the subject. "You off now?"

Any time. A baby abandoned at birth, as opposed to snatched after, was more uniform's territory. "Yeah. I was about to head home when the call came in."

"I dropped by the squad room earlier but you'd left."

"Oh?"

"Thought you ought to know Gould's been released without charge."

She'd half expected it. Apart from Natalie Beck's statement, they didn't have anything on him, yet. "Yeah, well, he isn't going anywhere."

The guv had. The phone was dead. As she checked it over, it rang again. She didn't recognise the number; the sexy voice was no problem. The timing was. She was standing in the pissing rain in the middle of Balsall Heath on a Friday night. "Can't talk now, Zach. Can I get back to you?"

"Sure." Doctor Caine sounded a tad miffed. "Only it's

business, not pleasure. And you did ask me to let you know."

Like the proverbial bad penny, Natalie Beck had turned up and was currently to be found at her mother's bedside. Bev ended the call, asked Oz to hang round and tie loose ends. She checked the mirror as she pulled out. Would always regret that. The final glimpse of the scene was a burly ambulance man kneeling in the rain, the baby's body in his arms.

Sod Drumsticks. She pulled over at the first tobacconist, was stubbing out the third cigarette as she arrived at the General. Wished to God it was as easy to put out the images in her head.

Natalie lay on the bed, inadvertently flashing a pink thong, her arm tucked protectively round her mother's waist. Bev watched for a few seconds through the glass pane in the door. It might've been a touching little tableau from *Casualty* or *ER*. She scowled. Or maybe not. Not when it also brought *Porridge* to mind. The last time she'd spied like this was on Callum Gould. In a police cell.

"Well, well, well. The prodigal returns." The door cracked the wall. The slam wasn't intentional but it was like a pistol shot in the stark room. "What, no fatted calf? No spit roast? Not even a turkey twizzler?"

The words emerged sneer-wrapped. Bev was more fired up than she realised. Might be down to a dead baby in a phone box, the kind of thing that could make a girl a tad arsie.

She strode in, noting that Maxine was still out of it. Or going for a BAFTA. But Natalie compensated in spades. She went through the whole silent-movie thing: wide black-rimmed eyes, fingers on lips, brow furrowed like a ploughed field. Easing herself off the bed, she nodded at the door. Bev followed, whirled at the last second. Couldn't swear to it but thought she saw the flutter of a moth's-wing eyelid. Had Maxine been following the action?

Natalie was propped against the nearest wall: ankles crossed, arms folded, chewing on her bottom lip. Little Miss Truculent. "Fuck's sake. D'you have to do that?"

"What?"

"Scare the shit out of everyone."

"Quaking in your boots, are you, Nat?"

The Beck girl sniffed. Could be churlish contempt or the new nasal piercing: a ring through the right nostril. Either way, it had affected her power of speech. Bev used the impasse for further study. Natalie's spotless white Vans were brand new, as was the Bench top.

She mirrored the teenager's stroppy stance, hoping the monologue would develop into a dialogue. "I would be." She paused. "Quaking, in my cool new trainers." Slightly longer pause. "If I'd buggered off while the cops were searching for my kid. Not knowing whether she's dead or alive. Looks bad, dunnit? Like you don't give a shit."

"What would you know?"

"So tell me."

Natalie snarled, "Talk to the hand." She pushed herself off the wall and headed down the corridor.

Bev called after her. "What's it feel like? Selling your baby's story?" The loping stride didn't falter, let alone halt. "How much they paying you, Natalie?"

Without turning, she stuck two fingers behind her back.

"Two grand?" Bev snorted. "A mate at the Beeb says it's worth at least twenty. Best check that with Tel, hadn't you, love?"

175

That brought a momentary pause. Enough for Bev to catch up. She grabbed Natalie's skinny arm and swung her round.

"Listen up, sweetheart. You can do what the fuck you like. But waste any more police time and I'll slap a charge on you so fast your feet won't touch."

"Sod off." Short and snappy; *so* not clever.

OK, kid, gloves off. Bev smiled, waited as a brace of nurses walked past, then tightened her grip, lowered her voice. "I thought we'd found Zoë's body tonight."

Natalie stiffened. Bev almost pulled her punches but a verbal fist was probably the only way to penetrate the posing. "All the way there, I'm feeling sorry for you." She released her hold on Natalie's forearm. "I get there and there's this new-born baby dumped in a pool of piss and blood on the concrete floor of a filthy phone box. See, Natalie, I can't get rid of the image, that God-awful stink. I'm real glad you didn't have to go through all that… But don't piss me around. I'm not in the mood."

Natalie slapped a hand to her mouth and ran outside, sobbing. Bev found her perched on the low brick wall. It had stopped raining but everywhere was damp. She'd get a wet bum. Shame.

"Cruel, you are," Natalie whined. "No need for that." Snot and tears glistened on the back of the teenager's hand.

Bev said. "Know what? I'm fresh out of sympathy." She lit a Silk Cut, didn't offer the pack. "You shouldn't have left without telling anyone. You shouldn't have ignored my calls." And while she was at it… "And you shouldn't have dropped Callum Gould in the shit." It was little more than a shot in the dark, instinct more than anything.

"Pulled him in, 'ave you?" The question was way too casual.

Bev crossed her fingers. "Highgate nick. Charges any time."

"Good. Bastard raped me." Bev listened hard, but there was little conviction in the voice.

"Did he, Natalie?"

"Giss a smoke."

Bev stashed the pack in her bag. "Did Callum Gould rape you?"

The teenager turned her head away. Bev waited, partly to give her an opening, mainly because a departing ambulance with flashing lights and wailing sirens would've drowned out any words.

She took a deep drag and spoke through the smoke. "Serious allegation, kid. Bloke could go down for years."

Natalie swung her leg to a silent beat.

"'Course, you're under a lot of pressure. Could be you made a mistake."

The leg stilled momentarily. Bev reckoned she might've hit a nerve. "You'd probably get off lightly at this stage. But drag it through the courts… Unless you're absolutely positive, of course." She held her breath, hoping for a reply. Would've passed out if she'd held it any longer. "Judges are coming down heavy these days on women who lie about rape."

She'd offered more openings than the job centre. And she'd be better off talking to the sodding wall. One last drag, then she flicked the dog-end into a waste bin. It was cold and dark, her stomach thought she was fasting and this was going nowhere. "You still staying at Roper's place?" Blank look. "Case I need to contact you." Another prompt. "Case there's news on Zoë."

Natalie gave a desultory nod. "Yeah. If I'm not here."

Bev saluted, turned on her heel, shouted over her shoulder.

"Give your mum my love."

"Yeah, no prob…"

She was in the girl's face in a second. "Maxine *is* faking, then? What's going on, Natalie?"

The gap was long enough for a year abroad. Finally the teenager spoke. "Honest. She's not opened her mouth since I got back." She was visibly shaking; a pear-drop tear ran down her cheek. "I've been cuddling her, stroking her hair. I know it sounds daft but I talk to her, tell her lots of little things, pretending she can hear and we're having a little chat. But it's like she's not there." She lifted her face, a plea in her eyes. "They don't know what's wrong and I'm worried sick."

Bev was a sucker for a sob story and the emotion appeared genuine enough. She handed over a crumpled tissue. She couldn't leave her like this, but she was famished. "Come on. I need a bite."

25

Oz had the mobile in his hand ready to call again. He hit the first two nines before catching the faint wail of a siren in the distance. He hung up, debated whether to call Bev. She'd be with the Beck girl now and there was nothing she or anyone could do. Except wait for an ambulance that was also too late.

The baby's mother had been alive – just – when she'd been found. A student had turned down an alley to take a leak, stumbled over what he thought was a roll of carpet someone had dumped. Oz had taken the statement. For worn Axminster read girl bleeding to death. God knew how she'd got here. Wright Street was a good mile and a half from the Wordsworth. It looked like she'd wedged herself between a bin and a rubbish bag. Oz couldn't bear the thought that the location had been deliberate. Not that there was a wide choice. The narrow alleyway ran down the sides of two businesses: an Indian restaurant called Jewel in the Crown and a hairdresser's, Curl Up And Dye.

He shook his head, recalling the small frame, the lifeless eyes. Though the girl had just given birth, she'd been little more than a kid. Oz had sisters, reckoned she'd been around Amina's age: thirteen. He took a deep breath. It was one of those times he wished he could go off and get rat-arsed. The student said he'd be hitting the nearest bar. Oz couldn't blame him. The second the young man had registered a bare leg and the stench of blood, he'd called the emergency services, then did what little he could to comfort the victim. He'd been holding her hand when she'd taken her final breath, berated himself that he hadn't caught her last words.

Blue flashing lights appeared at the top of the road. Oz stepped out of the shadows and held out a hand to guide the ambulance crew. He felt sick, but knew he wouldn't throw up. He already had.

Ronald's Golden Arches just off New Street brought a sparkle back to Natalie's eyes. Two Happy Meals and the girl's cheeks had a hint of colour. Bev picked at chicken nuggets and super-sized chips. A thin coke was no counter-balance for the fatty diet. The place was packed with kids too young to be let into pubs, just old enough to be let out on their own. She nearly choked on a chip. That was a laugh. Most of the little dears would rather eat shit than be seen with a parent in tow. Assuming there was still a parent in the picture.

Bev glanced round, barely concealing a scowl: junk food and juveniles. Not quite how she'd imagined the night panning out. Bumping into Zach Caine and undergoing an in-depth examination wasn't even near the table now, let alone on the cards.

A considerably more chipper Natalie was on the other side of the yellow formica prattling one minute about *EastEnders* and *Neighbours,* the next about whether she should get another piercing or go for a tattoo. Bev just couldn't get a handle on her. At every encounter Natalie Beck was a stranger. More than that, she could change in the blink of an eye. What was that line from Eliot? Something about 'dying to each other daily'?

"I wouldn't swear to it, like. Not in court." Natalie dunked a chip into a tub of plastic purporting to contain sauce.

Bev's coke went all over the place. "What?" She'd almost missed a pearl among the pigswill.

"Gould." She reached for another chip, not looking at Bev. "I wouldn't go to court."

"You saying it wasn't rape?" The street-kids at the next table were agog. Bev glared till they got the message: butt out.

Natalie leaned forward, lowered her voice. "He was dead rough, but…"

"You're dropping the allegation?"

"S'pose."

Bev shook her head. Better late than never, but the girl could've cost the man his liberty. She'd give the guy a call later, put him out of his misery. "Why, Natalie? Why make up a thing like that?"

"He hurt me, Bev. I wanted to get back at him. To tell the truth… " Bev raised a sceptical eyebrow. "I don't give a stuff about Gould. Nothing matters. Nothing at all 'cept getting Zoë back…"

It was the first time she'd mentioned the baby.

"See, I pretend little Zo's on holiday, away at the seaside for a few days. I daren't think about what's happening. If it's not in my head, it isn't real. Know what I mean?"

She was in denial. Natalie had buried her head – Bev kicked the sand. "Staying with her dad, is she?"

Any grains of truth were engulfed by bullshit. "How many times you need telling? I don't know who her dad is."

Bev reached for Natalie's hand. "Just tell me. Is it Terry Roper?"

"I don't know! Right?"

She was out the door before Bev had buttoned her coat. As to Terry Roper being Zoë's dad, it was neither confirmed nor denied. Far as Bev was concerned, the jury was still out.

Bev was in the shower. Singing. Charlotte Church was safe.

"…beautiful morning, beautiful day, wunnerful feeling, everything's…"

She sounded like a scalded cat on heat – but the sun was shining, it was a day off and fun-time Frankie was coming over later. Bev stepped out, did the toga thing with the towel and hopped on the scales. That can't be right. She lost the towel. Better.

The wardrobe was a mess after her earlier *What Not To Wear* session. She scratched her ear, considering the options. Best have an away-day from the blue. Frankie'd started calling her Rita, as in meter maid. She grabbed black denims, teamed it with a tight black t-shirt. Must remember to suck in the slightly-more-than-a-six-pack.

She looked in the mirror. Not worth putting her face on till they'd given the house its makeover. She'd give herself one before they nipped into town. The plan was to hit Morgan's, then grab vids, vino and pasta fixings on the way back. Saturday. Sorted. Sweet.

The doorbell rang as she hit the stairs.

The old codger's face looked as if it'd been ironed. Badly. Like a Greek, he was bearing gifts. The bony fingers could've doubled as twigs. "Took it in for you yesterday. Postman wasn't happy 'bout leaving it on the step."

Bev accepted the brown-paper parcel with a smile. This was her first encounter with the lesser-spotted neighbour. Or in this case liver-spotted.

"Thanks very much, Mr…"

"Tommy'll do." Shame. She had him down as Albert, as in Steptoe – scrawny neck and bristly chin, striped pyjamas flapping like pigeon wings under a grey mac.

"Bev." She smiled. "Bev Morriss. Can I get you a cuppa tea or somethin'?"

He winked a milky-blue eye. "*Somethin'* would do."

Her smile was even less certain; as for a comeback, she was floundering. It sounded like the old guy was hitting on her.

He tapped her arm. "Don't mind me, Bev. Love a laugh, I do."

Fucking hell. She lived next door to a geriatric comedian with Casanova tendencies.

"I'll not trouble you now, love. Plenty of time for that later." He tapped the side of an old Roman nose. "Get to know each other a bit better, eh?" The new dentures didn't quite fit. Tommy looked like a horse sucking a lemon sherbet.

"Can't wait." She gave an outrageously lewd wink, then closed the door. She was still grinning when the mobile rang. The call wiped the smile off her face.

"Why the hell didn't you tell me last night, Oz?" She felt a cold fury as she took in the details of a young girl's needless bloody death among a load of rubbish bins. Talk about human waste.

"I left a message." The lips were taut. She could hear it.

"Not good enough, mate."

"Why? What could you have done?" She didn't like the tone.

"Not the point."

"Yes. It is. Unless you've taken to raising the dead."

It wasn't said in jest. It was cold. As ice. She was about to mouth off, then paused. Maybe he was right. Maybe she was miffed and shooting the messenger.

She tried making light of it. "Not up to the big one. Still working on water into wine."

"Come in handy, won't it?"

She smiled despite the deadpan delivery. It faded when she registered the dialling tone. The answer phone was in the hall. She pressed play, listened as Oz's voice, disembodied and emotionally detached, described the girl's discovery and death. He sounded shattered and not in the sense of tired. It had hit him hard and she'd kicked him while he was down. "Oh, Beverley. Brain. Mouth. Get it right, girl."

She wandered through to the kitchen, still mulling over their terse two-way, wondering if it was too late for a damage-limitation call back. Bread into toast first. The parcel caught her eye as she strolled back to the phone. Deciding to open it beforehand was classic displacement activity, but the prospect of more crossed words with Khanie didn't appeal. Could be he was just tired of her. And she didn't want to think about that.

It didn't rattle or tick. And it was too light for a book. She used her teeth to tear the sellotape, then ripped the paper like a kid with a Christmas present. The gift box was classy and distinctive. She knew instantly where it came from. Agent Provocateur. Shopped there too if she was feeling flush. She lifted the lid and smiled.

Oz was a dark horse at times. He shared her penchant for naughty knickers. And these were very naughty. French. Ivory silk. Like the ones languishing around packing-case city.

Like but no cigar. As she lifted them from the tissue paper she spotted a big difference. Small difference, actually. With the best will in the world and the harshest corset, she'd never squeeze her size-twelve bum into a ten. She frowned. Oz knew that. She riffled the paper, looking for a card. Nothing. The address label was typed, Birmingham postmark. She sighed. Bullet. Bite, Beverley.

"Oz?" The mobile was under her chin as she buttered toast. "You sent me anything in the post?"

"I see you every day. Why would I do that?"

Good point. Except a potential audience of cops would be so un-cool. "That a no?"

"Yes. Why?"

She hesitated. "Nada." Could they possibly be from Zach Caine? Not a thought to share. "While I'm on, mate, sorry 'bout…"

"Forget it. Look, I was just on my way out."

Her Motorola slipped and landed in the Marmite. He was so going to think she'd hung up on him.

Mid-morning and Natalie Beck was still in bed. No room service here. No breakfast, come to that. She'd spent the night at Terry Roper's two-up-two-down in Selly Oak. Tel did as much work in the kitchen as she did in the board-room. She'd not slept well, was feigning it now. Tel was on the phone in the bathroom and he'd drop his sneaky voice even lower if he thought she was earwigging.

She reckoned he was a scrote in more ways than one. It wasn't just keeping her in the dark about the cash. She suspected Bev Morriss was on the button there. Tel was well minted at the moment and she'd only seen fifty quid. Nah. Besides that, Natalie reckoned Tel was getting his leg over someplace else. And that wasn't fair on Max. She might not know her own name right now but that was no call for Terry Roper to go sniffing round elsewhere. Natalie knew he wasn't getting it from her, she hadn't let him anywhere near in months. And Tel had the sex drive of a Grand Prix.

She lifted her head off the pillow, still only caught the odd word. Sounded like he was cooking up another deal with the tabloids. If she didn't get a bigger slice of the cake this time, there'd be hell to pay. There was a whiff in the air: someone should tell him not to be so generous with the after-shave. She lay back smartish, pulled the duvet over her head.

"Hey, doll. I'm nipping out. Get you anything?"

Yeah, a private detective. She groaned, mumbled "No, ta." He took the stairs two at a time; she waited till the front door slammed before springing out of bed. He kept his room locked but she'd had a spare key cut weeks back, just in case. She'd gone through every pocket last night while he was getting hammered in the Selly Tavern. Apart from the fact he must have shares in a condom factory, the search had revealed sod all.

She prowled the small bedroom, working out where to start. The place gave her the creeps. It hadn't been touched for years. Talk about time warp. The furniture was out of the ark. As for the wallpaper: purple roses. Puh-lease. But she was on a different kind of paper trail: credit-card statements, cheque stubs, receipts, letters, anything that'd point the finger.

The chest of drawers was the size of a planet. Uninhabited. A trawl turned up only a cheesy line in Superman boxers, a job lot of grey silk socks, more shares in the condom factory and a bit of loose change. She dragged a stool over to the wardrobe. Should get some clothes on, really. Her fcuk t-shirt wasn't up to the job. She stood on tiptoe. What a surprise. Big boys' wank mags. She shook her head. The guy was so obvious.

"Lost something, doll?"

Her footing. She hit the floor bum first. Shit. "Tel. Thought you went out."

He was leaning against the door, chewing gum, getting

an eyeful. She tugged at the t-shirt.

"What you doing, Nat?"

Dusting? "Just looking." She gave a girlie giggle. Nerves. Tel was putting the shits up her. Never done that before.

"For?"

She shrugged and watched as the chewing gum appeared like an anaemic slug between his perfect white teeth.

"I'll let it go this time, Natalie. But bear this in what passes for your mind. If I find you going through my things again, you'll get a slapping you wouldn't believe."

He strolled over, held out a hand. She made to rise. "No. Get yourself up, doll." He prodded her bare thigh with his boot. "Key. Now."

She slipped it in his palm. "Sorry, Tel."

Sorry she hadn't found anything. Sorry he knew she'd been looking. Still, the key bloke had been doing a bogof: buy-one-get-one-free. Would've been stupid not to. Wouldn't it?

26

Loose end or what? Bev pulled a face, ended the call. Frankie was running late. Running round after Poppa Perlagio, more like. Giovanni wouldn't let Frankie out the house if he had his way. Even inside, he'd cocoon her in cotton wool if she'd let him. A widower now, Gio loved his only kid to bits but boy, it could be a pain. Bev had his paternal seal of approval because she was a lady cop, mature, sensible. Yeah, right.

An hour to kill. She drifted among a mini-maze of packing cases. Frankie'd urged her to make a start but it had as much appeal as walking on spikes. She wandered to the window, tapped her fingers on the sill. Her mum had advised her to get nets. Yeah. That was up there domestically with a hostess trolley and matching Tupperware. Mind, she could do with a broom. The pavement and her concrete lawn were carpeted in mouldy-gold leaves. She glanced up as a youngish couple emerged from the house opposite, laughing and chatting. He carried a baby in a sling on his chest. She pushed a kid in a buggy. Rare sight, that. Nuclear family: dying breed. Not like the proliferation of single mothers.

She shook her head. It saddened her: absent fathers, broken homes, damaged childhoods. Kids needed a mum and dad, decency and discipline. It was all very well Blair banging on about respect. What about self-respect? The courts were full of yobs who didn't give a shit about themselves, let alone society. She was sick of dealing with the fallout: street gangs, gun law, ordinary folk scared to step out of the house during the day, never mind after dark.

What good was a sodding asbo against that? Family values and a clip round the ear might do it. She rolled her eyes. Thank you, President Morriss.

She turned to face the room but her thoughts were elsewhere. Mr and Mrs Nuclear Family had brought the singular Becks to mind, and the baby. She'd already checked in twice; nothing had moved. The weekend team was poring over every report, every witness statement, every word that had been recorded since day one. A fresh pair of eyes, a new slant might just pick up a lead that had been overlooked. As well as the bums-on-seats stuff, there'd be a team on the beat. She'd authorised another street canvass on the Wordsworth: officers with clipboards stopping and questioning anyone with a pulse.

Come on, Bev. Day off. Remember?

Eenie, meenie, minie, mo. Her finger landed on a case marked 'ODDS AND SODS'. Crap and tat. She teased open the lid, caught sight of a Bay City Rollers scarf and a Rubik cube. Life's too short; she'd book a skip on Monday.

She glanced at her watch. Elevenses. Great. Could do with a break.

Quick phone call before she forgot. She'd already tried Callum Gould's number a couple of times, last night and this morning. He had a right to know Natalie Beck was dropping the rape allegation. And if she could spread a little cheer as she went along her way...

She smiled, but her good deed was not to be. Gould wasn't in. And she was out of milk.

There was a shop on the corner so why was she in the motor? Nice day for a drive didn't cut it. She asked herself again, finally acknowledged what it was about. A niggle at the back of her mind was growing. A quick check was all it needed.

Bathed in the golden glow of a bright autumnal sun, even the Wordsworth looked less like a slum. Jee-zus, Beverley. Poetry in motion. She wasn't stopping. Her destination was *in* Balsall Heath but not *on* the estate. She'd checked the A-Z.

She shoved in a CD: Stevie Wonder, *Sunshine of your love*. Least she could do was provide a bit of backing. By the time she pulled up her brain was almost a niggle-free zone. She'd been doing the mountain-molehill thing again.

Gould's house was tall, narrow, redbrick Victorian. The kind that little kids clutching thick crayons in chubby fingers drew when they first went to school. No smoke from the chimney, though. Bev locked the MG, took a closer look.

It was unseasonably mild but she felt the stirring of a faint chill. *The Guardian* was still in the letterbox; curtains upstairs and down were drawn. A dog barked even before she lifted the knocker. It was a big dog or it had a microphone. She took a deep breath, hammered on the door, jumped back smartish. It was the hound of the sodding Baskervilles. The wood was going like a wobble board. The tap on her shoulder made her jump even more. She swirled round, half-expecting Christopher Lee. Or Rolf Harris.

It was the Queen of Bling. "And you are…?" She was a walking jeweller's: bangles, chains, chandelier-earrings. Even a couple of fillings flashed in the sun.

Bev showed ID, explained she was after a word with Callum Gould. The woman appeared to give it some thought. It wasn't easy to tell because the face had been lifted; the scaffolding was probably round the back. The leathery complexion was the shade of strong tea, not a good look on top of a teenage-thin frame. Bo Jangles obviously dieted within an inch of her life.

"It's not like Callum to leave the dog." The woman could've been talking to herself. "He normally asks me to have her."

"You live next door?" To the she-wolf?

"Over the road, actually." The hand she offered bowed under the weight of the rings. "Jackie. Jacqueline Jackson." She gave her fingers a surreptitious wipe on pink animal-print leggings.

Not surreptitious enough. That sort of thing really pissed Bev off. "Any idea where he is?"

"He's not in trouble, is he?"

"Not at all." It went against the grain but she gave a bright smile.

"You wouldn't say if he was." The snarl was lop-sided.

"Do you have a key, Mrs Jackson?"

"Do you have a warrant, Sergeant Mason?"

Getting the name wrong was probably deliberate. She let it go. She needed JJ on side. Quick change of tactics. "It's just that I've left mine at home."

"What?"

"Key." Bev went for coy, shuffled her feet, gazed at the ground. "Callum's not mentioned me, has he?"

Jackson looked uncertain but that was more or less permanent.

"We've not told many people," Bev gushed.

"*You're* the woman he's seeing?" With several thousand volts, she couldn't have sounded more shocked.

Good job it was a scam or Bev would've been well offended. "I said I'd pop round, feed the dog but ..." She spread empty palms. Nice touch, Beverley.

There was a glint in the green irises. "Lovely, isn't she?"

The she-wolf? Bev nodded; weak smile, wary eye. Nice

touch? Maybe not.

"Tell me." Jackie ran a skeletal finger along a razor-sharp jawbone. "What's her name?"

Bitch? "Never forget a face," Bev busked. "Names?" She arched a hand six inches over the top of her head. "Crap, I am."

"You surely are."

Glances locked for a few seconds. Bev thought JJ was going into spasm then realised it wasn't a hissy fit – the woman was shaking with suppressed laughter.

Bev had the grace and sense to look a tad sheepish.

"You lying mare," Jackson sniggered. "I wasn't born yesterday. Callum's lady friend…" She paused. "Sonia's a six-foot Jamaican."

"Worth a try."

"Wait there. I'll get the key."

Jackson was back in a less than a minute.

"Why'd you change your mind?" Bev asked.

"If you're that desperate to get in, there must be a bloody good reason, right?"

Bev shrugged. She'd look a right tit if Gould had nipped to the shop.

"Anyway." Jackson smirked. "If you try anything, Jude'll have your leg off."

Jude was a cross Doberman cross. Bev kept her distance while JJ slipped a leash round the dog's neck.

"I'll take her round the block. Be back in five."

It took less than two. Nothing appeared out of place initially. The house was a shrine to Ikea and earth tones. Gould hadn't slept in his bed.

Bev found his body in the never-land nursery. Sleeping pills and Scotch had put him out of his misery.

"He could've lain there for days if you hadn't gone round."

Bev snorted. "That supposed to make me feel better?" Her DM sent gravel flying. "Tell you what, guv. It's not working."

She was phoning from Gould's place. A crime team was inside. The pathologist had been and gone. It looked like a clear case of suicide but she'd not take anything for granted ever again. If she'd followed through last night, maybe Callum Gould would still be alive.

Anyway, he'd left a note. His final words weren't dramatic. They weren't even original. "Life's a bitch. And then you die…" Bev reckoned that said it all. And left out everything.

"He took his own life, Bev. You're not responsible."

Cop-out. They'd all played a part as far as she was concerned. Gould must've been living on a knife-edge. They'd sharpened it and Natalie Beck had shoved it in. No wonder the guy's dog had been pissed off. She could hear it baying from across the street. Jackie had taken it in but its future looked no rosier than Gould's.

Bev glanced up as a seagull screeched overhead. Seabirds in the city weren't uncommon. The sound pleased her every time she heard it. Not now. It simply evoked a stretch of sand with a line of buried heads.

"Bev?"

She took a deep breath. "Still here, guv."

"Look, the man was under pressure. His marriage was down the pan, his job on the line. He'd been on anti-depressants for more than a year."

"Great. Just what the doctor ordered, then. A false rape accusation."

"No one forced the tablets down his throat."

"As fucking good as." Natalie shovelling a Happy Meal

193

down her neck came to mind. "What'll happen to the Beck girl?"

"Nothing."

"Come on, guv. She more or less admits making up the rape stuff."

"And we charge her with what? Wasting police time? The might of the West Midlands' finest versus a traumatised under-privileged kid? That'll do us a lot of good."

Bev clenched her fist but knew the big man was right. They'd be portrayed in the media as uncaring heavies and Natalie as a cerebrally challenged teenager whose tenuous grasp on reality had been further loosened by the cruel loss of her baby. If she was pursued through the courts, she'd get a caution, at most. And none of that was going to bring back Callum Gould.

On the other hand, if Natalie's claims hadn't been levelled in the first place...

"I'm going round," she said. At the very least, Natalie needed a few home truths.

"You're not." It was an order, not an option.

Reluctantly, she agreed. She'd probably end up landing one on the lying little sod. Best to wait till her blood was off the boil.

"Get off home, Bev." Byford's words were gently spoken. "There's nothing you can do there."

Here. There. Any-freaking-where. What was it Oz said? Unless you've taken to raising the dead.

"Here you go, my friend." The tray held a dinner fit for a cop. Perlagio pasta and spicy meatballs, heavy on the parmesan, saucy little pinot on the side.

"Marry me, Frankie," Bev said. "I'll have a sex change."

"Won't stop you snoring."

"Wear plugs."

Bev pressed play on the DVD. It was Frankie's choice. *Desperate Housewives* did zilch for Bev but she owed her mate big time. Frankie'd spent half a day helping sort packing cases and putting the place almost to rights. She'd let herself in and made a decent start before Bev returned from the Gould debacle – late, owing to the MG throwing another wobbly.

They'd not talked much about the teacher's suicide; Bev could barely bring herself to think about it. But Frankie was there for her. That was worth more than any number of words, however well meant.

Wisteria Lane's horny housewives were less than absorbing. Frankie's mind wandered long before the end. "Where are all your photo albums, Bevy? I fancy putting a montage together tomorrow. It'll make you feel at home."

Bev grimaced. She looked like a gargoyle in most pictures, but Frankie loved doing that sort of thing and was clearly on a mission.

"That case in the back." Bev waved a fork in the general direction. "The one with Photo Albums written all over it."

"Nice one, Bev. So why's it empty?"

They downed trays in synch and headed for what might one day be the dining room. Not so much as a strip of negatives in the packing case, where there should've been twenty, thirty albums, many donated by Emmy – snaps capturing everything from Bev's first breath to her last day at school.

"Must be around somewhere." Frankie sounded uncertain. She picked up bad vibes like a magnet.

Bev knew her face was being searched for pointers. She sat cross-legged on the floor, ran a mental inventory, picturing each room. She was certain the photo albums weren't in the house, yet in no doubt they'd been in the box. But Frankie didn't need the hassle. "'Course they are, Frankie."

The pictures were around. Just not around here.

Such deep blue eyes. They followed him everywhere. The Beast scanned the photographs he'd displayed so carefully, his glance resting on a particular favourite here and there. He'd cut out the nobodies in the shots; even so, the pictures almost covered an entire wall of the lock-up. He was rather pleased with the effect. The candles were arranged like runway lights. He lit the wicks with a long taper and carefully dropped the black silk robe, his naked body bathed in gold. He moved this way and that, his shadow, dark as blood, seeping across her face. He stood hands on hips, letting her feast those baby blues on his nakedness. He moved a hand, fingers stroking his cock, cupping his balls. Careful. Not yet.

He imagined her opening his gift, leered as he pictured her wearing the knickers. That's if she lost a few pounds. He sniggered. He'd bought the wrong size deliberately. Little hint. The Beast went for slim pickings. He lifted a hand to his ear lobe, stroked there too. Wondered if she realised her earring was missing. He'd sent enough messages, dropped enough clues. She'd pick up on it soon. He wanted her to know, wanted her running scared. He wanted a thrilling hunt, before moving in for the kill.

And this one would die.

He strutted nearer to his favourite picture, stared at her face, stroked the outline of a cheek. The eyes were so striking, so… arresting.

He smiled at the notion. "Catch you later, babe."

27

Natalie Beck's face stared dolefully from the hall mat when Bev drifted downstairs next morning. The girl, with a picture of Zoë in one hand and the baby's teddy in the other, was splashed across the *News of the World* front page. Bev's mouth thinned as she skimmed the story. 'Tears of tragic mum' was the gist. Even though the baby could still be alive. Unlike the currently decomposing Callum Gould. The teacher's overdose didn't get a mention.

Frankie was already at the kitchen table, making Nigella Lawson look frumpish. "Why didn't you tell me?"

Bev gave an uncertain smile. It was only a few hours since she'd worked it out herself. She'd been up in the night searching the house for the missing pics. She'd obviously woken Frankie. Bev wasn't ready yet to share her fears; Frankie worried about the dangers of Bev's job enough. "Tell you what?"

Frankie sashayed to the fridge, opened the door and grinned like a game-show hostess. "That you're on a liquid diet." Apart from a carton of semi-skimmed milk, the interior resembled an off-licence.

Relieved, Bev lifted a finger, hunkered down and scrabbled in the back of a cupboard. Keeping the Best Before date well hidden, she dolloped out a generous helping of Coco Pops.

"Needs must," Frankie mumbled through a full mouth. "You not having any?"

"Nah. Not hungry." Soon as she'd fixed coffee, she joined Frankie at the table.

The cereal bowl was empty apart from half an inch of sludge at the bottom. Frankie pushed it to one side. "Haven't had Coco Pops since I was a kid." Her tongue flicked across her top lip. "Don't remember them tasting like that."

"In a good way?" Bev ventured.

Frankie waved an undecided hand.

Bev smiled weakly and sipped coffee. They chewed the cud for a while, innocuous chitchat mainly. Bev's concentration level wasn't high, her mind elsewhere. Good job she was adept at dissembling.

Frankie clicked her fingers. "Control to Detective Sergeant Morriss. Come in, please."

"What you going on about?"

"You, Bevy. The lights are on but nobody's home."

Frankie didn't just look concerned, she looked hurt. The last thing Bev wanted was to upset her best mate. Should she confide in Frankie? Even though she wasn't a hundred per cent certain that her suspicions were correct? She leaned forward, elbows on table.

"That's the problem, Frankie. I have a feeling someone has been home." Frankie's eyebrows met as she frowned a question. Bev lowered her gaze. "I think I might have a stalker."

"*What?*"

She described how she'd turned the place over looking for the AWOL albums. Frankie wiggled her shoulders, her mouth turned down. Not exactly conclusive.

"It's not just that," Bev said. "Some of my underwear's missing." She'd checked it all, found more than one item gone. "And some of it's been replaced." She told Frankie about the gift in the post.

"Shit, Bev." The huge brown eyes narrowed to slits. "Anything else?"

Bev shook her head. She wasn't even sure why she'd checked the jewellery case. It wasn't as though she owned much. Maybe that was why she knew, and valued, every piece. Especially the gold studs her dad gave her before he died.

There was only one now. But a missing earring would be too much information. Frankie looked scared enough. Mind, she had just spotted the Best Before.

Monday. Early. Highgate. The search for Zoë Beck was entering its tenth day. Reluctantly, Bev wanted to come off the case, reckoned she had the leverage. She was grabbing a word in the guv's office prior to the early brief, had just informed him about her uninvited guest. "Put me back on Street Watch, guv."

"No way." Byford slumped in his chair, a faint twinge at the temple. The big man's face was impassive but the Waterman in his fingers was in imminent danger of snapping.

"But…"

He'd not even considered it.

"But nothing." He took a file from a foot-high stack, a weekend's worth of paperwork. It was an unsubtle brush-off, but she sat her ground. She'd had longer to think it through. If the so-called Beast had her in his sights, the sick fuck must have been in hers. Their paths must have crossed. If she backtracked, maybe she could pinpoint when and where. Anticipating a negative reaction from the guv, she'd already photocopied key reports.

"I've not given up on Zoë Beck, guv, but I'll be a damn sight better use on Street Watch." Any number of cops could lead the hunt for the missing baby; in the hunt for the rapist it looked like she *was* the lead. Why couldn't he see that? "The bastard's toying with me, playing games, wants a partner."

"For Christ's sake. You'll offer yourself as live bait next."

"Good thinking." She'd not actually considered that.

"Don't be ridiculous." He lifted a finger. "A, there's no proof your intruder is the rapist." Another finger. "B, if he is, he sees you as prey, not playmate. And C…" He hesitated.

She rushed in. "And C, I reckon I've rattled his cage." She leaned forward, hands on desk. "So give me a bigger stick."

"And C…" Byford glanced pointedly at his watch. "I say so. Post-brief, bring DI Powell up to speed." Byford pointed to the door. "He's the officer in charge."

It was still dark outside and the window reflected a Morriss eye roll and particularly pissed-off lip curl as she stamped from his office. Byford braced himself for a slammed door. It could've been tissue paper, she closed it so gently. He should've known. Bev was both unpredictable and impetuous: a dangerous combination, especially if the rapist was targeting her.

Far from being intimidated, she'd appeared exhilarated at the possibility. Byford had caught the flash in her eye, the flush on her cheek, as she'd urged him to release her from the Beck case. The big man massaged his temples. He wouldn't put it past her to go big-game hunting on her own. But if she went on a one-woman safari, she'd be open to attack. And if she flouted his orders again, he'd bloody well kill her himself.

He needed someone to watch her back, knew she'd never countenance a minder. Still, she didn't need to know everything.

He put the phone down a couple of minutes later and reached for the drawer. Damn. The pack was empty; the Nurofen was no more. And he had the mother of a migraine.

The sun was getting off its butt at last, releasing mauve-pink tendrils across a blue-black skyline. Bev reckoned the view out there had more going for it than the static action in the incident room. A duty inspector whose name escaped her was droning on about the weekend's non-developments. Talk about déjà vu. Ten days in and only the stats were different. She tuned out as her glance fell on the baby's photograph.

Bet you are, too.

Bev was no Doctor Spock but even she knew how quickly babies changed. OK, Zoë hadn't been gone a fortnight. But what if she was still missing after three months? Six months? A year? Assuming, of course, she was still alive...

That cheerful thought led inevitably to the poor bloody baby, and young mother, who'd died on Friday night. Bev rubbed a hand over her face. The story had led TV news bulletins most of the weekend, but no one had come forward to identify, let alone claim, the bodies. Unbelievable. Family honour? Disowning a daughter who'd died in childbirth? She hoped she was around when the relatives were finally traced.

The duty inspector must have signed off. Darren New was talking at her. "What you reckon, sarge?"

"Sorry, Daz, say again."

"*Crimewatch?* Worth another approach?"

"Good thought, mate." She'd already floated it to one of the producers but the next slot was a month off. Please God, let there be a break before then. Not that the exposure was all it was cracked up to be. Powell's appearance had generated more than a hundred calls, but there was sod all to show apart from a hike in the phone bill.

"If there's nothing else we'd best get on." She was perched

on a desk and casually uncrossed stockinged legs. The linen skirt rarely lived up to its knee-length description. And Oz was at the front. Not that he was looking at her. He was tapping a finger against tight lips.

"Natalie Beck, sarge."

"What about her?"

"Anyone see the coverage in yesterday's papers?" Most heads nodded. "It was all me, me, me," Oz explained for those that didn't. "She barely mentioned the kid."

Bev'd been so incensed with what she saw as the girl's part in Gould's death she'd only skimmed the *Screws* story. "What's your point, Oz?"

"I think the whole thing stinks. That baby's been missing for a week and a half and we haven't found so much as a fingernail." True, and given crime-scene expertise highly unusual. "No one's seen anything, heard anything or is saying anything." A dozen pairs of eyes focused on Oz, keen to know where he was going. "That's incredibly good fortune – or exceptionally clever planning."

"You think…?"

"I think we need to talk to the girl."

Bev was vaguely aware of a door opening, a figure approaching from the side. Oz was in full flow. Without turning, she lifted a hand to halt the latecomer.

"You said yourself, sarge: the snatch was no random spur-of-the-moment thing. We've been looking for someone on the outside. But maybe it was an inside job. And you don't get any closer than the mother."

A slow handclap broke the silence. The late arrival, control co-ordinator Jack Hainsworth, had not appreciated the offhand hold-up from Bev. "Glad you've got it sorted, sunshine." He offered her a piece of paper. "Best find this one now."

28

The bare bones were carbon copy: a baby girl abducted from her cot in the early hours of the morning. In every other respect the contrast was off the radar. Brindley Place was as far removed from Balsall Heath as Barcelona from the Bullring.

Bev gripped the wheel and hunched forward as she scanned the surroundings. Squad cars lined Broad Street and uniformed officers were already throwing police tape round the waterside development. She cast her mind back ten days. The start in the Beck case had been a damn sight tardier, thanks to Les King. Bet the lazy bugger would've got his act together faster if the call'd come from this neck of the woods. The guv didn't want King back at Highgate. It was to be hoped the fat sod had a big garden.

Oz indicated a space, moaned as she clipped the kerb. She ignored him; they'd still be sitting in traffic if he'd been driving. She'd got them here in seven minutes. Now they dodged human traffic: office workers, school kids, sales assistants hurrying or not to various destinations. Theirs was Windsor Place, a block of luxury apartments overlooking the canal. The address had meant nothing to Bev but the name rang a loud bell. David Carver was the English lecturer at Queen's College. She'd interviewed him in connection with Street Watch.

A woman constable opened the door, told them crime-scene officers were already on site. She led the way into a room larger than Bev's entire ground floor. The Carvers sat like mismatched bookends on a sofa the shade of unsalted butter. There was enough space on the soft leather between them to accommodate another two adults.

David Carver turned his head but Helen appeared oblivious, staring blankly into the distance, picking compulsively at the sleeve of her jumper.

Bev gave the plush surroundings a cursory glance as she approached. The apartment put her in mind of a wedding cake: all frills and flounces, whites and creams. A studio portrait of the couple and, presumably, their missing daughter dominated the space to the right. The baby was probably the most beautiful she'd ever seen; even in profile the child looked angelic. The photograph was about the only personal touch in what could have been a show home. No, Bev thought, the place was too pristine for casual callers.

She reached out a hand. "Bev Morriss. We have met."

"I remember," Carver said. "You were very…" He struggled for a second. "Professional."

She acknowledged the remark with a brisk nod. "I'm only sorry we're meeting again under such sad circumstances." She glanced at his wife. Helen Carver was in a world of her own, still staring ahead, still tugging at her sleeve. Bev looked closer. Mrs Carver had applied full make-up. It wouldn't've been Bev's priority, or most women's. Still, doubt, benefit and all that: trauma took different people different ways. It'd knocked the shine off David Carver. The man the kids called Heathcliff looked as if he'd been roaming the moors in a gale.

He gestured at a couple of deep armchairs, talked her through what he knew. He'd gone to bed at eleven, Helen a few minutes later; Jessica had woken for a feed around two. They'd found the empty cot at 7.45. "That's it." He spread his hands in appeal.

"Who fed the baby, Mr Carver?"

"I did."

Three heads swivelled as a tall elderly woman carrying a tray came into the room. Helen Carver remained immobile, apparently unaware.

"This is my mother," David Carver said. "Veronica Carver."

Bev reckoned the old woman looked more like the help: black skirt, white blouse, tight bun. "Mrs Carver. You were the last person to see Jessica?"

"The last of the people in this room." The correction was administered quietly but firmly. Veronica poured coffee from a silver pot as she spoke. It meant no eye contact; Bev wondered if it was deliberate. "Jessica was absolutely fine. She took virtually the whole bottle, then fell asleep as normal." Her hand was steady as she passed cup and saucer.

"You usually get up in the night to feed her?" It was hard not to show surprise.

The old woman gave a slight nod, tight smile.

Bev glanced at the baby's mother, decided on a change of tack. "None of you heard anything?"

Mother and son shook their head.

Bev looked again at Helen Carver: no one in, lights out. Bit like Maxine Beck. The similarity didn't end there. Take away the layer of Max Factor or whatever, pile on the pounds and a decade or so, the woman would pass for Maxine in a dim light. Amazing what money in the bank and a few decent breaks'll do.

"Anyone notice anything out the ordinary in the last few days?" Bev asked. "Dodgy characters hanging round? Unexpected callers? Anything suspicious?"

Vacant looks, closed mouths. The distant sound of a washing machine going into its spin cycle broke the silence. Domestic non-bliss.

Bev told the Carvers what to expect over the next few hours: a full-scale search of the building and immediate area; a media appeal as soon as it could be arranged; a family liaison officer to be assigned.

"We don't need a stranger in our home, thank you." Veronica Carver plucked a thread of cotton from her skirt before smoothing the material.

Bev glanced at David Carver, who gave a one-shoulder-couldn't-give-a-monkey's shrug. "We'll see how it goes, then," Bev said.

David rose, went to a sleek pale-wood unit, shelves and drawers. "You'll need this."

It was a smaller version of the studio portrait. Bev passed it on to Oz, then placed herself in Helen Carver's eye-line. "I know this is a tough time for you, Mrs Carver." It was bloody tough for Bev. Whatever she said would sound crass, even though she meant every word. "I promise we'll do everything in our power to find Jessica." And it wouldn't just be down to cops this time. Brindley Place, the whole of Broad Street, swathes of the city centre crawled with CCTV. It'd be a sodding miracle if the kidnapper wasn't on camera. "Trust me, we'll leave no stone…"

Bev jerked back, totally unprepared. Helen Carver had taken a swing that missed by an inch.

"Trust you? Don't make me laugh." But Helen Carver was. Hysterically. "Find Jessica? Like you found the other baby? Wonderful." She spat every syllable. "Can't wait."

"Helen, don't…"

She slapped furiously at her husband's hand. "How dare you. How dare you tell me *don't*."

He glanced at Bev. "Sorry, sergeant, my wife's…"

"What?" Helen screamed. "Your wife's what? How the fuck would you know what your wife is?"

Bev watched, open-mouthed, as Oz rose and took the woman's hand. "Mrs Carver, Helen, you're overwrought. Take some deep breaths; try to calm down. Jessica will need you in good shape when we bring her back."

When. Not if. Maybe it was that, maybe the sincerity in his eyes. Helen Carver's ragged emotions teetered for a second before she staggered to her feet. "I need to lie down. Please excuse me."

"Sarge." A head round the door: Ross West, one of the crime-scene officers. Bev joined him in a soulless lobby where he lowered his soft Edinburgh burr. "No sign of forced entry. Three sets of prints, far as I can tell. We've bagged hairs, fibres, all the usual…" There was something else. He beckoned her to a door on the right, stood back to let her enter first.

The nursery was another tier of wedding cake, the cot a four-poster crib, the only soft toy a polar bear. "What you got, Ross?"

The young man pulled back a sheet. Bev stiffened. There was another colour in the room. Red. Bright red. And still wet.

29

The blood was Helen Carver's. Not the baby's. Apparently mad with grief, the young mother had slit her wrist. Clearly the wound wasn't life-threatening, merely adding to a lattice of scars that criss-crossed both arms. According to David Carver, his wife was a serial self-harmer, the legacy of a childhood blighted by sexual abuse. Little wonder she habitually wore long sleeves. Bev's sympathy was in short supply. Her priority at the moment was the missing baby, not what she saw as the hysterical mother.

"She's barking, if you ask me." All that pristine perfection and immaculate grooming was mere window dressing; Helen Carver's foundations were cracking. David Carver had talked them through his wife's battles against depression and bulimia. The longed-for baby, Jessica, was supposed to have been a brand-new start. And, until this morning, he really thought Helen had turned the proverbial corner. Bev sighed, shook her head. "Woof bleeding woof."

Oz slowed for a red light on the Bristol Road, glanced across. "That's really harsh, y'know."

She waved a sausage roll, prior to taking a bite. "Sorry, Sigmund. But I reckon if my kid was missing, I'd be out looking for her, not making it all about me."

A half-shrug denoted doubt. "No one knows how they'll react till it happens."

She pointed the pastry at the passenger window. "Use the bus lane, Oz." Traffic was heavy. Mentally she put a foot to the mat. They were cutting it fine to make the news conference at ten. They'd already spotted God knew how many TV crews grubbing round down Brindley Place. Highgate was going to look like a Hollywood lot.

"Want a bite?" She clocked a Khan eye-roll. "Suit yourself." She brushed a few crumbs off her skirt. "Reckon she slags him off like that all the time?"

When Bev first met the Carvers, back in October, they'd seemed like Mr and Mrs Cornflakes ad. But given what else she'd witnessed lately, who knew jackshit about what went on in other people's lives?

"No idea." He overtook a well-preserved Morris 1000 convertible. "I can't begin to imagine the pressure they're under."

She had an inkling; she'd witnessed the Becks' ordeal. She closed her eyes, almost overwhelmed by the scale of the job ahead. Sweet Jesus, give us a break. Let the bastard be on security tapes.

"Talking of me, me, me," Oz said, "what about the Beck girl?"

Natalie would be informed of the development, of course. And they'd need to establish pretty damn presto if anything linked the families. David and Veronica Carver had already scotched the suggestion. Now under sedation, Helen was in no position to scotch or substantiate anything. As for Oz's thinking that Natalie Beck knew more than she was letting on about Zoë's disappearance, it looked like another theory blown out of the water.

Bev gave a dismissive sniff. "Seemed like a good idea at the time."

"I still reckon it's worth a word." Cool voice but he gripped the wheel like a vice.

Given Jessica's abduction, interrogating Natalie wasn't top of Bev's to-do list. Over the next few hours and days, hell breaking loose would look like a stroll in the park.

"I wouldn't bust a gut on it, Oz."

If one missing baby was big news, two were global.

None of Highgate's conference rooms could accommodate the media turnout. The entire shooting match had decamped to premises up the road, a spartan hall used for yoga classes. The way it was going, Bev reckoned she'd be signing up for meditation. A trestle table had been erected at the front; Byford and Bernie Flowers were behind it. Talk about sitting drakes. Bev leaned against a side wall, observing the action, trying to ignore the smell of stale bodies, cheesy socks and cheap air freshener. Thankfully the news bureau had only ever needed to borrow the place three times: the night of the Birmingham pub bombings, the day a terrorist cell was discovered in Small Heath, and now.

"What are we dealing with here?" Nick Lockwood fired the first question as soon as the guv threw it open. Given the size of the story, Bev reckoned the Beeb would already be mobilising its bigger guns. London faces have more clout than regional bods. Presumably the journalistic equivalent of calling in the Met. Bev glanced at the guv, wondered briefly what the journos' reaction would be if just for once he gave it to them straight: no police-speak, no fudge, just a plain and simple 'fuck knows'?

Byford laid down his pen, linked his fingers. "It's impossible to say at this stage."

She lifted an eyebrow: posh version, then. Either way they didn't have a clue. Common sense suggested a link between the abductions, the same perp responsible for both. But what if the second snatch was down to some nutter? Not so much carbon copy as copycat?

Or maybe they should take another look at a possible medical connection. What if Oz had missed something first time round? She'd read a case only last week about foetuses and newborns being stolen for stem-cell research, organ supply. OK, Birmingham wasn't back-of-beyond, but even so... Way it stood, they couldn't afford to discount anything. The guv was winding up the spiel along the same line.

"...as always, we have to keep an open mind."

The bland statement elicited a collective groan, then a chorus of competing voices.

"Surely you're linking..."

"You must have..."

"What about CC..."

"What's the thinking on...?"

Byford quelled further queries by raising both hands. Vague mutterings and dark scowls suggested the horde wouldn't be fobbed off this time by a bog-standard public appeal. Her thinking was right. Even before he'd finished, journalists were on their feet, throwing pointed questions. One was louder. And sharper.

"Who'll be taking over the inquiry, superintendent?"

Bev winced as Byford snapped a furious "What?"

"Standard procedure, surely. You've had a crack. Clearly a bigger whip's needed."

The lank hair was no longer tied back and the gold-framed specs were absent, but the breathtaking arrogance was all there. Bev put name to know-it-all face: Colin Squires, Sky News.

The newsman flicked a page in his notebook. "Are you aware the MP Josephine Kramer is tabling a question in the House? Police incompetence, public accountability..."

The WAR front had died down recently; the honourable member for predictability had found herself another wagon with a band. Bev tucked hands under armpits, out of harm's way. The guv's flush suggested he was struggling to keep a lid on it as well. He gave Squires a scathing look, then rose, scraped back the chair. "I've got work to do. A baby's missing out there."

Whoops. Bad slip. Hopefully no one would...

"One baby, superintendent?" Squires drawled. "Maths not up to scratch either? What's the line? To lose one is unfortunate, but two..."

Bev pushed away from the pillar. Far from exiting stage left, the guv stormed into the pack, heading for Squires. Fired up wasn't in it. Spontaneous combustion threatened.

Byford grabbed the guy's lapels, shoved his face close. "You supercilious piece of shit."

Suspended animation. Not a sound. Not a flicker. Bev held her breath; reckoned she wasn't alone. The guv wasn't shouting but every word reached the cobwebs in the rafters.

"We're talking tiny babies missing here, parents' lives on hold. And you're making cheap cracks. People are going through hell. Tell me, Mr Squires, where's the humour in that?"

The newsman tried making light of it. "Chill, man. I didn't mean any harm."

"Your kind never do," Byford spat, releasing his grip.

"Truth hurts, does it?" Squires casually pulled the material back into shape, but his face was the colour of a dirty sheet.

"You wouldn't know the truth if it smacked you in the teeth." The guv clenched a fist.

Bev darted in, grabbed the arm. "Come on, guv, he's not worth it."

Byford hesitated, aware presumably he'd already gone too far. The hacks still hung on every word; cameras captured every frame. The exchange was *so* not Byford. Even Bev would have thought twice with the media around.

"Scoring points off me, sonny, is pathetic. I'm doing everything in my power to find *two* missing babies. I don't have time for games. Sod off and play with yourself." He ignored the sniggers, jabbed a finger in Squires's chest. "You're no longer welcome at my news conferences."

"You can't…"

"I have."

Every glance followed as Byford stalked from the hall. It was a one-off performance and drew a unique response: tentative clapping from a handful of hacks swelled into a wave of applause. The pack had turned on one of its own. The guv might still get a savaging in the press but for now he was getting a show of respect.

Bev hoisted her bag and followed in his wake. Miracles did happen. How about a couple more, Big Guy?

"Oh my God." Natalie sprang up from a sagging sofa, flung a hand to her corrugated forehead. She'd been lying back watching the usual parade of losers on daytime TV: loud women with cellulite of the brain and ugly geezers with ball-breaking beer bellies. Mostly they'd shagged family or their best friend's wife/husband/Alsatian. Natalie couldn't get enough of it. Normally she switched off mentally during the news but not this time. A picture of Zoë had flashed on the screen. Then she'd looked closer.

"No fucking way." Another baby. Gone.

Terry Roper wandered in, jaw-cracking yawn displaying back teeth and residual tiredness. Late morning, he was clad only in headphones and black boxers; it didn't take a genius to detect where the iPod nestled. "Wassup?"

Natalie jabbed a finger at the box. The pictures, voiced by an unseen reporter, showed the news conference, then shots of the canal and Brindley Place, finally a split screen showing both Jessica and Zoë.

Roper snatched at the cans. "Fuck's going on?"

Natalie darted round the room. "What's it look like, moron?" She found the phone and furiously hit buttons. By the time the switchboard located Bev, Natalie had worked up enough steam to power The Rocket. "How'd you think I feel seeing that on the telly?"

"Hold your horses," Bev soothed.

"Sod off."

Instant calm. Well done, Bev. The girl's outrage was justified, though. Somewhere along the line, communication had broken down.

"I did send someone to have a word, love." And they'd be getting it in the neck.

"Don't *love* me. It's a fucking disgrace."

Her distress wasn't all due to the way the news had been broken, Bev thought. Up to that point, Natalie probably still clung to the hope she'd get Zoë back. With the abduction of a second baby, she'd think the odds had lengthened out of sight. She'd have shot either messenger, Bev or the media.

"I'm truly sorry." What more could she say?

Wind. Sails. Natalie spluttered. "Yeah, OK…"

Roper, who'd had his arm round Natalie listening in, was not placated. He grabbed the phone. "What the hell's going on?"

"You talking to me?"

"Sarky cow. Listen up…"

"Butt out. Put Natalie on. Now."

Natalie staggered back as he thrust the phone in her face. She gave him the finger as he stamped out, heading upstairs. "Sorry, say again."

"The other family, Natalie. The Carvers. Do you know

them at all?"

"Yeah, sure, go to the same cocktail parties. 'Course I don't fu…"

"Don't mess about. I'm serious."

The teenager paused this time but the answer boiled down to the same negative. "Name don't mean a thing. And I only go to Brindley Place to get bladdered – not hobnob with the neighbours."

"Did the news carry pictures of them? The parents?"

"Nah, don't think so."

"You might know them by sight. I'll arrange a meet." Bev scribbled a note.

Natalie jumped when the front door slammed. Roper passed the window, pulling on a leather jacket. She shook her head. Typical Tel. Guy does a runner just when she needed a bit of support. "Zoë's never coming back now, is she?" The voice was flat, the resignation heart-breaking.

Bev closed her eyes, wished she were there. What could she say? Chin up? It'll all come out in the wash? Yeah, right. It'd be cruel to tell her what she was desperate to hear. The abduction of a second baby meant there was either a crazy copycat criminal out there or the original kidnapper had upped an evil game. Either he wanted Jessica as a playmate for Zoë or he needed a replacement.

Angel was crying. For the first time in the baby's life, no one came to console with soft words and soothing fingers. The mousy woman was in the same room, staring through the window, but light years away.

She hated television. Never watched. Was desperate for access now. She'd just heard the news on Radio Four, The World at One: a baby missing in Birmingham. It didn't make sense.

215

Angel was screaming now, red-faced and squirming.

"Shut up!" The woman's raised voice, as much as the rare tone, stilled the nerve-shattering wails momentarily. Then the baby's cries increased in volume. The woman stroked her temples, her own eyes tearing, pulse pounding in her ears.

Quiet, she needed peace and quiet. She needed to think, had to think clearly. She left Angel on the changing mat, hurried to the haven of the nursery, closed the door on the squalling baby.

No scenario she came up with explained what they'd said on the radio: baby snatched, parents distraught, police exploring a possible link with an earlier abduction in the city.

How could it be? What was happening? She forced herself to take slow deep breaths: in to a count of ten, hold for five, out to ten. By the time her heart rate had slowed and the dizziness faded, the mousy woman had arrived at a decision. She had to know. There was only one way to find out.

Right now, though, the baby needed her. She inclined her head, listening. The house was quiet. Not a peep. Angel must have cried herself to sleep. For the first time, as she dashed from the room, she omitted her normal ritual. The rainbow swung anyway in the draught from her wake.

30

Bev dunked a seriously flushed face into a nearly overflowing sink. The women's loo at Highgate wasn't the classiest venue in which to cool down, but it was all she had after hours spent orchestrating the search in and around Brindley Place. She felt a tentative hand on her back, heard DC Carol Mansfield ask if she was OK. She nodded briefly, then raised her head, water cascading down cheeks and chin. Carol passed a handful of paper towels.

"Do-it-yourself christening." Bev winked. "Fancied a new name."

Carol didn't need to know she'd been bawling her eyes out for the last five minutes. The enormity of the crimes, the scale of the task facing the squad, had crept up on her during the afternoon. Two tiny babies snatched while sleeping in their own homes. It was evil, wicked beyond belief. And still not a lead in sight. Scalding tears had threatened and she'd slipped out of the incident room. Big boys don't cry. Nor did Bev. Not in front of the hard men.

"Dunno 'bout christening," Carol shouted from a cubicle. "More like baptism of fire. Has it been this mad since the off?" She was among fifteen officers temporarily assigned to the hunt for the babies. Byford's call.

"Bedlam now, Caz." Everything was times two: non-stop phone calls, a million sightings, door-to-door inquiries, street interviews, exhaustive checks. Everywhere the public looked, Jessica Carver's beautiful face appeared alongside Zoë Beck's. The images dominated news coverage and were posted at strategic points all over the Midlands.

"String the bastard up, I say." Carol emerged with a scowl.

She had a boy and a girl, both at primary school.

"By the balls," Bev concurred. "When we've collared him."

"Or her."

They exchanged glances in the mirror. Bev tamped down a mental mug shot of Myra Hindley. Carol averted her gaze, washed her hands. "Doesn't bear thinking about," she said. "The Carver baby's the spit of my Naomi when she was born. It's a lovely photo, consid…"

Bev lifted a finger. The call she'd been expecting. She scrabbled for the phone at the bottom of her bag, nodded a couple of times, felt the hairs rise on her nape, her pulse rate go up as well. "Be right there, mate."

She caught Carol's curious stare in the mirror. "The christening?" she said. "From now on I'm Bond. Bev Bond."

"Yeah?" Carol drawled. "So who's the bad guy?"

Hidden cameras, surveillance monitors, eyes-in-the-sky. Big Brother's not the only one watching; the world and his uncle are in on the peep show as well. Bev had read the figures, done the math. The latest official guesstimate reckoned on more than four and a quarter million CCTV cameras in the UK – one for every fourteen people.

According to her Highgate spies, a damn sight more than one had captured the perp. Bev was both stirred and shaking by the time she hit the video suite.

"What you got, mate?"

Ivor Gask whistled through a gap in off-white teeth. He was Bill Gates to a tee: bad haircut, worse dress sense. Bev suspected it was deliberate. He fancied himself as a techie wunderkind.

"Are you sitting comfortably?" He grinned. "Then I'll

begin…" Tapering fingers flexed like they were about to tickle a Steinway rather than hit a few buttons. "I've butt-joined relevant sequences," he explained. "Save you ploughing through a load of crap."

"Great." She took a perch, blew on a cup of steaming Bovril grabbed from the machine en route.

"We've got him entering Windsor Place."

"Leaving as well?" A tingle started in her fingertips.

Ivor pushed out his bottom lip. "Nah. I got one of the lads down there to check. Camera was smashed."

"Bit risky."

"No proof it was down to your man. Could've been any-one."

She didn't argue. Ivor's prickly reputation made John Two Jags look like a UN peacekeeper. But the chance of some passing yob putting out the lens just when the kidnapper needed to keep his head down was as likely as Bev making chief constable.

"Let's have a butcher's, then." She hunched forward.

Ivor talked her through a series of shots that started on Broad Street, took in Windsor Place, Brindley Place, Centenary Square, Chamberlain Square, New Street, Corporation Street, the Bullring. As an illustrated tour of the city, it was great.

"I'm looking at the guy with the hood?" Her hesitant supposition was about as clear as the figure on the screen.

"Duh." Ivor slipped his fingers beneath a pair of braces. Bev tried to ignore the reindeer motif.

"Sorry, mate, but I haven't seen a feature yet, never mind a face."

"He's definitely the guy who got in, right place, right time."

Bev sighed. Far as she could see, it was fifty-fifty whether *guy* was even the right gender. The figure was swamped in baggy dark clothing and could just as easily be female. The occasional clip when the head was uncovered was little better. Either the camera angle was too high or the light level too low.

Silhouettes and shadows.

"Overwhelmed, aren't you?" Ivor sounded as pissed off as she felt.

"Guess I was expecting too much." Like a signed confession.

"Still stuff here to view, sarge. I might come up with a bit more later."

She flashed a smile. He was doing his best; it just wasn't good enough. The hooded figure appeared on tape from approximately eighty-two cameras. There were no distinguishing features on a single frame.

Highgate's canteen was not haute cuisine, unless its lofty location on the seventh floor qualified as a culinary criterion. Bev was two-thirds of the way through a solitary meat pie and chunky chips. A portion of mushy peas paid lip service to eating greens. The steak was on the chewy side but still more palatable than the lonely lump of parmesan in her fridge; the ambience slightly preferable to an empty house.

She brushed an unruly fringe out of troubled blue eyes. The day's frenetic pace had until now pushed Street Watch and stalker-thoughts out of her head. Not that she'd be allowed to act on them – not with a second abduction on the go. There was no way the guv would take her off the baby cases.

She drew her mouth down, gazed through the window, took fleeting pleasure in the city-at-night panorama: tower-block pinball machines, streetlights strung like tangerine beads, flashing neon and Dinky-toy traffic. She snorted. The Lilliputian lyricism didn't alter the fact that sleaze balls and lowlifes still clung to the city's underbelly. You just couldn't see them in the dark.

Like the so-called Beast of Birmingham.

She shoved the plate of congealed cholesterol to one side. Not that fear of personal attack was denting her appetite. She never took unnecessary risks and was well able to kick ass. And break bone. Rough justice was no justice, but she couldn't guarantee not dishing it out to an arse-wipe who'd already ruined the lives of three girls. Anyway, if he took first pop, it'd be self-defence, wouldn't it?

"Penny for them?" Byford.

She started guiltily. Thank Christ he couldn't read her mind all the time. "Cost you more than that, guv."

The left eyebrow arched a *doubt it* as he placed a metal tray on the plastic table. "Late supper."

She took one look at the melded macaroni and over-baked beans and pulled a face. "Late? Past it, if you ask me, guv."

"I didn't." A smile flickered as he sat.

She watched as he toyed with a forkful or two. Reckoned he must get fed up cooking for one all the time. She surely did. What the guv needed was a good woman.

"Fancy a drink after this, Bev?" Good job her open mouth was empty. "I'm not asking for your hand in marriage. Try not to look so shocked."

They often had a quick jar in The Prince of Wales but the invite, just when she was playing mental cupid, was spooky. She shook her head. "Sorry, guv. Miles away."

He lifted an imaginary glass. "Well?"

These invites were getting like buses. You wait ages, then

a stack comes along. She'd already turned down Oz tonight. Not just to give him a taste of his own medicine, more a case of a back-burner to-do list coming up to the boil.

"Sorry, guv. Something on."

"Fair enough."

She'd wait for him to finish, though, didn't like to think of him eating alone.

They ran through the state of play and took a quick look at tomorrow's fixtures, then Byford helped her into her coat and they made their way to the car park.

The Midget was in the far corner. Must remember the garage booking first thing. Gawd, her mental notebook was almost out of pages. She was about to get in when Byford called across. "Have you spoken to Mike Powell yet?"

Whoops. She was supposed to have brought the DI up to speed on her sinister secret admirer. "Sorry, guv. Went clean out my head. Today was a bugger."

"First thing, Bev. Don't let it slip." He tapped the side of his fedora. "Watch your back. And don't do anything stupid."

Read her mind? The old devil could probably write it.

No perv in the privet, no stalker in the shadows. Shame. Bev had been well psyched for fisticuffs before slapping on the handcuffs. Now settled at the kitchen table, sauvignon to hand, she was poring over the Street Watch files.

She'd already ticked one box. Doubtless Powell would throw a hissy fit if he found out, but she'd just put the phone down on Laura Kenyon. They'd been talking tattoos. The girl told Bev she'd had the heart design applied at Skin Deep in Northfield. Bev's own heart had sunk at that point. Not like Rebecca Fox, then, who'd been tattooed by Luke Mangold himself at Pain and Ink in Digbeth.

But on the off chance, Bev asked Laura if she'd sussed out any other tattoo places, before. And what do you know? Bingo.

Did Bev have another winning line? She glanced at the wall clock. Half nine. Not too late. She took a sip of wine and pictured Kate Quinn as she dialled the girl's number. Kate put her in mind of Alice, as in Wonderland. Must be the headband and long blonde hair. Wasn't down to attitude; Kate was demure rather than daring. Saying boo to a timid goose would faze Kate, never mind dissing a homicidal queen.

Bev had already called the Quinn household three times in as many days. She'd leave a message tonight, if need be. Hadn't so far because the conversation would be tricky; she didn't want Kate on her guard.

"Kate?" Yes! "Bev Morriss."

"Sergeant Morriss. How are things?" The girl's slight lisp made her sound younger than her years. Kate certainly looked younger: eighteen going on thirteen. Could explain why the mother was so protective, and Kate so passive. Then again, Bev had known neither till after the rape.

"Cool," Bev said. "You?"

"Same old, same old."

Bev smiled at the unwitting irony. She had a list of buttons to push to get Kate talking, lull her into a false sense of security before hitting her with the real thing. She mentally skimmed various topics: music, films, college, books, fellas, clothes. Sod it.

"Your tattoo. Where'd you get it done?"

"I beg your…"

"The tattoo. Tell me about it."

"I told you…"

"Tell me again."

"I don't…"

"The truth."

Bev held her breath. Come on, girl. Every instinct told her this was important. Something or someone had to link the three victims. She'd combed every report, every witness statement, every hand-scribbled note. No other connection even came close.

"Just a minute." The girl must have covered the mouthpiece. Bev heard two voices, both muffled. "I have to go."

"Kate…"

"Bye."

Bev ended the call, drained the glass, tapped her fingers on a file. There was another way to find out. If the mountain won't come to Morriss… See you tomorrow, Mohammed.

In the hours since the newscast, the mousy woman had tried the number twenty, no, thirty times. Now tossing and turning, restless and almost beyond reason, she recalled each failed attempt: where she'd been standing, which room, whether Angel had been crying. Instead of sheep, she counted the phone calls. Eyes tightly closed, precious sleep still eluded her. Almost afraid to look, she glanced at the clock's digital readout: 03.00.

She'd tried desperately to come up with an explanation for the second baby's disappearance; there had to be one. Surely it was only a question of time before she found out, before he got in touch. So why couldn't she sleep? If she didn't get her rest, she'd fall ill. Then where would they be? She had to stay strong for Angel.

Angry now, she threw back the duvet, stole silently to the nursery. Even in the nightlight's soft glow the baby looked flushed, damp tendrils of silken hair sticking to her tiny skull.

Dear God, don't let the child be ill. It brought back the horror of the miscarriages, the stillbirths, then the brain tumour that killed her husband. She could not go back to that arid existence.

She knelt at the side of the cot, clung to the bars and prayed harder than ever in her life. Hot tears raced down her cheeks, cooling fast as they trickled over her breasts. The rainbow swayed in the disturbed air but she was oblivious to its gentle motion. It was unlikely, anyway, that it could have worked its customary soothing magic.

Dear God, don't let anything go wrong. Not this time.

31

Pain and Ink was tucked away in a Digbeth side street directly opposite the café where Bev'd already met Luke Mangold twice. The area wasn't particularly dingy, just dodgy, with most shops shifting sex toys and adult mags. One window had busty mannequins in crotchless knickers and studded dog collars. It was all a bit in your face. And a lot of it was probably round the back, too, in the line of lock-ups she'd just clocked.

Despite a Closed sign on the door, Mac's was patently open for business. The young guy who'd served Luke last time was wiping down the counter and in the far corner a couple of old blokes were nursing thick mugs of tea, poring over the racing pages in the *Sun*.

She ordered a bacon bap and a coffee. "It's Will, isn't it?"

He gazed at her for a second or two. "Yeah?" So much for her striking personality.

"I was in here with a mate? Luke Mangold? Few days back?" The old-mates routine often paid off.

"Right." The smile hit his eyes as he recalled. "The football lady."

She turned her mouth down, waggled fingers. She'd been called a lot of things in her time but…

Will flipped a rasher of bacon, wiped fat on white trousers. "You're a bit early for Luke."

"Know what they say about worms and early birds." Going by the startled look, proverbs were not one of his strengths.

"I'll bring it over when it's ready."

Dismissed, she took a seat by the window. The décor

hadn't registered before, but the blue and white stripes made sense, given Will was a Blues fan. And not just into the beautiful game: the walls were covered in posters of movie stars, Arnie, Brucie, Charlie. Not a chick in sight.

Trade was not roaring. Apart from the ageing tipsters, Bev was it. She lit a Silk Cut, the fumes joining a heady blend of chip fat and onion rings. Taking a drag, eyes creased against the smoke, she glanced across the road, fully aware the tattoo parlour wouldn't open for another three hours.

"Here you go." Will placed a mug on the red plastic cloth. "The food'll be along in a tick."

"Cheers." She watched him stroll back to the counter, tore her gaze from tight buttocks and returned her focus to the tattoo parlour.

The garish shop-front was full of torso-size posters. Spotlights picked out the complex designs: pouncing tigers, crouching dragons, coiling snakes, plus a bunch of skulls and scorpions. Impressive, if you liked that kind of thing. She attempted a smoke ring, considering. It was too macho to float her boat; like the surrounding culture of sex shops and escort agencies, all a bit sleazy-cheesy. Not that Pain and Ink appeared to offer anything but what it said on the can.

Mangold's alibi was tighter than a cheap facelift. But he wasn't the only guy who wielded the needles over there. And knowing now that Laura Kenyon and Rebecca Fox had visited the place, and suspecting still that Kate Quinn had, Bev reckoned the parlour was worth a closer look.

"You look as if you're casing the joint." Will was back with her bap.

It was as well she wasn't actually on surveillance. She stubbed out the baccy and reached for the brown sauce, masking mild amusement. "What makes you think that?"

"You were givin' it the eye, like."

Magic eye, maybe. It was that all-important need to get a feel of the place. "Should I be? Know something I don't, do you?"

"Thought you were Luke's mate." The smile was a tad cocky. He'd clocked her little white lie. Not just a pretty face, then; shame about the Birmingham accent.

She shrugged, took a sip of coffee.

He sat down, leaned in close. "Are you a cop? I fancy joining the police. Giving it a go, like."

A go? Made it sound like Monopoly. She bit into the bap. Saved answering.

"When you were in here with Luke, I thought you were asking about a tattoo."

"Why's that?"

"He often brings clients over."

"Go on." This guy could be useful.

"Some of them get freaked. Reckon it'll hurt like shit. Luke generally talks them round. He's really good with people." The Brummie accent broadened as he relaxed but his voice was the last thing she was interested in.

She kept hers level. "See a lot of him, do you?"

He shrugged. "He eats here most days. Sometimes I take coffee over there."

She removed an envelope from her shoulder bag. His eyes doubled in size as he spotted the police insignia in the corner. "I knew it. You *are* a cop."

Well done, Sherlock. "Just look at the pics."

She studied his face closely as he scanned each print. Rebecca Fox had definitely frequented the place. Will's black-coffee eyes lit up when he saw her. He couldn't swear to Laura Kenyon. If pushed, probably not. As for Kate

Quinn, Will more than confirmed Bev's suspicions. The girl didn't have one tattoo; she had two.

"Fact. She sat right there." He pointed next to Bev.

"You a hundred per cent certain on that, Will?"

"Hundred and ten. Full of it, she was. Showed me the tattoos and everything."

Bev stuffed the envelope in her bag, scraped back the chair. "What's your full name, love?"

"Will Browne. With an e."

"You've been a real help. Thanks a bunch." She stood, took a fiver from her purse, laid it on the table. "Keep the change."

He rose, rocked on his Reeboks, positively glowing. "Is there a reward, like?"

She paused at the door, flipped the sign so it read Open. "Service is its own reward, sunshine."

Natalie Beck had caught a bus to the General, hoping to grab a bit of peace and quiet. Tel was driving her doolally. She sniffed. That was rich, considering the doctors now reckoned her mum was off her trolley. They wanted Maxine in some loony bin in Erdington. She scowled at the consultant's retreating back. Wanted the sodding bed, more like.

She put on a posh voice, waggled her head from side to side. "Your mother needs psychiatric assessment, Ms Beck. We can't do nothing for her here."

The arrogant git said arrangements would be made in the next day or so. What the frigging hell did that mean? She tucked her hand round Maxine's. "Come on, mum. Don't leave me on me own. I need you."

Maxine lay on her back, eyes closed. Natalie sighed, squeezed her mother's fingers. She was running out of things to tell her. She'd talked her through the soaps and *HELLO!* and that. She kept off the subject of Zoë. If the docs were right and trauma was doing Max's head in, it'd be the last thing she'd want to hear.

Maybe a bit of music would get her going. All their stuff had been lost in the fire but she'd nicked a couple of CDs off Tel that her mum liked. It was a toss-up between Simply Red and Elton John. She sneered: each to their own. As she slipped Elton into the Walkman, her elbow caught the other case. It hit the floor with a crack. Shit. Tel'd kill her. Maybe she could stick a bit of tape over it.

She opened it warily. Sod's law. It fell apart in her hands. The notes slipped out and a bit of paper fell on her lap. At first she thought it was the receipt. It wasn't.

It was an address in Edgbaston, a telephone number. And a woman's name.

Natalie punched the air with a fist. Gotcha.

Bev dithered outside Powell's office. She felt like a schoolkid caught smoking behind the bike sheds. Maybe she should shove a book down her knickers. No point prevaricating. The DI had a right to know about the new lead, even though he'd likely bollock her for following it.

She lifted a hand ready to knock. Sod it. She needed a drink first. Great minds and all that: Carol Mansfield was just feeding coins into the machine.

"Sarge." Carol plumped for hot chocolate.

"What's new?"

The DC grimaced. "Apart from Helen Carver popping a load of pills?"

"You're joking."

"Hardly."

Carol moved aside as Bev searched for small change at

the bottom of her bag. "How is she?"

"I just got back from A & E. She'll be OK. The husband half-expected something of the sort. Been watching her like a hawk."

"Hawkeye obviously needs glasses." She took a cappuccino from the slot.

"The guy can't see through doors, sarge."

They walked the corridor as Carol talked her through it. Apparently Helen Carver had locked herself in the bathroom and swallowed the contents of the cabinet. Slight exaggeration. David Carver had rushed her to accident and emergency where she'd had her stomach pumped. All being well, she'd be allowed home in a few hours.

"Must help if you have more than one kid." Carol remarked.

"How d'you mean?" Bev couldn't imagine bringing up a budgie, never mind a baby.

"Well, even if you lose one, you've got to keep going for the sake of the others. Otherwise…" She sighed, left it unsaid.

The thought that someone like Carol could even contemplate suicide gave Bev pause for thought. She couldn't conceive of taking her own life because a loved one had lost theirs. Or maybe there was no one close enough to care about that much? Nah. Bollocks. She'd adored her dad, worshipped the ground he walked on, but she'd never once considered topping herself when he died.

She felt Carol's fingers on her arm. "Thing is, sarge. Till I had kids I'd no idea how strong the bond is. The love's so intense it's scary. You know what they say…"

She knew she was about to find out.

"A woman might die for her man. She'll sure as hell kill for her kids."

Bev wasn't convinced. She knew a few mothers who knocked seven shades of shit out of their precious off-spring when they hadn't had a fix. And a few more who hired them out to the highest bidder – child prostitution and kiddie porn being nice little earners.

She opened her mouth but Carol spoke first. "I'm expecting a call, sarge. Best fly."

Bev'd meant to ask Mansfield something; by the time she remembered, the DC was out of sight. She took off in pursuit, didn't get far.

"Morriss. My office. Now."

A book down her knickers would've been pissing in the wind. The DI's icy blast could blow a hole in the British Library. Powell lounged back in padded chair, legs on desk, ankles crossed. "You were ordered to see me first thing. Since when's lunchtime first thing?"

Since two babies were snatched and headless-chicken mode would be less pressure. Nonetheless Bev winced inwardly. Powell wasn't even banging on about the tattoo connection. He was exercised about her stalker. The guv must've had a word.

"I was on the way to fill you in." She shuffled her feet, tried not to look shifty.

He turned, glanced at the sky through the window. "See that?"

She squinted, shook her head.

"Herd of fucking pigs on a flypast."

"Red farrows?"

"Not clever. Not funny." His biro bounced off the desk.

Please yourself. Wasn't one of her best.

"I want a detailed report. There." Next to the dove-grey leather loafers, she presumed. "In thirty minutes."

"You'll be lucky."

"You refusing?"

She sighed. It went against the grain but... "Look, sir, it's not worth it. A few photos missing? Pair of knickers?"

"Aren't you forgetting something?"

The earring. She rubbed a hand over her face. "All I know's this." She made the points with her fingers. "No one's been in the house in the last few days, there's been no more dodgy post, no funny phone calls. And no one's on my back. Nothing." She shrugged. "Maybe it was a goon having a laugh."

He steepled his fingers. "No tail? You sure?"

The affected pose and a hint of something in the voice rang a faint alarm in her brain.

"Deffo. Why?"

He spread his hands, but a glint in his eyes set off another alarm or increased the volume of the first. Had the bugger put a shadow on her? A professional was more difficult to spot. She dismissed the thought as quickly as it occurred. The DI had only been in the loop a few hours. But the big man had known almost from the start. Her heart sank. If her suspicions were correct, it had to be down to the guv. Great to know he had so much faith in her.

"It still stinks, Morriss." Powell lowered his legs. "The missing earring bugs me."

Bugged her a tad, too. She gave a *so what?* sniff.

"Christ, woman." He uncurled a paper clip. "If there was a chance a rapist was after me, I'd be shitting myself."

"Yeah, well, you would." Take that any way you like.

He cleaned a fingernail with the clip "On the other hand, a good seeing-to might sort you out."

Her blood boiled, her face would be crimson; at least the voice was cool. "Like to put that in writing?"

233

He flipped the clip towards the bin. It pinged and hit the carpet. "Gonna slap in a complaint? Go crying to the bosses?"

She took a step nearer. "I fight my own battles."

"Then you know who's your worst enemy."

She turned, headed for the door.

"You are, Morriss."

If she stayed a split second longer, she'd deck him. Right now she couldn't talk to the prat, let alone tell him about the tattoo parlour. She'd put it all in the report, sling it on his desk in twenty minutes.

She was in the corridor when he shouted her back. "I've had Luke Mangold from Pen and Ink on the phone. Ring any bells?"

Peals. She gave a tight nod, couldn't trust herself to speak. And it's Pain, not Pen. Get it right.

"Wanted to know why the cops were keeping an eye on his place. Know anything about that, Morriss?"

Will Browne must've spilled the beans, along with the bacon fat. Reluctantly, she opened her mouth to speak.

"Save your breath, Morriss. I'm not completely stupid. I didn't like Mangold's attitude. I invited him in for a little chat." He glanced at the Rolex on his wrist. "Should be here any time."

Wow. This she had to see. "Can I…?"

"No." He brushed past her. "It's not your case. Butt out and back off."

She waved as he stormed out. Two fingers. Fuck it. She didn't care a monkey's: at least *someone* would be following a lead with potential legs. Not true. She cared. Sometimes you just had to let go.

32

Natalie Beck sprawled, legs splayed, on the floor of Terry Roper's dingy bedroom. The carpet was threadbare and the sixteen-year-old looked almost as careworn. She held a piece of paper in trembling fingers. Not the scrap hidden in Roper's CD case. This one had been screwed into a ball and chucked in the grate in his room. The buy-one-get-one-free key she'd hung on to had paid off big time. Unlike her previous find, this was a till printout.

She'd been staring at it for ages. Despite the creases and fag ash, every item was legible. It was the meaning that was difficult to understand. The basics were straightforward enough: bread, milk, tea and so on, though the quantities were an eye-opener. As for the TV dinners, someone was gonna end up square-eyed. Still, Tel was no Gordon fucking Ramsay. No. It was the other stuff that Natalie couldn't get her head round.

Pampers, baby wipes, cotton wool, a dummy and enough Cow and Gate to keep a baby ward afloat.

It'd be just about OK, except for one frigging great daddy-long-legs in the ointment. The date. November 20.

Tel had splashed out on a load of baby gear a week after Zoë was snatched.

The skin round three of Natalie's nails was torn and bleeding. She worried a fourth. Since she'd first smoothed out the receipt, the ugly truth had begun to dawn. It glowed behind her eyeballs now, a huge red fiery sun. It was just so fucking hard to credit that anyone could be so twisted. Imagine nicking a baby to milk cash out of the telly and the papers. Big question now was, which of his tarts had he conned into looking after Zoë?

She toyed with the idea of giving Bev Morriss a bell. Nah. This was Natalie's baby – literally. She'd play it her way. She jumped to her feet, staring around. There were other places still to search. If it all stood up, one thing was sure: Terry Roper was going to pay for what he'd done, every day of the rest of his miserable snivelling life.

Bev crossed paths briefly with Luke Mangold as he arrived at Highgate for his parley with Powell. She reckoned it was the nearest she'd get to the guy. For now. She'd armed the DI with a report on the link between the three victims and the tattoo parlour. It was in his hands, literally and meta-phorically.

Mangold made eye contact as he held the door. "Fancy seeing you here." He tipped his panama, gave a lazy smile. "Ever fancy a tattoo, it'll be my pleasure. Cut price." The voice held not the slightest trace of menace, so why the spine tingle?

She gave a mock salute, brushed past. Oz was kicking his heels, loitering with intent by an unmarked police motor. He opened the driver's door for her.

"And they reckon chivalry's dead," she drawled as he slipped into the passenger seat.

"Just wounded." Oz sniffed. "All those kicks in the balls."

"Very deep." She raised an ironic eyebrow. "Remind me to make a note."

"Assuming you still can," he muttered.

And the hits kept on coming, all the way to and down Broad Street. Bev left the motor on a temporary parking site that had been set up off Brindley Place. It was the closest they'd get to the Carvers' apartment block without walking on canal water.

The hunt for baby Jessica was only thirty hours old but already officers' faces wore the same haunted expressions she'd seen during the operation to find Zoë Beck. Bev walked the scene, stopping now and then to question or answer a searcher.

The task was infinitely more complex here than on the Wordsworth, the area bigger and more developed with a variety of premises: commercial, residential, business. And given the canal and its towpath, the terrain was more challenging. Dogs, divers and fingertips had to cover every inch.

It was dark by four-thirty – sky and spirits.

"I'm heading back." The paperwork was piling up at Highgate. It was her big date with Zach Caine later but she wasn't in the mood for getting tarted up and heading back into town. On the other hand, she had to eat. She'd call Zach and offer a meet over a quick bite in Moseley. Take it or leave it. "You sticking around, mate?"

Oz shook his head. "Nah. I'm out of here."

Traffic was shite. They didn't hit Highgate till gone five. She was reversing into a tight space against the far wall when Oz asked if she fancied doing anything that night. The question didn't distract her, more the implication. After giving her a berth wide enough for the Queen Mary, this was his third invite in two days. She sniffed a rat, heard a crunch.

She flapped a hand as he tutted. "Fuck's sake, Oz. It's what bumpers are for."

"Right." He so didn't agree. "Anyway, fancy a drink or what?"

"Or what."

"Don't hold back."

She glanced across, caught a flared nostril. "*I* don't."

"Meaning?"

She turned in the seat, skewered him with a glare. "Straight up. Has the guv put you on my tail?"

He didn't say a word. Just as well. He was a crap liar. And the truth was all over his face.

"Sodding hell." She whacked the wheel with the flat of a hand. If anyone knew her capabilities in the d-i-y defence department, it was Oz. He'd witnessed the aftermath when she'd lashed out at a murderer, had recoiled from the sight of her bleeding knuckles after they'd rearranged the bastard's face. "I'm a big girl now. I do not need a frigging baby-sitter."

A muscle in his jaw was on a workout. "If the guy's determined enough, no one's untouchable. Not even you."

Patronising, arrogant, duplicitous git. She was seething, incandescent. "You are so right. Why didn't I think of that?"

He sighed impatience. "The guv asked me to look out for you because he cares."

What about you, Oz? "And I've got a death wish?" She turned her head away. "Wouldn't be so bad if you'd both been up front."

"Yeah, like that would've worked. Look at you."

"Fair enough." She capitulated. "Do whatever you like. But not tonight."

He reached to touch her arm. "Bev…"

"No." She pulled back. "I've got a date. I don't want you cramping my style."

He looked as if she'd slapped him in the face. Which is more or less what she'd intended.

The spat with Oz took the shine off the evening. Plus the fact that Bev arrived at La Plancha looking like she was there to read the gas meter. Having buried herself in paperwork at Highgate, by the time she surfaced it was touch and go if she'd reach the tapas bar for eight-thirty, never mind nip home first to change. She managed a coat of lippie and a quick comb through her hair but the crumpled navy trouser suit was hardly haute couture.

She spotted Zach Caine through the window as she approached. He looked lip-smackingly tasty in slate-grey cords and black trench coat. As the gap closed, she noticed a gold chain round his neck. She'd overlook it this time but men in jewellery were so last century. "Sorry I'm late."

He pecked her cheek. "No problem. Let me get you a drink."

The doc had reserved a table downstairs, which meant either he'd not been here before or like many a medico ignored the government health warnings. Twenty Marlboro and a Zippo next to the ashtray was confirmation he smoked. She watched as he went for drinks, weaving through a size-able crowd. The Spanish bar, all parlour palms, mirrors and mosaics, attracted a diverse clientele: students, family groups, girls-night-out types and love's young dreamers. She sighed. Which category did badass single cop fit?

She couldn't get Oz's pained face out of her head. In one way she'd regretted the remark almost immediately. Their liaison, for want of a better description, had always been fairly casual. Far as she was aware, neither she nor Oz wanted to be tied down. But of late there'd been a definite drift. Maybe it needed bringing to a head. The thought, too, that he'd gone behind her back to set up some minder deal with the guv still pissed her off royally.

"There you go." Zach handed her a glass of sauvignon blanc. She'd not stipulated size. Thank God it was a large one.

"Cheers." She sank half of it in a couple of mouthfuls.

"Rough day?"

She shrugged. "You could say that."

"Me too." And for the best part of an hour and a half he proceeded to tell her all about it: the ailing health service, government health policies, bird flu, MRSA.

Maybe a bloke so gorgeous was accustomed to his dates hanging on his every pronouncement. Bev almost asked for a couple of matchsticks for eye-props. By the end of the evening, she reckoned strong and silent was more her type. Like Oz?

Upside was, she'd satisfied the appetite; pigged out, more like, given she'd seen off the lion's share of six tapas dishes plus garlic bread. A lingering notion that she might as well satisfy a different urge by asking Caine back and having her wicked way went west when he pulled out his mobile and phoned for a cab.

"Don't know about you, but I'm on earlies tomorrow."

He knew jackshit about her. How could he? "Yeah, well, since you ask…"

"Sorry. Just a tick." She stared as he sent a message on his mobile. The smile suggested it was not business. He slipped the phone in his pocket and glanced round. "Looks like my carriage has arrived."

A black cab had pulled up; the driver sat on the horn. Caine stooped to peck her cheek. "Must do this again, Bev. What do you think?"

So she told him. Exactly.

Sometimes Byford thought he'd never sleep through a whole night again. Certainly the last ten had been badly disturbed. Soon as his head hit the pillow, images of Zoë and Jessica kept him awake. What restless sleep he did snatch was broken by dark dreams of Baby Fay. Now another fear

240

threatened his shaky peace of mind: that a rapist could be stalking Bev.

The call earlier from Oz Khan, though unwelcome, wasn't entirely unexpected. However low-profile the tail, he'd known there was a chance she'd spot it. Or in this case, sense it. By the sound of it, Khan had got it in the neck and less elevated parts of the anatomy.

Byford sighed, threw back the duvet, shucked into dressing gown and made his way downstairs. Again. He poured a finger of single malt, took it and his aching spine to the recliner in the sitting room. It was as good a place to think as any.

Getting Khan and DC New to keep an eye on Bev had always been a halfway-house strategy. Half-assed, too, given that meaningful protection required at least two minders 24/7. First thing, he'd call Bev in, force her to see sense. It would only be short-term, until the rapist was behind bars.

He sipped the scotch, recalled the conversation that evening with Mike Powell. The DI reckoned the tattoo lead still had legs, even though Luke Mangold had emerged from the interview smelling of roses in virgin snow. Still, the man had furnished Powell with a list of names, numbers, addresses: staff, clients, cleaners, suppliers, anyone who'd been within spitting distance of the premises in the last six months. Mike had been upbeat, sensed they could be closing in. Byford drained the glass, hoped to God they were on the right track.

The greatest danger walking back was dodging the vomit. Like most places, Moseley had its share of binge drinkers. What was that all about? Bev liked a glass or two, but what was the point in getting so bladdered you barfed?

She passed a few lovers linking arms, and sidestepped a particularly ardent pair mouth-to-mouth in the middle of the pavement. It brought home her solitary return to a lonely bed. Again. Maybe she should give Oz a bell…?

No, Beverley.

She eased the key in the Yale, registered three facts simultaneously: the door wasn't locked, the hall light was on and there was music playing. She stiffened, heart thumping. Back off or burst in? No contest.

Coming. Ready or not.

Clutching her keys as a lethal weapon, she stormed in. Adrenalin flooded every cell. Sod flight, she was up for a fight. She hit every room, checked every inch of floor space. All senses on alert to detect the merest hint of an intruder. She detected a faint unfamiliar smell, not one she could immediately identify.

Fists clenched, she clomped to the music centre, yanked out the plug. Fucking track must be on continuous play. It wasn't her CD, though she was familiar with the song: *If you don't know me by now*. Frankie sang it at most of her gigs. This was the original by Harold Melvin and the Blue Notes.

"Fucking comedian," she snarled.

She searched the house again and again until finally convinced she was alone. Far as she could tell, nothing else had been touched, let alone taken. She poured a stiff armagnac, took it with her as she went round for the fourth time, now checking every door and window, sliding bolts and turning keys. The locks were being changed first thing; it was the earliest date she'd been able to get. She'd been a fucking idiot not to insist on the work being done immediately. Maybe Oz was right? Maybe she did consider herself untouchable?

She took a shower to cool down, clear her head. That fucking song was still going round and round in there. The second line a mental mantra: *you will never never never know me…*

"Don't bank on it, fuckwit."

Teeth cleaned, hair brushed, she slipped into a black satin nightie. A little calmer by the time she entered the bedroom, she reckoned tonight's arrogant display was the latest move in the bastard's sick game. It was a mind-fuck. Yeah, well, it hadn't…

She screamed as she saw it. He'd left it under the duvet. A polaroid. The bastard had been in La Plancha. Bev was smiling at Zach. Only Zach was no longer in the picture. Just a jagged edge where he'd been sitting.

The Beast's sly smile was involuntary. The snatched shot didn't really do her justice but the thought behind it amused him. He stroked a finger along her cheek, pressed the photograph against his lips. The chase was so much fun.

More exciting than the kill? He'd find out soon enough.

He added the latest picture to the gallery on the lock-up wall. It wasn't his favourite. He preferred those where he could see into her eyes. The blue seemed to hold such depths.

33

Wednesday November 25. Twelve days since Natalie Beck had last cradled her baby in her loving arms. She cried now as she pressed Zoë's photograph against her flat chest. It wasn't the picture the public knew so well. It was one of forty-seven images Natalie hadn't set eyes on since a couple of days after her mum had picked them up from Super-Snaps.

As she drifted aimlessly round Roper's kitchen, Natalie cast her mind back to those first desperate hours of the police hunt. She and Max scurrying like scalded ants, desperate to find a photo to give Bev Morriss. They could've searched till the cows moved house, never mind came home. They'd been looking in the wrong place. She'd just found them in Roper's bedroom, stuck up the chimneybreast with masking tape. Terry Roper made a lousy Father Christmas.

Natalie perched her narrow backside on the kitchen table. She'd thought it through, *so* didn't like where it was going. She didn't yet know why Roper had nicked the pictures – but they weren't the only items she'd found gathering soot. She'd also come across a bank statement that showed a whopping great deposit. Fifty grand. Paid in by Tel.

Not media money, either. Before Zoë disappeared, there'd been no story.

The teenager lit an Embassy, squinted as smoke drifted into her eyes. A cluster of disparate images floated inside her head. She sifted them, watched as they started to settle. The pieces were beginning to fit together but the puzzle wasn't complete. Roper was spending more and more time out of the picture. To make sure the gap wasn't permanent, she'd lifted his passport. Just in case.

Natalie stubbed the fag out on a greasy plate, lit another. The scrap of paper she'd found in the CD case was in her pocket. Not that she needed it. She'd called the number so often she knew it by heart. She tried again now. Same story. Someone picked up, never answered. Natalie listened to the soft breathing, sensed the tension. She curbed the urge to scream obscenities, gently replaced the receiver. She could be wrong.

Taking another deep drag, she flicked the butt in the sink, then grabbed her bag, checked the contents. Everything she needed was there. Her slow smile was ironic as she slipped into a pink faux-fur coat and out on to the early morning streets.

As Natalie Beck hopped on a number 50, Bev was closeted in the guv's office at Highgate. She'd just furnished him with an account of last night's not-so-happy homecoming. Byford made it clear he wanted a police guard on the house and a personal protection officer on her.

"Long as it's only off-duty hours." Bev's muttered response sounded like a token protest even to her.

The guv's eyebrows formed upside-down v's. He raised a mug of mint tea. He'd expected a harder time.

There was no choice. Though she'd never admit it, Bev had been well and truly freaked last night. She'd given the guv a diluted version, concentrated on her concern for Zachary Caine. Soon as she'd stopped shaking, she'd put a call through to Zach. He was fine, thank God. Nothing amiss. Even so, security at the hospital would be stepped up and for the time being they'd keep an eye on the doctor's house.

For the guv's ears, she'd made light of her own ordeal. As far as she could. The weight still dragged her down. She'd caught herself glancing in mirrors, convinced her face would reflect the lingering fear. A rare emotion for Bev, and one to which she had no intention of getting attached.

Within the hour the early brief was done and dusted, tasks assigned and actions initiated. Bev bumped into Oz en route to the incident room. She smiled as they went through a silly excuse-me dance in the middle of the corridor. Oz didn't return the smile. His face was set in a dark scowl she'd not seen before, wasn't keen to witness again. Almost without thinking, she reached a hand to touch his arm but he didn't so much pull back as recoil.

"Oz?" She'd come so close to calling him in the early hours, desperate for a comforting touch; his touch. As dawn light filtered through bedroom curtains, she'd arrived at what for Bev was a momentous decision: when the case was over, she'd tell him what had happened and how she felt. At the moment it was all too raw.

"What?" Peremptory. Indifferent.

She knew she'd hurt him, didn't realise how much. She glanced round, moved a little nearer. "Look, sweetheart, I…"

He made a barrier with both hands. "Leave it. Get it into your head. It's not always about you."

Tears pricked her eyes. "Suit yourself, sunshine, if that's the way you want to play." A hasty retreat into the comfort of the Bev Morriss levity shell.

He lifted his head for the first time during the encounter. "I don't. Not any more."

She watched as he turned and walked away. Gutted. Now she had an idea how it felt. Not that she had time to explore.

"Sarge. You're needed. Quick." Darren New approached at a fair old lick from the opposite direction.

Bev cleared her throat, brushed a finger under an eye. "Shoot, Daz, before you blow a gasket."

"The Carver baby. A punter reckons he seen her. Like five minutes ago."

Natalie Beck had taken two buses to get there – a class pad in Montague Place, Edgbaston: white, double-fronted, tall casement windows, holly bush heaving with berries outside the porch. Not what she'd imagined. She'd ambled past a couple of times, given it the odd glance. Now she was giving it both eyes from the bus shelter opposite. Shelter? That was a laugh. The sky was holiday-blue but the cold was freezing her ass off. She tightened the belt round the pink coat and dug gloved hands into deep pockets.

Now she was here she was having third thoughts, cold feet to go with her icy bum. She'd dawdle across glowing coals if she was a hundred per cent sure Zoë was in there. But the place, the whole neighbourhood, was well posh. The wide rush-hour roads were clogged with big shiny motors, people-carriers and that, mums taking snotty kids to the private school round the corner. Didn't anyone walk round these parts?

Natalie sparked up; she'd lost count of the fags she'd smoked. The modest pile of butts at her feet was the conservative tip of an iceberg. A bloke with boot-polish hair and a Burberry standing next to her coughed, cut her a filthy look. She waved the smoke in his face. He could take a running jump over the exhaust fumes. Anyway, she needed something to take the edge off her nerves.

And she was scared. Shit scared. There was no hint, no tiny sign that she was right. Still, she'd come this far. She could wait a few more minutes. Fools rush in…

She almost missed it: movement at an upstairs window, curtains being drawn back. She homed in, agog for more. No one. Nothing. Whoever it was certainly hadn't hung round for the view. But someone was inside. Right, bring it on, girl. She ground the nub end under a pixie boot, then walked fifty metres up the road before crossing. This time when she passed she'd concentrate on the upstairs room.

But what she saw threw passing right out the window. She turned into the gates and crunched her way up the short gravel drive. Sunlight had caught on something shiny dangling from the ceiling of that upstairs room. She'd not been able to make it out properly, but it looked like sequins. And she reckoned that could be a kid's mobile. So there had to be a baby in the house, didn't there?

Natalie lifted the heavy brass knocker, keenly aware of the hammering her heart was giving her ribcage. Big question, only question: was it her baby?

The incident room buzzed, yet Bev had rarely heard it so quiet. Twenty or so officers crowded round a computer screen. On the monitor a photo of a woman and baby alongside the canal not far off Brindley Place.

"Where's it from?" Bev hunkered down for a closer look.

Darren glanced at his notes. "Old geezer name of Harold Devlin. Bird watcher. Spots the woman and the kid on the towpath. Reckons there's something dodgy so he clicks off a few shots. He's got a digital – just emailed them."

Jack Hainsworth anticipated the question. "Team's out there as we speak."

Bev clenched her fists, registered damp palms. Sweet Lord, let it be Jessica and let them get there in time. She glanced back at the monitor, fought to keep her voice steady. "You said *them*, Daz?"

Darren clicked the mouse, brought up four more photographs. As in the first, the baby was asleep in a sling round the woman's chest. The woman's face was partially obscured by tree branches.

"Can you go in on the baby?" It was a cliché that all babies look alike, but from this distance and angle Bev was having difficulty distinguishing the features.

"That's as far as I can go, sarge."

She grimaced. Not far enough. It could be the Carver baby but she couldn't swear to it. "OK. Let's hit the road."

First off, Natalie reckoned the woman who answered the door was the cleaner. Mousy wasn't in it: dowdy, shapeless, old-beige-bag-on-legs.

"Not today, thank you." She went to close what was only a face-width gap.

Natalie inserted a slender foot. "I ain't selling." She forced a friendly smile. Though not word-perfect, she'd practised the lines. "Tel… Terry Roper sent me."

The Mouse bristled. Even the thin frizzy hair seemed to stand on end. "I don't know anyone of that name."

But she did. When it came to lying, Natalie was a virtuoso, the old bag a novice. The eyes were the giveaway. Natalie could see panic, confusion and fear.

"I think you do." Natalie searched the plain washed-out face. Had she seen it before?

"Move your foot or I'll phone the police."

Natalie pushed her foot further in, held the Mouse's dull brown eyes in a defiant stare. "You do that."

The woman looked away first. "What do you want?"

"Answers." Natalie pointed. "Inside."

The hall was big enough to live in. Not that she'd want to. Massive staircase, galleried landing; Christ, it was like one of the spreads in *HELLO!*

"Wait in there." The Mouse pointed to a door on the left.

Natalie strolled in, glanced round. She reckoned the antiques were genuine and the paintings the real deal. Huge great logs in the fire. Shame they weren't lit; it was well nippy. She heard footsteps going upstairs, doors closing, a toilet flushing. She sat on a wing chair, sank back into deep cushions, scrabbling round in her bag for chewing gum. She'd have lit a fag but she'd smoked the pack.

Where the frigging hell was the old cow? What was she doing? If she thought keeping Natalie hanging round would put her in her place, or off her stride, she was dead wrong. Way Natalie saw it, she had nothing to lose. She was itching to get it over with, couldn't see the point in pissing about.

"Right, what do you want?" Maybe the woman felt the same way. Natalie hadn't heard her come in but she stood now in front of a huge gilt mirror on the wall over the fireplace. She looked the same but she'd sharpened her act. The words were clipped, full of contempt as she looked down on Natalie, in every sense.

Natalie didn't like it. She affected indifference with a yawn the size of a black hole, rubbed thumb and fingers. "Cash."

The woman laughed. Big mistake. Natalie sprang out of the chair and into her face. "What's funny?"

The woman stepped back, trembling hand at turkey neck.

"See, Tel's running a bit short. Needs another fifty grand." Natalie held the woman's startled gaze with unwavering eyes. She was making it up as she went along, busking with a full orchestra. The bullshit sounded so good, even Natalie believed it.

"Then Terry Roper can come here and ask." The eyes were steady this time. She was a quick learner, Natalie'd give her that. And that was all.

"Suit yourself." She sniffed. "Get the baby."

What little colour there was drained from the woman's face. "Never. You're mad. Completely insane."

Natalie's eyes flared; she felt the heat rise in her face. She grabbed the woman's cardigan, hauled her closer. "I'm not asking. Get her. Now."

"For God's sake! Let me go!" Good job the house was detached. The neighbours'd be banging on the walls. "There is no baby here."

But Natalie had smelt the truth in the woman's hair, the delicate heady scent clinging to her clothes. "Fucking liar."

The woman tore herself from Natalie's grasp. "I'm telling you, there is no…"

The walls were thick and the doors were closed but the sound carried into the room from upstairs: the angry squalling of a fractious baby.

"Yeah, right." Natalie spat in the woman's face and spun on her heel. She was halfway up the stairs when the woman screamed from the hall.

"Fifty thousand! It's yours! Anything you want!"

Fists tight, Natalie turned and snarled through clenched teeth. "I want my baby, you moron."

The words were like bullets. "*Your* baby…" The woman flinched, backing away as if she couldn't believe her eyes, needed a better view.

Natalie had to force herself not to squirm under the intense scrutiny. Seconds passed as the plain face twisted, trying to come to terms with the shock. The screams from above fell silent. Maybe it focused the woman's thinking, but what she said had the opposite effect on the teenager.

"You can't just change your mind like that. You gave your word."

Legs shaking, eyes boring into the woman, Natalie slowly started to descend. "What did you say?"

34

Brindley Place was teeming: shoppers, tourists, workers, oldies with time on their hands and cash in their pockets. The squad had fanned out, most taking the towpath, others infiltrating the crowds. Bev was co-ordinating the operation via police radio. The idea was to get the woman in their sights, not to approach.

Bev was in position on a bridge spanning the canal, just downstream from the Carvers' apartment block. She'd drop by shortly, tell them what the increased police activity was about. Hopefully she'd have something more than words to give.

Jazz riffs drifted from a nearby bar, competing with the strains of *God Rest Ye Merry Gentlemen* courtesy of the Salvation Army. The winter sun glinted brilliantly on oil rainbows floating on the canal. Bev held a hand to shield her eyes as she scanned towpath and canal banks.

"Could be anywhere by now." She tried to keep the frustration out of her voice. "Why didn't Devlin follow her if he was so bloody worried?"

"Come on, sarge, he's seventy if he's a day." DC New stamped his feet to ward off frostbite.

"Yeah, yeah." She sighed, her breath a plume of white smoke. "You spoke to him, Daz. What did he reckon was so dodgy?"

"He reckoned she looked scared. Like someone was following her? When he shouts to ask if she's OK, she takes off like a bat on speed."

Wasn't a lot to go on. Bev's high hopes were losing altitude when the call came through.

"Sarge. We've got her. Le Bistro, back table. What you want to do?"

The mousy woman was sobbing now. Her nose bled, could well be broken; the cheek looked equally painful. Natalie's stinging slap had left finger-mark stencils. She'd slung the woman a damp cloth to staunch the flow. They were in the kitchen, both in shock, both in tears as the painful details emerged about the woman's literally barren existence.

Her name was Sally Barnes. She had suffered many failed pregnancies; the last miscarriage had led to life-threatening complications; her womb had been removed shortly after. Wealthy but desperately lonely since her husband's death, she had kept on her managerial post at a job centre that Terry Roper sometimes attended. That desire for human contact had brought a sick monster into her life.

Plausible and charming, Roper had inveigled his way into the woman's trust. It didn't take long before he was promising her the one thing she thought money couldn't buy.

Further, he conned her into believing Natalie was in on the baby-for-sale deal, and that the media appeal and press interviews were all part of the scam aimed at adding credibility to the child's disappearance. The money, he said, was to finance a fresh start abroad for him and Natalie.

The teenager felt light-headed, queasy. The enormity of Roper's crime blew her mind. Yet Sally Barnes was clearly telling the truth. The woman was devastated and it was about to get worse. Natalie almost felt sorry for the pathetic dupe. Then she remembered the anguish, the horror, the god-awful pain of the last two weeks.

"What about me?" she asked. "Didn't you just once think what it was doing to me?"

"I had no reason to. He told me it was your idea. I thought I was doing you a favour."

Natalie gagged, ran to the back door, flung it open and threw up. Pale and trembling, she staggered to the sink, made a cup with her hands, gulped water.

"I should have known." The woman's voice was resigned, distant.

Natalie turned, water dripping from her chin. "Fuck you on about?"

"When the other baby went missing. I knew it would jeopardise everything. It was going too far. I was desperate to speak to him. He didn't take my calls, of course."

Natalie hadn't thought of that. Had Roper taken the other baby too, for another scam? Greedy bastard.

"What will happen now?" The woman stared down, tracing a finger along the edge of the table. Though she'd asked the question, she must know the answer.

"You'll get back every lousy penny," Natalie said. "I'll see to that."

"I don't care about the money." Her creased face crumpled further, her shoulders sagged. "Please… I'm begging…"

"Get the baby." Bloody woman was lucky to be getting off so light. One call and the cops'd be round like a ton of bricks. But losing Zoë'd be punishment enough. It was Roper who'd wish he'd never been born.

"I'd rather die than live without her." Looked as if she was about to.

"Tough." Natalie jabbed a finger at the ceiling. "Get her or I will."

Barnes sat still, unblinking as tears ran down her cheeks, mixing with the blood that trickled from her nose.

Natalie pushed herself up from the sink, strode past. "Suit yourself." She was almost at the top of the stairs when she felt a tug on the hem of her coat.

"Think of the baby, Natalie. Think what's best for Angel."

The girl half-turned, brow furrowed. "You what?"

"Let me keep her. I'll give her a better…"

Natalie probably didn't mean it to happen. She'd already decided to grab Zoë and get the hell out. She'd heard about a red mist before the eyes, but until the woman's final words she'd never known what it meant.

Gripping the banister, screaming, she swung a leg and smashed a boot into the woman's face.

Sally Barnes seemed to hang in mid-air, but it was an illusion. Although Natalie could still see the woman's suspended form even after the sickening crunch when her skull hit the hall tiles.

The unknown woman, babe now in arms, was drinking coffee. Bev kept a low profile outside, watching through Le Bistro's window as she waited for Carol Mansfield. Caz had been with Powell the day they interviewed David Carver and had seen Jessica in the flesh. A positive ID before going in could save them all a lot of egg-stained faces.

Dazza was on the phone: Carol had been out since first light knocking on doors in Windsor Place, should be with them any time. Continuing the covert surveillance, Bev thought the woman looked ordinary enough: thirty-ish, short blonde hair, make-up a touch over the top; more Coco the clown than Chanel. If she had snatched the baby, her body language was giving nothing away. You'd think she'd be a tad on edge. Bev chewed her lip. Everyone was desperate for a result. Too desperate?

"Sarge." A slightly breathless Mansfield loomed.

Bev nodded a greeting. "She's by the far wall over to the

left."

Carol took half a minute or so, ostensibly studying the menu on the window. "Can't tell. The baby's facing the wrong way."

"Wrong way?"

"The birthmark."

What birthmark? Bev frowned. Of course. That day in the loo at Highgate, Carol had started to say something about the baby. "You were going to tell me. Shit. I should've picked up on it."

"Sorry, I…"

Bev lifted a hand. "Not your fault." I shouldn't have let it slip. "Where's the mark? How big?"

Carol drew her mouth down. "Poor little mite. From one side, she's perfect. But all over the right side of her face there's this massive damson stain, like a bruise that'll never fade."

The Carvers hadn't even mentioned it. Bev closed her eyes, unaware she'd spoken the thought aloud.

"The mother's in denial, of course." Carol sighed. "The elephant in the sitting room thing."

Bev nodded. "Don't mention the war."

She filed worrying thoughts for later. First things first. The woman was still in situ. "Come on. I'll get the coffee. You know where to sit."

They didn't drink the espresso. The woman lifted the baby just as Bev placed the tray on the next table. The only mark on the child's face was an impression of the crocheted shawl on which she'd been sleeping.

That was only one reason why the coffee remained untouched. The other was a call to Bev's mobile from a hysterical Natalie Beck.

35

Barely alive, Sally Barnes peered through a slit in her eye-lids. Warm foul-tasting blood streamed from her split lips and shattered nose. Through a red veil, she could just make out Natalie's form slowly descending the stairs, both hands clutching the banister as though her legs were about to give way. As she came closer, Sally could see a pierrot face, all eye-liner, tears and snot.

Sally parted her ragged lips, desperate to speak but unable to form words. Maybe Natalie sensed it. She went closer, knelt, lowered her head, hair reeking of sweat and smoke. Sally closed her eyes, imagined the baby's tiny delicate skull, her sensuous soft pink flesh. She knew she was dying, wanted Angel to have everything: the house, the money, the investments. There was no one else. She loved her so. She opened her mouth again. She had to see Angel just once more...

Natalie recoiled. The woman's face had caved in, white bone visible through glistening blood. She gagged as she felt Barnes's hot moist breath in her ear. She tried, really tried, to make out what the woman was saying but the words were lost in shallow breaths. Dying breaths?

She sprang to her feet in panic. She had to get Zoë and leg it, no questions asked. She hit the stairs running. It was freezing; the place was like a morgue. Her hands shook so much she could barely grasp doorknobs. She tried three rooms before finding the nursery.

Standing on the threshold, breathing in baby smells, Natalie was overcome by emotions she never knew existed. She'd come to believe she'd never see her baby again. Now she was inches away. Slowly she tiptoed to the cot, hardly daring to breathe, gazing down through a blur of tears. Zoë was asleep, tiny fingers clutching at a sheet. Gently Natalie lifted her baby, held her gently against her breasts, swore she'd never let her out of her sight again.

But a woman lay dead or dying at the bottom of the stairs. What was the sentence for murder? Life? No way was Natalie going to take the fall. Think, girl, think. She hit on an idea, examined it more closely. Maybe it had been in the back of her mind all along. Why else bring the knife?

Carefully she tucked the baby back in her cot, accidentally sent the mobile spinning as she straightened. She saw what it was now. A rainbow. Weren't they supposed to be lucky? She snatched it, stuffed it in her pocket. Natalie needed all the luck she could get.

She ran back to the kitchen, pulled on gloves, frantically scrabbled in her bag. The blade was sharp and shiny. Tel looked after his toys. She laid it to one side, took out the bank statement and till printout. She'd intended shoving them in the woman's face if they got into a slanging match. No one could argue with evidence. They proved Roper was in it up to his neck. And she'd bury him.

Could she do it? It wouldn't be easy. But what was the option? Losing Zoë? Yeah, right.

Twenty minutes later everything was ready. Natalie made the first of two phone calls. Whatever happened now, it was out of her hands.

She watched through a narrow gap in the nursery's curtains. The baby was asleep, thank God. Natalie couldn't stand still, willed herself to stay calm, at the same time wondering if it was too late to do a runner. She could still get away with it. She'd wiped her prints, planted the paperwork, didn't think there was anything incriminating.

But that wasn't enough. Roper was going to pay.

Bastard should be here by now. She crossed her legs to stop the trembling. Luring him in was always going to be the trickiest part. She'd played the innocent during their short terse dialogue. He'd fired questions; she'd feigned indifference. She'd kept cool, even though sweat oozed or dripped from every pore. She was banking on the keywords *money* and *cops*. Either usually punched Roper's buttons.

A scarlet two-seater pulled up at the kerb. Couldn't be Terry, unless he'd splashed out... She gasped, stuffed fingers in her mouth. Roper stood by the driver's door, scanned the street in both directions, then stared at the house.

She pulled back sharply. Close to panic, she made the second call.

She'd left the front door slightly ajar. Couldn't risk him not having a key. She was on the landing now, standing in the shadows, holding her breath as the heavy wood inched slowly open. She watched as he took a tentative step into the hall. How could a man who looked so good be so evil? She itched to pummel him, smash his lying teeth.

After the initial wariness, he swaggered in as if he owned the place, shouted Sally's name as if he owned her. The act was short-lived. He soon saw where she was, saw that she was in no condition to answer. She lay in a pool of blood and piss at the bottom of the stairs. Her face looked like a pomegranate and there was a knife through her heart.

Roper froze. This wasn't in the stage directions. He was almost at the door when Natalie made her entrance.

"Going somewhere?"

He spun round, nearly lost his footing. "Fuck're you doing here?"

Her slow steady descent continued. "Took the words out of my mouth."

"I'm off."

"I don't think so."

"Did you…?" He glanced at the body.

She stepped over it, couldn't avoid treading in the blood.

"'Course I didn't." She glanced down, cool, calculating. "Got here too late, didn't I?"

"For?"

"Sounded dead scared on the phone, she did. Come as soon as I could, like. But she was already…" Her boot pointed at the body.

"So who…?"

"Why, you, of course, Terry."

The laugh was weak and uncertain. "You're mad. Totally barking." He stared at her. "You're serious."

"Deadly. She was there, you're standing over her with a knife. What's a girl to think?"

"You'll not get away with it."

"Wanna bet? See, she'd had a change of heart. Guilty conscience, like. Specially after you took the other baby."

He took a step towards her, fists balled. "Slut."

"She was gonna grass you up. Get you sent down. She called me to come and collect Zoë. 'Course, what happened before I got here… I can only guess. Heard you shouting and her screams, like."

She caught his move in the corner of her eye. Her fingers were already round the handle of the kitchen knife in her pocket. "Back off." He stiffened, the blade inches from his face. Seeing him there, remembering what he'd done, the lies, the deceit, she'd have his eyes out if he so much as twitched.

He stepped away. "Listen, Nat. We can work something out. Go away, maybe…"

"Oh, you're going away, Tel." She tilted her head at the body. "Recognise the knife?"

Not until he knelt for a closer look. He was silent, probably examining shrinking options. He rose, trying for a rueful smile. "I was gonna tell you."

"Tell me what? That you stole my baby?"

"Think of it as borrowing. I'd've tipped the wink to the plod. You'd have got her back. We'd've been quids in."

Natalie's grip tightened on the knife. If the cops didn't turn up soon she'd kill the bastard and have done with it.

"Anyway," Roper reasoned, "it's not like she isn't my kid as well."

"Don't kid yourself, arsehole. If you were her dad, I'd have given her away."

He was quicker this time. And an angry cry from upstairs distracted her. As she glanced up, he grabbed her wrist.

"I should've finished you in the fucking fire." Saliva hit her in the face as he spat the words.

She jerked away, slipped in the spreading pool of blood and toppled back. As she hit the tiles, Roper fell on her. The blade glinted between their bodies. It was the last thing she saw before a fade to black.

Bev hit the blue light, put her foot down. Traffic on Broad Street parted like waves. Carol Mansfield was on the radio putting out an all-units call. A dead body at 6 Montague Place was all she had. All Natalie Beck had gabbled before collapsing into hysterics.

"Know which one it is?" Bev asked.

"Second right, off Askew Road." Bev took the corner on two wheels. Carol didn't open her mouth; white knuckles said it all.

Bev registered the big houses, the wide tree-lined road,

gleaming motors. What was the Beck girl doing in a place like this? She pulled up behind a red sports car outside number six.

The door was open. Bev slipped on gloves, pushed it further. "Sweet Jesus."

Three bodies were sprawled on a red carpet: an unknown woman on her back at the bottom of the stairs, a man close by spread-eagled over a third body. Bev lifted her hand to halt Carol. Talk about crime scene. It was a bloodbath.

"Get on the radio, Caz. The full works." Carol knew the drill: pathologist, police photographers, SOCOs, uniforms, detectives. So why no action?

The DC tilted her head. "We can't just leave it crying, sarge."

Bev hadn't even heard the baby. "Just make the call, Carol."

It'd be on Bev's head if evidence was contaminated. She kept close to the wall, watched where she placed every foot. As she approached, she realised she'd been mistaken. It wasn't a red carpet. It was a vast pool of blood. She was wrong, too, on the body count.

The girl trapped under the man was still very much alive.

"Took your time, didn't you?"

36

The blade had missed Terry Roper's heart by an inch. He'd live. And then get life, if Natalie Beck was to be believed. Roper was under police guard in hospital. A couple of detectives were there too, waiting to question him.

It was two hours since Bev had entered Montague Place. She'd taken a short hurried statement, then made way for SOCOs, who'd be there for at least the rest of the day. Before the interview could be resumed, Natalie had showered and changed into fresh clothes, courtesy of a skinny probationer. Natalie's gear was with forensics.

Midday now, Bev faced the Beck girl across a metal table in Interview Two at Highgate. Carol Mansfield had notebook and pen; the tape was running.

"Take it from the top," Bev prompted.

As far as it's possible on a high-back chair, the girl sprawled, legs spread, arms tight across her chest. "Not till I get my kid."

Bev closed her eyes, swallowed hard as she re-played the scene at the house. She'd gone up to the nursery, gazed down on a red-faced furious scrap of humanity writhing in a sodden nappy, damp hair plastered against hot skull. She'd gently lifted the baby, amazed when the crying ceased. She'd held her close for a minute or two, stroking her head, whispering, soothing, thinking hard. The look on Natalie's face as Bev placed the baby in her arms was a picture she hoped she'd never forget. The look when the social worker took Zoë away, one Bev wished she'd never seen.

"A few things need sorting first." Understatement of the year.

Bev had a quick look at her notes. According to Natalie, Roper had stolen the baby for cash. Sally Barnes paid fifty grand, then had a change of heart. She'd summoned Natalie to fetch Zoë, intending to call the cops, turn Roper in. But Roper must've got there first. The woman was dead when Natalie arrived; Roper then attacked her. They'd stumbled; he'd fallen on the blade; she'd blacked out.

"It's all there," Natalie drawled. "How many times you need telling?"

"Till it adds up."

The teenager glared, sullen, hard-faced. A tiny muscle twitched in her left eyelid like a burrowing tick.

Bev leaned back, hands on head. "I've got all the time in the world, Natalie."

The teenager's exasperated sigh stirred papers on the table. "Listen up, then."

Bev watched closely as Natalie ran through it again, picking at her non-existent nails throughout. It tallied almost word for word with the previous account. Which meant either she was telling it straight or she'd learned lies by heart.

"Nice try, love."

"Meaning?"

"Yesterday. I wasn't born." However much she might want to believe it, it was too neat, too pat. Bev rose, circled the room. She could go along with Roper being behind the cash-for-baby scam. No doubt the slimy bastard was evil. But he wasn't thick. Why leave a bank statement lying around that house? Crime scenes had unearthed it, along with a supermarket receipt that showed a stack of baby items. Convenient or what?

"Why'd Sally Barnes change her mind all of a sudden, Natalie?"

She shrugged. "Said Terry had gone too far. Nicking the other baby."

Bev stopped pacing, zeroed in on the girl, waited till she looked her in the eye. "Are you saying Roper took Jessica Carver?" It was the big one. Sally Barnes was beyond help but the Carver baby was still missing. Was there another desperate woman out there? Another deluded dupe with more money than moral sense?

"Ask him." The girl broke eye contact. "Bastard'll deny it like everything else."

Bev balled her fists. Couldn't ask Roper his name till he was out of danger. Three heads turned as a uniformed constable came in carrying a sheet of A4. "Ta, mate. Can you bring us some tea, a few sarnies?"

Bev took her seat at the desk, her mouth tight as she read the few lines of type, passed the paper to Carol Mansfield. "You sure you don't want a solicitor, Natalie?"

"Yeah. Ally McBeal."

"I'm serious." She paused. "OK. Let's go through it again. What happened when you arrived at the house?"

"He was standing over her with a knife. Then he come at me."

"How'd you get in?"

Split-second hesitation. "Door was open."

Bev nodded. "You saw him stab Sally Barnes?"

"Yeah. Horrible, it was." The shudder was a nice touch.

"Had two blades, did he? One in each hand?"

Natalie frowned, played for a little time. A shrugged *dunno* was all she came up with.

Bev leaned forward, deliberately invading the girl's space. "Was Sally Barnes still alive when you kicked her teeth in?"

The girl jerked her head away, but not before Bev

glimpsed a flash of fear in her eyes. "What you on about?"

She waved the sheet of A4 at the girl. "Chips of bone embedded in the toe of your boot, Natalie."

"I didn't kill her. He come in and finished her off. Then he turns on me." She grabbed Bev's arm. "You've got to believe me."

Bev looked down until the girl removed her hand. "It's not going to happen, Natalie. There'll be phone records, fingerprints…" Not to mention the blood-stained rainbow they'd found in the teenager's pocket. Along with a crock of bullshit.

"No." Natalie shook her head vehemently. "There ain't no prints."

"Wiped them, did you?" That'd explain the damp duster under the sink. What do they say about a little knowledge? She snorted. Watching a few episodes of CSI doesn't make anyone a forensic hotshot. "It'll be better for everyone if you tell the truth, love."

Natalie slumped, the image of truculent teenager made flesh. "Not till I see my kid."

"Carry on like this, and she'll be older than you before you set eyes on her." Bev paused. "Except for prison visits."

"Fuck you." She dashed an angry hand at specks of saliva on her mouth.

"Whatever." Bev looked away, made a few notes, affected complete indifference. The silence was uneasy, unnerving. Like watching a bad actor dry on stage. When Bev glanced up, Natalie's face was wet with tears, her bony shoulders hunched and shaking as she fought for composure. Bev made no move to comfort her.

Eventually Natalie spoke. "Let me see her, Bev, please." She wiped slime from her nose with a sleeve. "I might remember more once I've seen Zo."

"More lies?"

She spread her hands. "Please, Bev. I'm begging."

"No."

Carol Mansfield passed Natalie a bunch of tissues. "Sarge?"

Bev gave a barely perceptible shake of the head. She watched as Natalie sat up straight and tightened her ponytail. Holding Bev's gaze, she said, "OK, then."

Bev gave an encouraging smile. Thank God for that. For a minute she thought she'd lost her touch.

"If I can't see my baby – go fuck yourself."

At that, Bev almost lost it. She itched to give the girl a good slapping. Instead, she took a deep breath, her voice blasé. "Callum Gould killed himself. Know that?" The teacher's suicide still hadn't made the papers as far as Bev was aware.

The colour drained from Natalie's already pasty face. "So?" The tone was uncertain this time, not insolent.

"So." Bev rose, slowly approached Natalie, leaned over and for the first time in the interview – any interview – she screamed at the top of her voice. "A man's dead because of your fucking lies! If you don't level with me now, I'll see it's laid at your door!"

It would never happen, of course. No one – as the guv put it – had forced the tablets down the guy's throat. But Natalie was already in emotional overload. Gould's untimely death was one more shock to her already creaking system. Cruel but fair. Bev backed off, headed for the door.

"Wait!" Natalie yelled. "I'll talk."

Bev locked glances with the girl before slowly resuming her seat. "This had better be good."

Natalie pointed at the tape. "Turn that off, then."

Bev considered the offer before reaching for the switch.

"Sarge?" Carol didn't add further protest. One word said it all.

Bev changed the subject without looking round. "Chase the tea, Carol."

The DC rose, stood in front of Bev. "Sarge."

Bev tilted her head at the door. When they were alone, she told Natalie she had two minutes. She listened as the teenager gave another version of events; this one rang truer. She'd kicked Sally Barnes down the stairs but only after the woman had spoken the fatal words: 'I'll give her a better life'. Prior to that, Natalie had meant her no harm. Unlike her intentions towards Roper. Framing him for the murder was Natalie's warped way of seeking revenge. She'd not stabbed Roper. It was a genuine accident. She wanted him alive, so he could pay for what he'd done.

A part of Bev understood the girl's actions. Roper had stolen her baby, then a sick woman had told her she wasn't a fit mother. Extenuating circumstances, a sympathetic jury – Natalie might get out after twelve years or so.

"Fix it for me?" Bev drew back as Natalie made another grab for her arm, wide eyes pleading. "You can fix it, Bev. Terry deserves everything that's coming. He torched Blake Way as well. Wanted us both dead."

Maxine Beck: another sorry victim in all this. Bev shook her head. "I can't…"

"'Course you can. It's his word against mine. I can lie for England."

As Callum Gould discovered. "Not against evidence, love."

Tears welled in the girl's bloodshot eyes. "But I'll lose her."

Bev looked away, saw the baby in her mind's eye, recalled the warmth of that tiny body as she cradled it against her own. With Maxine on another planet, Zoë would go into care.

"Please, Bev. You know how the system works. Get me out of here." The girl was on her knees, huge tears rolling down blotchy cheeks. "Please, Bev. Do it for Zoë."

She put her arms round Natalie's quaking shoulders, tasted blood as she bit her lip. Did she seriously consider it? Just for a second? Afterwards, Bev often asked herself the same question. Always came back with the same answer. No. Not for an instant.

She was an even better liar than Natalie Beck.

37

Highgate. Bev squatted on her office floor, back against the radiator, head in hands. It was coming up to six o'clock and minus five outside. Bitter, like her. This had turned into one of the blackest days of her life. And it wasn't over yet. She was steeling herself to pay a house call: the Carvers.

"Fucking job. Hate it."

"You do?"

She peered through her fingers. Byford hovered in the doorway, coat on, hat in hand. She scrambled to her feet, smoothing her skirt and grabbed a tissue from a box on the desk. Through a watery smile she managed a weak quip. "Talking to myself again, guv."

He came in, stood by her, fiddled with the fedora. "Everyone does, you know."

"You said it. Must be mad to work here."

"Don't be obtuse, you know what I mean." The right eyebrow formed an arch. "We all hate the job. From time to time."

Yeah, but she really really loathed it. That afternoon, she'd watched a sixteen-year-old kid, who'd not started out with a lot, lose what little she had. An inconsolable Natalie Beck was banged up in a police cell. She'd appear in court first thing, when she'd almost certainly be remanded in custody. Even if the magistrates took pity on her, she had nowhere to go. And no idea when she'd see Zoë again. The baby was in emergency foster care.

Byford strolled to his preferred spot on the windowsill. "The girl stabbed a woman through the heart, Bev." He must've read her report. As well as her mind.

"Yeah, I know…"

"But?"

"Nothing's ever black and white, is it?"

"Mostly it's all a mess."

She tugged at her fringe. "The kid'll end up adopted. Natalie'll spend the best years of her life behind bars. And Maxine… God knows what'll happen there."

"You're a cop, Bev. You haven't got a magic wand."

Just as well. Or Terry Roper would be slug turd. Cancel that. He already was. They'd not been allowed near the shit-for-brains so far. They only had Natalie's word that he was involved in the Carver baby's abduction. Like that was worth a bunch.

She blew out her cheeks. "Mums are supposed to tell you."

"What?"

"There'd be days like this." She gave a lop-sided smile at the thought of a bad day in Emmy's book: an unfinished crossword. "Come on, guv." She grabbed her coat from the hook. "I'm out of here."

Byford held the door. "Have you spoken to Larry yet?"

Was he avoiding her gaze? Had he only dropped by to check up on her? Larry Drake was the main man in personal protection. "Sure have. One of his guys has already checked the house." Baldwin Street's new locks and alarm were up to scratch.

As they crossed the car park she started whistling the *Minder* theme tune. He didn't say a word but she caught a fleeting grin on his face. "Sorry, guv, couldn't resist."

She scanned the car park, searching for the MG, then remembered it was in the garage having major surgery. She'd been allocated an unmarked Peugeot, so uncool.

At the motor, Byford reached out, brushed a strand of

hair from her eyes. The gesture caught her off guard. The silence lasted a second or two longer than it should. Had he crossed a line? And would she welcome that?

He smiled, tapped the brim of his hat, headed for his wheels, then turned back. "You never said."

"Guv?" She paused, key in lock.

"What you'd do if you weren't a cop."

She turned down her mouth, waggled a hand. "Lap dancer?"

Even at the best of times, Bev hated mirrors in lifts. The ones in Windsor Place were wall-to-wall and the last twenty-four hours had been a bugger. Not to mention the last two weeks. They'd certainly left a mark or two. She lifted a hand to her cheek: flaky skin, suitcase eyes. Early night after this, girl.

Shouldn't take long. The Carvers knew the score: uniform had kept them up to date. But as officer in charge, Bev felt duty-bound to show her face. Not that they were answering. She frowned, rang the bell again, held her breath as she pressed an ear against the door, straining to identify the faint sounds emanating.

A woman's voice, in the cadences of prayer.

Bev had God-bothered enough in her Catholic school-girl days to recognise a Hail Mary or four. If the Carvers could talk to the Big Man, they could give her a hearing. She hammered the wood with the flat of her hand.

She barely recognised Veronica Carver. The lines on the old woman's face were so deep they looked felt-tipped. The grey hair swung like steel cable.

"I'm glad you're here," she said. "I was about to call." After communing with Our Lady? The rosary in her fingers was a giveaway.

"Right. Great. Come in, shall I?" Bev rubbed her hands together. "Parky out here."

The woman moved aside, led the way into the large sitting room. Helen Carver lay asleep on the sofa. There was no sign of David. Veronica drifted over to a wing chair by the open fire.

Bev glanced through the window, glimpsed a dumb show of revellers geared up for a night on the town. Wouldn't say no to a drink herself. Might pop into the Boat for a quickie after this. The old woman was waiting. Bev hesitated. Made more sense if the Carver women heard it together. Wasn't exactly good news, but it was better than nothing. It was just possible Natalie wasn't lying through her teeth and Roper knew Jessica's whereabouts. Bev glanced at the sofa, raised a querying eyebrow. Veronica shook her head.

Bev shrugged. "Just want you to know, we'll be talking to a suspect first thing. It's possible he can tell us where Jessica is. It's important not to get your hopes up, though."

"Thank you." She smoothed a crease from her skirt. "As I said, I was about to call." She tilted her head towards the sofa. "I found her a few moments ago."

"Found her?" Bev froze, stunned.

"I'm afraid I was too late."

Bev raced over, knelt at Helen's side. Surely she was asleep? Hair tousled, make-up smudged, warm to the touch… Bev felt for a pulse. Nothing. It had to be another overdose.

Veronica sat stiff-backed, rosary in her lap. The old lady must be in shock. Christ, Bev was in shock.

"Do you know what she took, Mrs Carver?" Bev reached for her phone: Control could sort the arrangements. Veronica shook her head.

Bev glanced round, struggling to keep her cool. "Where's your son?"

"This is nothing to do with David."

None of this made sense. "Meaning?"

"Helen couldn't cope with… It was hardly Jessica's fault, was it?"

Bev had no idea where any of this was going. Silence was often the best way to find out. She took a seat, waited.

"Helen won't admit it, of course." The rosary slipped to the floor. Veronica made no effort to retrieve it. "She says it was to punish David. She found some earrings, you see."

Bev registered that the old woman was talking as if Helen was alive. Not surprising, given the body temperature.

"They belong to a woman David's friendly with. He was getting them repaired."

Bev was beginning to see a minuscule chink of light. David Carver had been questioned a couple of times in connection with Street Watch; the media reported that the rapist took trophies, earrings. "And Helen jumped to the conclusion…?"

Veronica Carver snorted. "Ludicrous."

Fucking tragic. "I'm not clear, Mrs Carver. What's all this to do with Jessica's disappearance?"

"Two birds with one stone, sergeant." She made eye contact, held it for three, four seconds as if preparing the ground for a dense pupil. "Punish a man you love by killing a baby you don't."

"Jessica's *dead*?" Bev swallowed hard. "She killed the child just to get back at her old man?"

"Not just that." Veronica frowned, impatient. "I told you. She couldn't bear to look at the baby. Hated Jessica's imperfection. That awful mark on her face."

Bev shook her head, didn't want to believe it. She ran the new data, desperate to comprehend it. Had Helen Carver seen Zoë's abduction as an opportunity to get rid of her own baby? Banked on the police lumping the crimes together? And when she learned that Zoë had been found safe and well, had it tipped her over the edge? Knowing there'd be no homecoming of any kind for Jessica? Knowing the police would widen the net?

"How?" Bev asked. "How did she kill her?"

The old woman looked down. "She drowned her in the bath, then disposed of the body in the canal."

Bev dropped her head in her hands. It was too much to take in. And it still didn't add up. So far Helen Carver had been spectacularly unsuccessful in topping herself. And what was it Carol had said after the last failed attempt? David Carver watches her like a hawk.

Lifting her head, Bev peered at Veronica, who immediately looked away. Her calm was preternatural.

"She's always been unstable, of course." The old woman rose, poured herself a scotch from a decanter on the sideboard. "It was only a question of time before she succeeded, I suppose."

Bev chewed her bottom lip. "That's why you'd keep an eye on her, right?"

Veronica shrugged indifference. "If someone's determined enough, sergeant…"

Bev searched the old woman's face. Didn't like what she saw. It struck Bev that the old bag was calm because she didn't give a monkey's. Or maybe the suicide was no great shock because she knew a damn sight more than she was letting on.

"Where'd you find her?"

A barely perceptible pause. "On the settee, of course."

"And the pill bottles, the packs, where are they?"

Confusion flitted across the face. Or was it anger? The old woman clearly didn't like her authority being questioned. She waved arthritic fingers. "I have no idea."

"You've searched the place?"

"Yes. No."

"Which?" Bev fired back.

The old woman took a lace handkerchief from her sleeve, dabbed at her temples and top lip. Playing for time? Or feeling the pressure? Bev sprang up, headed for a door.

"Where do you think you're going?" The voice was a whiplash.

"I'm gonna take this place apart, till I find what killed your daughter-in-law."

"You won't. And I'll sue you for any damage you cause."

It was the arrogance, the absolute certainty, as the old woman sipped her scotch, stared at Bev and pressed her thin lips into a superior smile. Bev saw the dark probability and leapt.

"How'd you get her to do it?"

"I beg your pardon?" It was the last thing she'd beg, going by the contemptuous drawl.

"Painkillers, paraquat, whatever she took… How'd you get her to take it?"

"I hope you can substantiate that remark." She glared at Bev. "For your sake."

Bev ignored the implied threat. "You and Helen close, were you?" The old woman shrugged. "Thought not," Bev went on. "So how come you know all this? I can't see her confiding in you."

"Let's just say I'm a light sleeper." She rose to replenish the glass, turned her back on Bev. "And she left a note."

Bev stretched out a hand. "Give."

Veronica waved dismissively. "I burned it."

"Bullshit."

"It would have been painful for David to read."

Bev glanced over her shoulder. "Where is he? You never did say."

"He's on a few errands."

Convenient. "Had to get him out of the way, did you? Wouldn't want your precious son implicated."

"He's not."

"Just you, then?"

She raised the glass, draining it. "Prove it."

At that moment, Bev knew for certain. Not every comma and crossed t. But in some macabre twisted way Veronica Carver had presided over her daughter-in-law's death. Either she'd coerced Helen into popping the pills herself, or she'd forced them down Helen's throat with her own bony fingers.

And from where Bev stood, it looked as if the old crone would get away with it.

38

Bev's footsteps rang out in the tinny acoustics of the multi-storey. From the street below, raucous laughter and a flat falsetto warbled, "I will survive." Don't bet on it, mate. With a vicious kick she sent an empty can clattering across the concrete. It was getting on for ten pm and tonight would not go down as one of her best.

Veronica Carver hadn't budged an iota from her fairy story. The old woman had cast a scathing eye over the evening's activities, including the removal of her daughter-in-law's body. Bev held little hope that the post mortem, scheduled for first thing, would reveal anything other than what it was: death by overdose.

Murder by proxy. Perfect crime.

Bev snorted. Ironic, considering that Helen had been so obsessed with perfection she'd killed a baby who couldn't live up to it. Veronica had wreaked a warped revenge. And it looked like the evil old cow would never face a court. Veronica, like Natalie Beck, had taken the law into her own hands. Only difference: the old woman's were a safer pair.

Bev nodded at the driver of a silver Passat parked in the bay behind. Number plate and description matched details of tonight's shadow that Larry Drake had phoned through an hour ago. She wasn't in the mood for small talk. She made for the Peugeot, sat for a minute or two catching her mental breath, then wrinkled her nose. Pool motors were a right pain: smelly and tacky, all fag ash and fast food. Thinking of which, she could murder a bag of chips. She'd pick one up on the way home. And looking on the bright side – she'd get the MG back in the morning.

Window down, she lit a Silk Cut, shuddered involuntarily as Veronica Carver's face flashed before her eyes; heard again the old woman's words: "Let's say I'm a light sleeper." She could picture the action: the old woman creeping after her daughter-in-law, witnessing the crime, working out how to turn it into Helen's death sentence. Maybe she'd taunted the younger woman, threatened her with the police and prison. Unless Helen did the decent thing.

Bev smacked the wheel. One thing she wasn't sure of: was the son in on it? She'd eventually reached David Carver on his mobile. The guy had sounded stunned, amazed. But then Heathcliff taught drama. And Bev had heard a female voice in the background. She suspected one of his lady friends was there, giving him an audience.

She took a final drag, flicked the butt, closed the window. Then tensed. Her hand froze on the ignition, heartbeat quickening. She'd caught movement. In the mirror. She looked again. Must be mistaken. Reflection, perhaps. She turned the key. A CD began to play.

If you don't know me by now...

Rustling from the back. Her eyes met his in the mirror, an unwavering stare through jagged holes in a black mask. He'd been lying in wait, biding his time. The shock was so great she nearly pissed herself. Cool it, girl. Show fear and you're fucked. "OK, sunshine, out you get."

"I don't think so."

Don't panic. Larry's guy was in the car behind. Two against one. "Hop out and we'll forget this ever happened." Like hell.

"You'll remember." A mocking whisper. "Every detail."

She hit the horn hard, glared at the mirror. Where the fuck was the minder?

"It was quick. He didn't suffer. Much." Cold steel against

her neck, then a warm trickle. "Start the car, Bev."

"Go to hell." His knife hand twitched. She nearly passed out in pain. Fingers trembling, she turned the key, reversed the motor, trying to think ahead. Stay calm, go by the book, establish rapport.

And there was something about the bastard's voice…

"Gonna tell me your name?"

"Next right."

She took it. "Still don't know what to call you."

"Give the dog a bone."

She'd heard it before. Recently? Think. She needed to hear more.

"Come on, you know my name."

"And the rest." Ice on her spine.

She needed more to go on; talk, you bastard. Sod the book.

"Get off on wearing frilly knickers, do you?"

"Wank off." The Birmingham accent was stronger. And the menace.

"The pair you sent don't fit."

"Lose weight," he sneered. "I'll help." The knife bit into her flesh.

But it was enough. The voice had told her what she needed to know.

"Thought you only went after blondes?"

"Oh, I will. When I've got you off my back."

Another jab of the knife took her breath away; a knee in her kidneys punctuating more words that confirmed her suspicions. And the food smells hadn't been trapped in the pool car. They were wafting off her attacker. As for on his back, she'd not even been close.

"Clocked you as filth first time I laid eyes on you. Should've kept your piggie snout out."

Then the wannabe cop, Will Browne, told her how she'd die and what he'd do before then.

Storefronts and shop windows passed in a blur. She focused only on what was ahead. Within minutes the city streets lay behind them. The last signpost pointed to Hollywood. No hills, no movie stars. The south Birmingham suburb shared the name, not the glamour.

The roads were narrower here, the lanes winding. He'd make a move soon; aroused, nervy, maybe distracted, he'd order her to stop the car.

"Pull over. Now."

She never had liked taking orders. She took a deep breath, braced herself and slammed her foot down. Not on the brake. On the gas.

The body was found at 11.37 during a routine security patrol. It took a further five minutes to establish identity. Kevin Melrose, a thirty-seven-year-old protection officer, married with two children, had been killed by a single stab wound to the heart. The implications were obvious and immediate.

Larry Drake, personal protection unit head, alerted Byford at home. By 12.05, every available officer and detective was either on the road or about to join the hunt for the missing Peugeot. Control was unable to raise Bev. She'd been out of radio contact for more than two hours.

In the nightmare, she was being raped. She fought to regain consciousness, struggled frenziedly to throw off the attacker. His body pinned her to the frozen earth as he thrust into her. Desperate to wake, she screamed, writhing in pain and terror. Something sharp pressed into her spine. She forced her eyes open, gulped for breath. And smelt cow-shit and petrol and fear and sweat.

Not a dream. They were in a field: long grass, thistles, straggly hedge. The car on its side a few yards away, a main beam casting light over a scene she wanted no part in. Filthy, shivering, half-naked, she could barely move under the rapist's weight. She had no recollection of anything since hitting the accelerator. Guessed the impact of the crash had knocked her out, and he'd pulled her clear.

This wasn't how she'd envisaged it panning out. Lamb to the slaughter was not her style. But this wouldn't be the final act. With absolute clarity and coldest fury, she determined that when this was over, he was going to die.

Operations room at Highgate. The place buzzed with barked orders, snatched conversation, radio static. Byford was heading the search, Jack Hainsworth co-ordinating. As SIO Street Watch, Mike Powell had been informed and was in a squad car heading towards the main search area.

The general location was down to data from CCTV. Cameras had also captured what looked like an ostensibly innocent encounter between the personal protection officer and an unknown assailant. The stranger, who'd kept his back to the lens, appeared to be assisting Melrose into the Passat. To the casual observer, Melrose then looked as if he was sitting at the wheel, waiting for a friend.

Bev's motor had been filmed exiting the multi-storey, and travelling along Broad Street. It had then been picked up at various points including the Bristol Road, Moseley Road, Kings Heath High Street. It was last recorded heading towards Redditch on the Alcester Road, the A435.

The most intense police activity was centred south of the city. The area was swarming with squad cars, unmarked motors and hard-faced cops itching to catch the bastard.

Byford's glance kept returning to a freeze-frame on the monitor: a shot of Bev in the car park, hands deep in pockets, that funny little half-smile on her face. Byford closed his eyes. Dear Jesus, keep her safe.

Fear and nausea threatened to overwhelm her. She gagged, gasped with pain. Blood ran into her eyes and mouth, warm and sticky. It felt as if a vice was tightening round her skull. She had to think. All that mattered was survival. She had to get out alive. Had to control this.

Black eyes stared through the mask's holes. She had to blank out what he was doing. Concentrate on what *she* could do. Training and experience kicked in. Go for the groin, the eyes, the knees. How? She could barely move and the pain was intense. Then she remembered what he'd done to the other girls: Rebecca, Kate, Laura. How he'd diminished them, damaged their lives. She would not be a victim. She had to act, seize the slightest chance.

The bastard was reaching a climax. It was almost over. A new terror ran through her. The knife? Where was it? He'd kill her if she didn't act.

Fear wasn't going to do it. Fury was the way. Cold and calculating, she worked out what to do. She'd have a second, maybe two. No more.

The call came via control from a motorist on his way home. A car in a field off the B291, looked as if it had ploughed into a ditch and gone over, no information on occupants or vehicle. Byford put the phone down, felt a stir. With neither number nor model, it wasn't a given; his gut told him otherwise. Road and map reference had been relayed to every car in the area. He rubbed knuckles into tired eyes. They'd find out soon enough.

Bev's image was still frozen on the monitor. Byford studied it for thirty seconds or so, realising – maybe acknowledging – that he no longer saw her as the lippy daughter he'd never had. He couldn't define exactly what he felt now. Paternal wasn't even close.

He grabbed his overcoat. He wouldn't get there first, but he'd get there.

It wasn't cold fury. It was animal instinct, passion for survival. Pinned down, in pain, Bev couldn't kick or punch. There was only one option. Adrenalin fizzed in every vein as she jerked her head up and sank her teeth into his face.

She aimed for the nose, found the lips. Biting through the mask in a gross parody of a kiss, she tore the flesh, thrashing from side to side like a pit bull savaging a child.

He howled, his hands flailing at her face. With his blood soaking through the mask into her mouth, she clamped her teeth tighter, reaching out, frantically scrabbling for a weapon. Her fingers found the hilt of the knife, fallen to the ground beside her. Tried to lift it. Christ. It was snagged. Tangled grass? She gave another desperate tug, groaning, hot furious tears wet on her cheeks.

Blood gushed from Browne's wound as he fought to get away from her teeth. He hurled himself aside, falling on his back with a gasp. It was the opening she'd prayed for. When he twisted back towards her, she was ready, slamming a knee into him, throwing a punch at his ruined face. Again and again she lashed out, then yanked off the mask, saw bloody flesh and glazed eyes. Why wasn't the bastard fighting back?

She staggered to her feet, waves of pain she'd blanked out now threatening to fell her. Still Browne didn't move. Slowly she circled him, swung a vicious kick at his ribs. As the body rolled with the impact, she saw the glint of the blade – the inch or so not embedded in his back.

She was only vaguely aware of the car, the new headlights. Sinking to her knees on the grass, burying her face in her hands, she sobbed uncontrollably in relief, in shame, in sorrow. She felt a blanket being draped around her shoulders, the gentle touch of a hand.

"It's over now, Bev. It's all over."

Even in the aftermath of horror and death, she registered the words and recognised the voice. For the first time in seven years, Mike Powell hadn't called her Morriss.

As she glanced up, the DI gave a tentative smile, then knelt on the frozen earth and held her in his arms until she stopped crying.

39

"I spy with my…"

Emmy Morriss's little eye searched for inspiration. A starkly clinical private room in Edgbaston's Nuffield Hospital didn't provide a lot of scope. Especially after seven days' play.

"Mum," Bev sighed. "I swear if it's b for bed again, you're gonna end up in the next one."

"Glad to hear you're feeling yourself." The guv hovered in the doorway, both hands clutching his fedora.

"That's b for boss, then, is it?" She threw Emmy a withering glance.

Her mum hastily gathered sewing gear, satsuma peel and a less than enthusiastic old lady. "We'll leave you to it, love. Grab some coffee, shall we, Sadie?"

Bev's gran mumbled like a kid missing all the fun. "See you later, Mr B."

"Best come in," Bev said. It was bound to happen sooner or later. She'd not allowed the big man anywhere near since the attack. Nor Oz, nor Dazza, nor Vince. Her mum, Sadie, Frankie, Carol – they'd been the ones on grape duty. She could handle them.

Mike Powell was the only guy who'd got past reception on the couple of occasions he'd dropped by. She couldn't explain why. It wasn't as though they had a lot to say. She supposed it was to do with him having been there, having comforted her when she felt like dirt on the bottom of a shoe.

Byford sat back in an armchair still warm from Emmy. "How you doing?"

"Tickety-boo." She saw his lips tighten. Physically she was on the mend. The aubergine bruises had faded to plum; they'd turn dingy green in no time. Blood tests for STDs were clear. She wasn't pregnant. The stitches had been removed from her neck; the scar would be a permanent reminder. Like she needed one.

"Want the truth, guv?"

"No point otherwise."

"I don't feel myself," she said. "I feel like shit."

He reached a tentative hand. "Bev…"

She jerked back, folded her arms. "What?"

"I…"

"Don't know what to say? Where to look?" She snorted. "No. Nor me."

He hesitated, then launched into an account of the week's highlights, events not emotions. She knew most of it, of course, but the monologue filled what threatened to be a spiky silence.

Terry Roper had pleaded guilty to child abduction and arson with intent to endanger life. The phone calls – hoax and malicious – were also down to him. He'd be looking at a six-year stretch. Natalie Beck and Veronica Carver were sticking to their stories; the crown prosecution guys would have to sift fact from fantasy. Police divers had recovered Jessica's body; Byford and Carol Mansfield had attended the funeral. Helen Carver's body was on ice, pending the possibility of further forensic tests.

"The Beck baby's with foster parents in Northfield," Byford said. "But Maxine's made headway since Zoë was found. There's a chance she'll get custody. She'll certainly fight for it."

Bev reached for a glass, slowly sipped tepid water.

"And…" This was new. He paused, hoped she was ready.

"Will Browne's body's being released for burial tomorrow."

If she didn't put the glass down, it'd break. "You're telling me all this like I give a shit?"

"Is that right, Bev?" He waited for her to look at him. She knew and took her time. "You don't care any more ?"

She broke eye contact. It was one big mess and she couldn't sort it. Will Browne was dead. And she was dead sorry. Sorry it hadn't really been her doing. The fatal stab wound was inflicted when he fell on the blade. Its lethal position was down to her frantic fumbling, and it getting caught in a clump of grass. Inadvertent, not intentional.

The Beast was dead and she was sorry she'd only mauled him. How sick was that?

"You've not answered, Bev."

How could she? Browne had violated more than her body. She'd heard about the sick fuck's lock-up in Digbeth, gagged whenever it sprang unbidden to mind. She barely knew who she was any more. Desperately needed some-one to tell her. Not so long ago, she'd have looked to Oz. But he was finding the attack and her actions difficult to handle. So Carol had told her – and had also told her about the sergeant's exams Oz was about to take. Best all round. Probably. Didn't mean it didn't hurt. But she was damaged goods anyway.

And was fucked if she'd show it. "Lob us a grape."

He sighed, passed her the bowl. "How long are they keeping you in?"

A shrug.

"When you coming back?" It sounded more than a query about returning to work.

Another shrug. Out of the corner of her eye she caught him clenching his jaw. The visitor was losing patience. How could she explain? About panic attacks in the day? And being scared to sleep at night, with Will Browne's ruined face in front of her every time she closed her eyes?

"Tell you who won't be on the welcoming committee," Byford said.

That piqued her interest. "Oh?"

The guv popped a grape in his mouth. "Les King."

Lazy Les. PC Plod who'd dragged his feet on the first day. "Still on gardening leave, is he?" Not that she cared.

"Bit more than that. Bastard's on a charge."

Criminally negligent, but that wouldn't land him in court. "What for?"

"You know those letters I got?"

Remember Baby Fay... One to the station, one to the guv's home. "He didn't?" She closed a gaping mouth.

"We got a camera installed at my place. Caught him red-handed." Byford gazed down at his own. "Should've occurred to me, really. King was around at the time. We never hit it off."

"'Specially after you nearly decked him the day Zoë Beck disappeared." The lop-sided smile was rare these days but it went unnoticed. The big man was miles away. And she'd bet a pony to a pound his thoughts weren't on the *Beck* baby. "What you thinking, guv?"

He met her glance. "Baby Fay. That we'll never know what happened, who abducted her, killed her. We all have them, you know, Bev." Her raised eyebrow inquired. "Bits of hell on the pillow."

She nodded. So how come hers were all over the sodding bedspread as well?

"Almost forgot." He dug a hand in a pocket, passed an envelope. "Vince Hanlon said to give you this. You won the Christmas raffle."

She tossed it unopened at her side. Another memory

from hell. Vince had been flogging tickets the night a terrified young mother had dumped her newborn in a stinking phone box in Balsall Heath. Relatives had flocked forward to bury the corpses. Not.

Byford rose, hat under his elbow. "You're bigger than this, sergeant."

That's what she'd thought, too.

"No one thinks any the less of you, Bev." She'd spot tears in his eyes, if she could see through the veil of her own. He turned at the door. "Browne isn't doing this. You are."

She stared at the wall. The big man was right. She'd vowed not to be a victim but, God, was it easier said than done. She heard his voice in low conversation in the corridor. Her fingers brushed against the envelope. The faintest of smiles tugged at her lips as she opened it. "Guv?"

He popped his head round the door.

She waved a couple of tickets. "Fancy a night out? West End job?"

"Sounds good." A sceptical voice suspected a catch.

"Front-row seats." She winked. "*An Inspector Calls.*" Best not mention Claridges. Bags of time to worry about that.

Byford shook his head, gave a slow smile. She'd get there; he knew she would. "Go on, then. You're on."

"Cool. Oh, and guv?" She threw a grape in the air, caught it between her teeth. "You're driving."

"Cool. Oh, and Bev?" The grin took ten years off him. "We'll take the train."

New Year's Day

Byford left the Rover in its customary spot, preferring to walk the final part. It was early morning and below freezing with a biting wind; dirty snow lay here and there. His eyes watered, which meant his first glimpse was blurred. Rapid blinking cleared the haze so that as he approached the angel came into sharper focus. She was no longer white and the marble was badly chipped. The once-beautiful face was pitted with age and erosion. Byford had removed the moss and lichen many times. It was one of the reasons he was here.

This was his eighteenth pilgrimage to the baby's grave. As far as he knew, he was now the only person who visited, brought Fay flowers.

Not this year.

Intrigued, he halted, peered closer, then continued the short walk. He took off his hat as he knelt on the frozen earth. There was no message, no name, no indication from whom the gift had come. As he stroked one of the tiny pink flowers, his lips formed a smile of sorts.

It was bitterly cold out here, but cacti were hardy and resilient. The big man was pretty sure this one would survive.

Author's note

Several spooky incidents occurred during the writing of this book. For instance, I alluded in the narrative to a real and shocking crime that happened nearly thirty years ago and – out of the blue and within twenty-four hours – there was a development that made every national news bulletin and newspaper in the country.

This and one or two other happenstance instances made the hairs rise on the back of my neck. Were they mere coincidences? Or portents? Or… what? They may mean nothing at all but for what it's worth, I share this one with you…

Rainbows, real and fabricated, are featured throughout the story. On the day I finished writing *Baby Love,* I printed the first hard copy. Chapter thirteen was coming off the printer when I turned to look through the window of my office. There, spanning a blue-grey sky was a spectacular rainbow, so perfect it could have been painted. A minute later and I'd have missed it. The timing, the chance of that was – to me – stunning. What a story, I thought. Who'd believe it? So I raced downstairs and took a photograph, just to prove it wasn't journalistic licence.

And even now every time I look at that rainbow I get goose bumps.

Baby Love is Maureen Carter's third Bev Morriss mystery from Crème de la Crime.

Also available are:

Working Girls

The sight of a teenage prostitute murdered in a Birmingham park breaks Bev Morriss's heart. To pin down the culprit she struggles to infiltrate the deadly jungle of hookers, pimps and johns - and takes the most dangerous gamble of her life, out on the streets.

Dark and gritty… an exciting debut novel… Reviewing the Evidence

ISBN: 0-9547634-0-8

£7.99

Dead Old

West Midlands Police think an elderly woman's bizarre murder is the work of teenage yobs, but Bev Morriss can't accept it. Her reputation hits rock bottom and no one is listening. Then the killer decides her family is next.

confirms Carter among the new generation of crime writers.
Julia Wallis Martin

ISBN: 0-9547634-6-7

£7.99

COMING LATER THIS YEAR
from Crème de la Crime:

No Sleep for the Dead
Adrian Magson

Another outing for crimebusters Riley Gavin and Frank Palmer.

Investigative journalist Riley has problems. Palmer disappears after a disturbing chance encounter, her love affair seems set to stay long-distance and she's being followed by a mysterious dreadlocked man.

Frank's determination to pursue justice for an old friend puts him and Riley in deadly danger from art thieves, gangstas, British Intelligence – and a bitter old woman out for revenge.

Published August 2006
Price £7.99
ISBN: 0-9551589-1-5

Behind You!

Linda Regan

Crackling debut novel by popular actress turned crime writer.

Christmas: a time of peace and goodwill.

Oh no it isn't, thinks Detective Inspector Paul Banham. Was the suspicious death at the pantomime an accident – or murder? Banham finds the theatrical glamour tarnished by rivalries, grudges and illicit liaisons; and then there's a second death. But the panto is sold out and the show must go on.

Published September 2006
Price £7.99
ISBN: 0-9551589-2-3

ALSO AVAILABLE
from Crème de la Crime:

A KIND OF PURITAN   PENNY DEACON
A subtle, clever thriller...
Daily Mail
ISBN: 0-9547634-1-6   £7.99

NO PEACE FOR THE WICKED   ADRIAN MAGSON
...the excitement carries right through to the last page... Ron Ellis
ISBN: 0-9547634-2-4   £7.99

IF IT BLEEDS   BERNIE CROSTHWAITE
Pacy, eventful... an excellent debut. Mystery Women
ISBN: 0-9547634-3-2   £7.99

A CERTAIN MALICE   FELICITY YOUNG
*a beautifully written book... Felicity draws you into the life in Australia...
you may not want to leave.* Natasha Boyce, Ottakar's crime buyer
ISBN: 0-9547634-4-0   £7.99

PERSONAL PROTECTION   TRACEY SHELLITO
a powerful, edgy story... I didn't want to put down... Reviewing the
Evidence
ISBN: 0-9547634-5-9   £7.99

NO HELP FOR THE DYING   ADRIAN MAGSON
*Gritty and fast-paced detecting of the traditional kind, with a welcome
injection of realism.* Maxim Jakubowski, The Guardian
ISBN: 0-9547634-7-5   £7.99

A THANKLESS CHILD   PENNY DEACON
*... moves at a fast slick pace... a lot of colourful characters... a good
page-turner... very readable.* Ann Bell, newbooks
ISBN: 0-9547634-8-3   £7.99

12
13 50
25 50